THE CURSED
SEBASTIAN STORM

MOONLIGHT FALLS BOOK TWO

COLETTE RIVERA

Some magic
changes you forever.

Edited by Abbie Nicole

Cover design by Sleepy Fox Studio

People depicted in the cover image and internal images are models and should not be associated with the book.

Interior Formatting by Colette Rivera. Stock Images: Canva Pro & Depositphotos

ISBN

Print: 978-1-991284-01-3

Kindle: 978-1-991284-02-0

Storm Family Tree
Selma Nock — Tony Storm
Nelson Storm   Sullivan Storm — Marilyn Dalton
Claire Bates — Simon Storm
Stephen Storm   Samantha Storm — undisclosed
Kira Storm   Sebastian Storm

Moonlight Falls Directory

Aydin	Diner Kitchen Hand
Beth	Souvenir Shop Owner
Carla	General Store Clerk
Carson Lee	Logging Foreman
Eleanor Ashley	Mayor
Elijah Gray	Researcher & Diner Waiter
Hazel Delgado	Gray Electrical Co-Owner
James Gray	Gray Electrical Owner
Jay	Town Hall Administrator
Kaylin	Diner Waitress
Luna	Diner Waitress
Melinda Gibbs	City Councilor
Mila Lopez	Librarian
Nora	City Councilor
Parker Hayes	Diner Chef
Princeton Taylor	Museum Curator
Sam Lee	Logger
Sebastian Storm	Owner of Storm Manor
Tony Harris	Elementary School Principal
William	City Councilor

MOONLIGHT FALLS

The Fall of Elijah Gray

The Seduction of James Gray
The Cursed Sebastian Storm
The Heart of Moonlight Falls

THE CURSED
SEBASTIAN STORM

MOONLIGHT FALLS BOOK TWO

COLETTE RIVERA

CHAPTER ONE

SEBASTIAN STORM CLOSED and locked the gate to Storm House. For the first time in six years, he was outside the wrought iron bars.

He barely glanced at the old Victorian house as he turned toward James's truck. He couldn't believe any of this was happening. The reality of his escape hadn't hit him, not fully, but he could feel it coming. Happiness was building inside him so quickly that it was almost sickening. And out of all the things he was escaping Storm House to do, he never thought it'd be to go on a date with James Gray.

"Let's go." James's excitement was palpable as he waved Sebastian to the passenger side of his truck. God, he was adorable. Sebastian never dreamed he'd be able to make a grumpy man like that smile so goofily.

Sebastian got in the truck. James started the engine with the push of a button and the magical battery sprang to life. There was no hint that the vehicle had been sitting neglected on the side of the road for weeks while James had been imprisoned at Storm House.

James pulled out onto the winding road, heading through the

tall trees toward Moonlight Falls. As they left Storm House behind, Sebastian's stomach twisted. His chest tightened and, for a second, he couldn't breathe. For years, he'd wanted nothing except to escape the property and his family's curse. Now that the moment was here, happiness wasn't the only emotion threatening to overtake him.

A hand clasped his knee. Sebastian looked over to see James's brow furrowed, his face calm and concerned.

"You okay?"

"I—" For a split second, Sebastian worried he'd burst into tears. "It's hard to believe I'm actually leaving." His voice betrayed him, sounding small and unsteady.

James squeezed his knee before returning his hand to the steering wheel. "I know, and I was only stuck for a couple of weeks. I can't imagine what driving away feels like for you."

Sebastian cleared his throat and turned to stare blankly out the window. "Yeah."

James was so understanding, and sometimes, Sebastian found it frustrating. James was so good all the time. Sebastian didn't always deserve the benefit of the doubt, yet James never hesitated to give it to him.

"If you aren't in the mood for a date, we don't have to go out now," James continued.

Sebastian pulled at the cuffs of the leather jacket he'd stolen from James. The sleeves were too short because Sebastian was taller and had longer arms, but he liked the jacket. It smelled like James, and his broad-shouldered frame meant his jacket engulfed Sebastian's narrow body in a way he found endlessly comforting.

"No, let's go now." Sebastian pushed his funny mood down. "We should be celebrating getting out of the damn house. Right?"

"Definitely." James's lips twitched into a smile.

Sebastian's heart ached. There was no way he was turning down a date with James Gray. He'd only been dreaming about going on one for most of his life.

Sebastian's crush on James began when they were kids and never really died. The feelings started before he even realized what they meant. Hell, James had been key in Sebastian figuring out he was queer. He'd been the source of the most angsty bi panic it was possible for a young boy to have.

Not that James knew any of this. Sebastian certainly wasn't going to tell him. James had hardly noticed him growing up, and Sebastian didn't need to make things weird.

It wasn't like he'd ever tried to talk to James back then. Crushes had been terrifying when he was young. He hadn't had the courage to approach anyone he'd liked until his last year of high school, and by then, James had been gone. Sebastian's self-confidence hadn't found him until he was in college, far away from Moonlight Falls.

Sebastian concentrated on the redwoods zipping past his window as James drove toward town. The sight didn't help his sinking mood. Happiness was slowly eclipsed by discomfort. He shifted in his seat. Sebastian had never liked these woods, never liked living at Storm House, even before he was imprisoned or knew about the curse. He'd hated being banished out there every summer, but he'd recently learned something to make him hate these woods even more, and once James found out, things wouldn't be so great between them.

Sebastian should have come clean with what he knew, but he was selfish. He wasn't good like James. He wanted their date and another night together. Screw everything else. He wanted things to be nice before they got ruined again.

Because things always got ruined, and Sebastian wasn't silly enough to hope anything good could last.

As they rolled into town, James pointed excitedly at Gray Electrical. For someone who spent ninety percent of his time scowling and grumbling, he could be adorably sincere.

Sebastian had always found James's prickliness hot. As a teen, it had been mysterious. He'd wanted to be the one to make James smile. Now, he was the one making James happy. He'd gotten that wish and discovered he loved making the man frown in frustration just as much.

They drove into the town center. The circular road lined with old buildings looked unchanged, giving Sebastian a disorienting jolt. It could have been six years ago, ten years ago, fourteen. He didn't like not being able to see the effect of time on Moonlight Falls. He'd hated so much about this place as a kid and had never intended to return.

"It feels good to be home." James's posture sagged with relief as he pulled into the back parking lot at Moonlight Diner.

Sebastian frowned at the other parked cars. "I don't understand how you love this place so much."

"What do you mean?" James turned off the truck and faced him. "The magic here just feels right. You're a Moonlighter. You know what I mean."

Sebastian rolled his eyes. Some of the citizens of Moonlight Falls believed this place called to them. They were townies whose families had lived here for generations, and they were all obsessed with the place. The Storms had been around just as long, but Sebastian had no idea what people were talking about. Moonlight Falls didn't call him home. It wasn't some comfort in the dark. The whole damn place was cursed, plaguing his very existence.

"Moonlight Falls is just a town." Sebastian unbuckled his seatbelt. Honestly, it was like most of the people here had been brainwashed into loving the dirt under their shoes, like being raised here indoctrinated you into a cult.

James looked mildly offended. "You don't like it here?"

"Why would I?" Sebastian got out of the truck. Seeing the diner and the little park beside it made him feel like a lonely kid again. What was there to like about that?

James frowned. It was his thoughtful frown, as opposed to his annoyed frown or his stressed-out frown. "Would you like to go somewhere else for dinner?"

Shit. Sebastian was ruining everything. He was supposed to be living out his teenage fantasy of a date with James—which had definitely included the diner as their date location—not bitching about how much he disliked Moonlight Falls. He knew James was practically in love with this town.

The town loved James back, so Sebastian couldn't really blame him. Mutual affection was a heady thing.

Sebastian walked around to James's side of the truck. "No, I don't want to go somewhere else. Being back in town is just freaking me out. It looks so much the same that it's like the last six years might never have happened. But not in a good way."

James pulled Sebastian into a hug, and for one long embrace, Sebastian forgot all his negative thoughts.

"Those years definitely happened. The curse is more than enough evidence of that, and dealing with it isn't over." James pulled back to look at Sebastian. "We can't leave the veins feeding off the fuel cell forever, so we've got to figure that out. And there's a lot of people mad at me. Maybe it's silly, but I want to do something nice with you. Something simple for us before we deal with the rest."

Sebastian nodded. His mind was caught on all the times James had said *we*. Moonlight Fall's golden boy didn't need to help him with the Storm House curse now that he was free. But the fact that he said he would, like it was the most natural thing, made Sebastian ache all over.

"You're right. We deserve this. Come on." He pulled James's hand, and they walked around the side of the diner to the entrance. "Just so you know, I expect a milkshake with two straws and a chocolate-flavored kiss on this date."

James chuckled. "That's very specific. Almost like you've been fantasizing about it."

Sebastian's cheeks burned, but he walked ahead so James

wouldn't notice. James was just teasing him. There was no way he knew how often Sebastian had pictured that scene. "Yeah, well, I've been fantasizing about ice cream and dairy in general since living without electricity for years."

Sebastian entered the diner and froze. There were people, of course there were, but the sight shocked him. Before James turned up, Sebastian hadn't seen more than one person at a time in six years. Before James, he hadn't spent more than a few minutes with anyone, and now, suddenly, four people were staring at him.

He shrank into James's leather jacket, hunching his shoulders.

"Hi," Eli called out, wearing a dumbfounded expression. His mouth hung open.

James rubbed the back of his neck. "Hey." He did his best to avoid his younger brother's stare.

Eli marched over and put a hand on his hip. "Don't you *hey* me," he growled in a loud whisper. "You haven't been home in weeks, and you're just going to walk in here like it's a typical Thursday?"

Pain laced Eli's words, making guilt wash over Sebastian. It was his fault James had been trapped at Storm House. His tongue bound, like Sebastian's, prevented him from telling anyone about the curse imprisoning them. He hadn't meant to get James trapped—it had been an epic fuck up—but Sebastian had still dragged James into his mess and put James at risk because he didn't know all the ins and outs of the magic he was messing with. And now James had to deal with the fallout.

"Sorry, Eli." James clasped his brother's shoulder. He was taller than Eli, who was slimmer than James's broad-shouldered, muscular build, but the brothers had the same nose and well-defined jaw.

Eli huffed.

"We want to explain everything." Sebastian tried to ignore the other three customers who were not so subtly watching their conversation. "I know James disappearing didn't make sense, but —" His words trailed off. He was surprised he'd been able to say that much. The silencing spell keeping the curse's existence secret was usually much stricter, not even allowing him to hint at anything being wrong.

"You and Parker should meet us at home after you get off," James continued for him. "We'll explain everything then, I promise."

Eli crossed his arms, pulling from James's grip. "What the hell, you guys? That's all you're going to say? We'll talk later? That is not enough to make me drop this. How do I know you'll even be home when I get there?"

"We'll be there," Sebastian promised. "This is all my fault. I'm sorry, Eli. I can't explain it all now, not here." He couldn't help glancing at the people at the back of the diner.

"Fine." Eli closed his eyes momentarily, then opened them with a forced smile. "Would you guys like some menus?"

James accepted the dark-blue laminated menus and led Sebastian to a booth by the window. He didn't choose the one beneath the photo of himself, showing him off as the local swimming champion. Sebastian would have teased James about the old picture and his obvious effort not to look at the display, but he found everything in the diner too distracting.

Being here was surreal. The smells, the sounds, everything from the pie cases on the counter to the photos on the walls were so familiar, but it felt like he hadn't been here in a million years. Like the last time he'd been to a restaurant of any kind was in another lifetime.

Sebastian slid into the blue vinyl booth across from James.

He gave Sebastian a sheepish grin. "Ideally, a date wouldn't begin with my brother giving us hell."

"Nothing about this situation is normal, James."

"You're right." He glanced down at the menu. "But I'm still so happy we're here. And once we figure out how to tell Eli and

Parker the truth about what happened, next time we come, it'll be perfect." His tanned cheeks turned slightly pink like he was hopeful and excited about the prospect of more nights at the diner together.

Sebastian squirmed, his stomach dropping. How was James so sure he wanted to take Sebastian out again? "I feel like the secret-binding is loosening," he said instead of acknowledging James's focus on dating. "That conversation was easier than any of our previous ones with Eli."

"That's true." James's eyes widened like he hadn't noticed the difference until now. He wasn't as used to magic dictating his words as Sebastian, who'd been painfully well-acquainted with its limits. "I wonder if getting free has anything to do with it?"

"It must," Sebastian agreed, even though he had no idea how.

His Uncle Stephen had said his mom was bound to secrecy, even though she was never physically trapped by the curse, so he didn't see how leaving the curse and the Storm property affected the tongue binding. Unless his mom's tongue had never been bound that tightly, and she'd chosen not to try and warn him about the curse, regardless of how much she was prevented from revealing it.

A group of teens entered the diner, the bell above the door ringing as their laughter filled the space. Sebastian flinched reflexively, his heart fluttering rapidly at the shock of the sudden noise.

"Are you all right?" James's brows drew together in concern, his lips turning downward.

"Fine." Sebastian smiled and forced an exasperated laugh. "Just startled me." He eyed the teens as they grabbed menus and went to sit at the other end of the diner. His heart continued pounding too fast. What the hell was wrong with him?

James ordered their chocolate milkshake and then dithered over what to eat. He was taking his dinner selection so seriously that you'd think it was the most importing thing he'd done that week. It was almost enough to make Sebastian smile and relax.

Sebastian ordered tater tots, jalapeño poppers, and waffles with whipped cream. He was going to make himself sick, but after years where his meal options were dictated by having no refrigeration, electricity, or ability to go to the store for perishables, he wanted to indulge in everything he'd been deprived of.

James laughed as Sebastian ordered, making Sebastian's heart sing. This was exactly the date he'd imagined for them when he was young. One where they ate ridiculous food and made each other smile.

Eli pressed his lips together like he was struggling to hold back anger as he noted Sebastian's selections and James's final decision to have a burger.

As soon as he walked away, James grabbed Sebastian's hand. "I still can't believe we're here or that my idea with the fuel cell actually worked."

He sounded almost giddy. Sebastian had felt that way too when he'd first stepped beyond the Storm House boundary. Was all of James's excitement for this date just post-escape euphoria that would die down? It would make sense.

Sebastian was less and less sure of things the longer he was free of his biggest problem. "I can't believe it either." Except he wasn't brimming with excitement. Fear that this could all get taken away snuck up on Sebastian unexpectedly. What if he got trapped again? What if this was all temporary?

What if James got tired of him when the giddiness wore off?

More people entered the diner, a family of four closely followed by an older couple. There were just so many people. So much noise. Sebastian found it unsettling not knowing if anyone was going to look at him or try to talk to him. And the idea that *more* people might come to the diner, filling all the available seats, made his chest tighten for reasons he couldn't explain.

He'd never been anxious like this. All he'd wanted for the past six years was to be around people, to be lost in a crowd, to go to a club and have his ears blasted with loud music as he danced with strangers. Why was he acting like this tiny group of low-key patrons at the diner scared him?

He tried to focus on the milkshake and how good the ice cream tasted. He tried not to look around and ignored everything but James's kind brown eyes. He looked good in the hoodie Sebastian had bought him. Well, the hoodie the personal shopper his lawyer had hired bought him, but whatever.

Even after all these years, James was still Sebastian's dream. His square jaw was more pronounced now than when they were young, his features bolder. He was hard and unrelenting and perfect. Not to mention, he wore the hell out of a leather jacket. The only downside to stealing it was that Sebastian couldn't appreciate James in it anymore.

Eli delivered the tater tots and jalapeño poppers with a cheery, "Here we are."

Sebastian flinched. He hadn't seen Eli coming. He didn't look up. Instead, he focused on the food, trying to get his twisting stomach to settle.

Eli's cheeriness had been overdone, no doubt to remind them he was pissed, but he was at work and forced to be polite. Given that, Sebastian wasn't expecting Eli's next words to come out so delicately. "It's really good to see you out, Sebastian."

He forced himself to look up, intending to roll his eyes or say something snarky, but the kindness in Eli's eyes did something weird to Sebastian's insides.

"Hope we'll be seeing you in town more." Eli offered a small smile before turning to the next table.

Fuck. Sebastian fought back tears like sap. Everyone in town thought he was a recluse who couldn't deal with people, but that wasn't true. It was just the curse trapping him at Storm House and the secret-binding making him lie that had created the illusion that he couldn't handle coming into town. So why did Eli's words touch him like he was taking some big step coming to the diner?

The bell above the door rang and more people came inside. Damn this small town for having nowhere else to go for dinner.

Sebastian's stomach was twisted in too many knots for him to eat. He ran a hand through his overlong hair, pushing it from his eyes. His skin itched and his pulse didn't want to settle. He put his head in his hands, elbows braced on the table. If his chest could stop seizing, maybe he could pull it together.

He didn't get what was happening to him. Why couldn't he deal with being in public? He wasn't a recluse with social anxiety. That was nothing but a lie.

An arm came to rest across his shoulders. "Sebastian." James's gentle whisper tickled his ear.

"Fuck," he swore, refusing to open his eyes or release his head from his hands. He didn't want James to see him like this.

"Why don't we take our food to go?"

Sebastian lifted his head. The lights were too bright. Honestly, who needed things to be this blinding, and why hadn't he noticed how awful the glare was before? Several people were staring at him. Did they realize who he was? Could they tell he was fending off panic?

"Can we get some boxes?" James asked Eli when he returned with the burger and waffles.

Dread washed over Sebastian. He didn't want to leave. He didn't want to be freaking out right now, unable to eat in a damn restaurant. But at the same time, getting away from the noise and unforgiving light seemed vital. He was glad he at least had a choice.

He'd never wanted to be alone, trapped far out of town with no one to talk to. Had he really gotten so accustomed to the forced isolation that the rumors about him had come true? He wanted to say no, but he didn't know how to explain what he was feeling, other than some sort of social anxiety.

James packed up their food and paid. Sebastian followed him outside. Relief hit almost instantly, and he hated it as much as he'd hated every lonely day trapped in that old house.

"We can head to my place." James paused outside the diner. "Or sit in the park."

It was dusk, late enough that the newly installed lights had come on in the town center. Sebastian couldn't remember how many shades were usually around town, but it wasn't like people avoided going out at night because of them. Storm House had always been plagued with scores more than anywhere else.

Not wanting to retreat completely, Sebastian said, "Let's eat out here. It's not that cold."

James carried their dinner to a picnic table by the swing set, directly under a large, bright light.

"Doesn't seem like this date was such a great idea." James fiddled with the lid of his burger container. "I'm sorry. I was too excited to think. You haven't been out in so long. I should have realized it would be overwhelming."

Sebastian's heart constricted painfully. "I wasn't expecting to react like this." He popped a tot in his mouth, taking a moment to enjoy the crunchy, salted potato.

Now that they were away from everyone, he was much calmer. Even the light above them wasn't as oppressive in the open space, and the subtle night sounds were familiar. He breathed more easily as the twinge in his chest disappeared, but he couldn't fully appreciate the calm feeling.

Sebastian had detested the silence of Storm House. The quiet had driven him to desperation countless times. It was messed up that something he'd hated now soothed him.

"It makes sense that your reactions have changed." James gave him a look full of unfaltering understanding. "Maybe ease into social settings gradually, see where your new comfort zone is. A date night at home would have been just as good. We can go watch a movie after dinner."

The prospect should have perked Sebastian up. How often had he wished he could watch movies or television over the last years?

"You really want to date me, don't you?" Sebastian couldn't help asking. James was a very serious guy, determined and single-minded when he was set on a goal. Sebastian had never thought that focus would be directed at him, especially not now that James was free to escape Sebastian and all his problems.

James frowned like he was surprised by the question. He set down the milkshake he'd been about to sip. "Yeah, I want to date you. I mean, only if you want to. I thought, now that we're free, things could be—but if you don't want to, I mean, I'm hardly your only option now."

Sebastian had no idea where the idea he wouldn't choose James had come from. He wanted James badly, to an almost desperate degree, especially after James had watched him silently unravel in the diner and treated the incident like it was totally normal.

"I want to date you too, James. There's no doubt about that."

James smiled at him. "Perfect." He picked up his burger and took a bite like all was right with the world.

This turn of events was a lot for Sebastian to get his head around. James didn't just want to fuck, which they had been doing rather spectacularly. For some reason, he wanted more with Sebastian. He wanted to *see where they went* like he was hoping for an actual future together, and not one centered solely around mutual orgasms. Sebastian was floored by the idea. He'd never hoped for a future with James.

He'd never let himself consider a future beyond Storm House. He'd been happy to take any small shred of joy he could find. Hooking up with James had been better than his wildest fantasies, but he'd never hoped for more. Yes, he'd said he'd take care of James, had been vulnerable with him, had made big promises to face fears with him, but that had all been born out of their fucked-up situation. Being imprisoned against their will had made taking risks seem less daunting.

Suddenly, something real together was a possibility, a relationship not built on circumstance, forced proximity, and shared trauma. Sebastian could have more than he'd ever dreamed of. All he'd ever wanted was his freedom. That would have been enough. But no, in addition, he'd been given things he hadn't even dared to ask for.

It was terrifying.

A future with James wasn't an idea he could get attached to. It wouldn't ever happen. They wouldn't last. He knew he'd lose James just like he'd lost everyone and everything else in his life, no matter what James said he wanted right now.

Sebastian and James together forever was an impossibility.

Things would change between them once James discovered what Sebastian was hiding. Sebastian wouldn't blame James for letting go of the idea of the two of them. Anything else was too much to hope for and way more than Sebastian deserved.

CHAPTER TWO

Despite the rocky start, dinner wasn't a total disaster. The tension eased, and Sebastian was able to enjoy the undivided attention of a man he'd never expected to think twice about him.

Of course, Sebastian had schemed to get James's attention. He hadn't hired James as an electrician because his business was in Moonlight Falls. It wasn't on a whim that he'd written to Gray Electrical, mysteriously asking for assistance from a childhood acquaintance. Sebastian's actions during James's first visits to the house had been calculated, tailored to intrigue James as much as possible. He'd needed James hooked so that when things got complicated, he wouldn't abandon Sebastian to rot in the godforsaken *manor* like some helpless victim in a gothic novel.

Still, Sebastian had never imagined his seduction would go this well.

It was fully dark by the time he got up to throw away their compostable takeout containers. Luckily, James had helped him eat the jalapeño poppers and tots. Otherwise, he'd have made himself sick trying to finish everything. Though, he supposed he could have put any leftovers in the refrigerator at James's house.

He was too used to being unable to save certain foods, always cooking and eating precise servings to reduce waste.

Sebastian walked back to the picnic table where James was waiting. "You know what, a movie sounds good."

He was about to step into the light when something flashed in front of him. He turned as a shade swooped down. "Go away." He shooed it with an outstretched arm, the gesture less than effective without the billowing sleeves of his purple robe.

The shade hissed and lunged at him. It latched onto the exposed skin on his wrist with its sharp teeth, clamping down hard. Sebastian gave a shout of pain and surprise as he tried to shake the beast off.

James jumped up from the table. "Get into the light."

Sebastian staggered to the side. Blood ran down his wrist onto his hand. The shade seemed larger than usual, it's body more solid and imposing. It emanated shadow, tendrils rolling off it and darkening the night around them. Sebastian stumbled into the light, but the shade was unaffected by the brightness.

More shades appeared in the sky. James swore as he tried to help Sebastian free his wrist. The beast had a vicelike grip that they couldn't pry open without risking more damage to Sebastian's arm.

The shades above them swooped around the light fixture. It looked like they were trying to attack it but couldn't get close enough, like it had been warded. Apparently deciding destruction wouldn't work, they arranged themselves in front of the light, blocking it out as more shades joined them.

"Why isn't the light affecting them?" Panic took hold of Sebastian as more of his blood spilled from the shade's jaws.

"I don't know." James stepped back and summoned sunlight, sending a flaring orb right into the face of the shade attacking Sebastian.

It had no effect. Sebastian had never seen a shade so immune to light.

"I need to go brighter." James grimaced, already straining with the effort.

"No!" Sebastian shouted. "You drained yourself less than twenty-four hours ago. Don't you dare."

Sebastian hadn't done any magic since freeing himself from the curse. Now seemed as good a time as any to test if his strength had returned. He said the words to summon fire. Sparks flared and flames erupted in the shade's face. It hissed, releasing Sebastian as the fire took hold.

The beast exploded into tendrils of black smoke. With nothing left to feed it, Sebastian's fire went out. The shades overhead paused, staring down.

"Come on." James put an arm around Sebastian and guided him around the back of the diner to his truck. Once they were in the cab, James inspected Sebastian's wrist. "I don't think you'll need stitches, but I'm no doctor. Let's go home and bandage you up. Then we can head to the hospital in Apple Valley."

Sebastian held his sleeve back, trying not to get blood all over James's leather jacket. "I don't think I need the hospital." He winced in pain. He was pretty cut up, but he refused to see the injury as anything dire.

James was already backing up. "We'll be home in two minutes."

The drive was as quick as promised. James turned into the driveway of a tidy two-story home on the south side of town. It was the perfect picture of domestic life, a simple garden of dormant rose bushes, a clipped lawn, and a small picket fence. James clicked open the garage door with a remote and pulled in. He was out of his seat and opening the passenger door before Sebastian could collect himself.

Sebastian didn't pay much attention to the home's interior as he was led upstairs. James pulled him into a bathroom attached to what was presumably his bedroom, directing Sebastian to the sink to wash himself off. The water stung like hell.

James helped him dry and wrap his wrist, putting pressure on it. Sebastian took off the leather jacket as carefully as he could.

"Some of these are still bleeding," James said, strain visible as his mouth formed a tight line.

"It's okay." Sebastian didn't want to cause undue stress. He knew James was afraid of anything bad happening to him. The bite wasn't serious, but that didn't mean James's reaction wouldn't spiral. "Why don't you try the spell you used in all our blood-magic rituals to stop the bleeding?"

"That's a good idea." James's face relaxed a fraction. He uncovered Sebastian's wrist and performed the spell, which clotted the wounds and prompted Sebastian's natural healing to start.

The cuts weren't going to close and disappear before their eyes. That kind of magical healing wasn't possible, but something was much better than nothing, and after a moment, the bleeding seemed to stop.

The spell working confirmed that the bite wasn't that bad. Simple magic like that wouldn't help a more severe injury.

James delved into his first-aid kit and pulled out some bandages. "I've never seen shades act like that."

"Me either." Sebastian wasn't going to deny how worrying the behavior was. "They were way stronger than usual."

James grunted in agreement, most of his attention fixed on covering the larger cuts on Sebastian's wrist. After wiping the remaining blood away, James wrapped the wounds with gauze. "We can still get a doctor to take a look."

Sebastian examined his bandage. "I think we're good after that spell."

James nodded reluctantly. "Okay, but fuck. You really didn't need this on top of everything else."

"It hasn't been my best night. But we still got free today." Sebastian refused to accept everything going wrong since leaving Storm House as a sign. It didn't mean anything.

He was overwhelmed by the events of the last day. The

transfer spell, the explosion, being crushed by shades, James almost draining himself to death. Too much had been packed into those twenty-four hours, and after all of it, his future yawned in front of him, blank and uncertain like the biggest horror of all.

He had no idea what would happen next or what he wanted to happen. He didn't know if his anxiety in the diner would come back every time he was in a situation like that. He didn't want to think about any of it.

"Yeah, we're still free," James agreed, though he didn't look as happy about it as earlier. His posture was tense and worry lined his eyes.

Sebastian didn't like to see James stressed, but he was glad he'd suffered the bite, not James, especially after how much James had risked fighting against the horde of shades at Storm House.

"Come here." Sebastian pulled James close, knowing James was likely worrying as much as he was. They could be quite the pair.

James melted into Sebastian's arms, cradling Sebastian around the waist. They might be plagued with fears, but they could still comfort each other. The promises they'd made at Storm House weren't empty. Sebastian wanted to keep them and hoped James wouldn't change his mind about wanting him so he'd get the chance to try.

"James?" Sebastian whispered.

James pulled him tight, kissing his cheek like he understood what was behind the plea. "I've got you, Sebastian." James's voice was tinged with desperation, almost like he was reminding himself things were all right.

Sebastian needed the reminder too. He needed James's closeness while he could still have it. He tilted James's face upward and kissed him.

James groaned, the sound raw. It fueled Sebastian's need to connect with James and revel in the fact that this man liked him, wanted to protect him and build a future with him. Even if all that scared Sebastian and felt out of reach, he wanted to live in a world where it was all possible, even if that world only existed for as long as this kiss.

James pulled Sebastian into the bedroom and guided him to sit at the end of the bed. "Nothing else bad will happen to either of us. Not after beating this curse." It wasn't a promise James could make, but his adamant tone showed how much he cared about Sebastian. At least right now.

"No, I won't let it," Sebastian promised in return, determined not to let his problems cause James any more grief.

James stood between Sebastian's legs and leaned in to kiss him. Sebastian accepted needily. He didn't think he'd ever get over touching or being touched by James. After so long alone it was hard not to constantly wrap himself up in James. He needed affection more than ever, and he'd always been touch-starved. Only in these intimate moments did Sebastian let himself loose. He pulled James to him like he'd never let go and lost himself in feeling wanted and cared for by another person.

The two of them coming together was so much more than sex. Not that Sebastian would admit that aloud. He was terrified of James finding out how intense his reactions were. Having James's naked body pressed against his was about more than getting off. More than finally having sex after six years of isolation. More even than finally getting to kiss the person he'd crushed on for most of his life. Touching had become primal. Being skin on skin created a life force of its own, and Sebastian thought he'd die without it.

He yanked James's shirt up, needing to be closer.

"Careful." James touched Sebastian's wrist before taking his shirt the rest of the way off, followed by Sebastian's.

Sebastian had forgotten his injury. He was already hard, squirming where he sat. His hunger for James would never be satisfied. Maybe that was down to the isolation or the fact that

Sebastian's sexual experience had been limited before his imprisonment, but sex with James was different from anything he'd had before.

Twenty had been too young to be cut off from the world. He'd only started coming into himself. His intimate experiences had been fumbling and exploring without a lot of thinking. That sex had been fun, but it should have been the beginning for him, not the sum of his experience.

This was so much more than fun. No one turned Sebastian on like James. He'd acted like seducing James was a game because part of him had needed to see it that way so the risk of rejection wouldn't stop him in his tracks. But they were past that now, and James couldn't seem to get enough of him either.

Sebastian pulled James onto the bed. "Please." He could never help begging.

James's reactions were worth it. Sometimes he got this look like he was in awe of Sebastian, like he thought Sebastian was special. He was doing it now, his fingers tangling in Sebastian's curls like he was afraid to let go.

They kissed like two people who'd just survived the most traumatic event of their lives. Not the most recent shade attack. That was just a momentary scare. The curse was the real terror.

Sebastian managed to keep his injured arm out of the way, but only just. He wasn't thinking about anything but touching the man in bed with him as much as possible.

"Please," Sebastian begged again. He needed James closer. Needed to be consumed by him but couldn't find the words to convey his exact desires.

James seemed to understand him anyway. He undressed them both and settled on top of Sebastian like he was meant to be there, only breaking their kiss when they were heaving for breath.

James pulled back and looked down at Sebastian as if he were about to devour him. It was exactly what Sebastian wanted. He ran a hand over James's lean muscles, his chest and defined pecs, his tight stomach, and down to his thick cock. James closed his eyes at the touch, rocking into Sebastian's fist, rubbing tantalizingly against Sebastian as he moved.

"James, I need you," Sebastian whispered. He needed to be held more than he needed air. He wanted James to crush him into the mattress and fuck him forever. He never wanted to be alone again, to always have James touching and kissing him, to not have a single moment apart. It was unhealthy and consuming, but Sebastian didn't care.

He knew he couldn't have James for the rest of his life, but it didn't stop him from wishing. "Please, James," he begged without a shred of shame.

"I've got you." James kissed down Sebastian's body with a fervor that said his need was just as consuming. His mouth was wicked, biting and sucking every bit of Sebastian he could reach.

Sebastian writhed, his breath heaving. His whole body tingled and sparked. He buried his hands in James's hair, not restricting his movements, just needing the extra connection.

James groaned when his mouth reached Sebastian's leaking cock. "Already so wet for me."

Sebastian's cheeks burned.

James licked the precum off Sebastian's stomach. Sebastian shivered and moaned as James sucked him down, but James didn't keep his mouth on Sebastian's cock for long. He hitched Sebastian's legs up, hands under his knees, elbows braced on the bed, practically bending Sebastian in half. James moved his mouth lower, licking and kissing Sebastian's balls before turning his attention to Sebastian's hole.

The way James ate him drove Sebastian out of his mind. It made him feel so cherished he feared he'd burst. It felt so good to be spoiled and lavished with pleasure. To be connected to someone so intimately and to have that someone be James.

James licked and kissed, giving Sebastian endless open-mouth caresses, pressing his tongue into Sebastian's entrance and moaning every time Sebastian pressed himself harder against James's mouth. James seemed determined to get Sebastian off by eating his ass and nothing else. He could have, but Sebastian didn't want to come before James was inside him.

"Fuck me," Sebastian gasped. "Now. I need you."

James released him, sitting up on his knees. "You're so hot when you're desperate."

Sebastian huffed, but it came out more like a moan.

"Don't worry, I won't make you wait." James smiled, running a hand down Sebastian's chest. He climbed off the bed and opened his bedside table drawer. He quickly rolled on a condom. Back on the bed, he lubed his fingers and began working Sebastian open. "There you go. Just what you need." His expression was hazy with lust but not without tenderness. It was a look Sebastian had never seen before.

Sebastian nodded in agreement. James was what he needed. His breaths came out in a steady pant, sweat lining his brow. "*James*," he pleaded just as he thought he'd die of anticipation. James's fingers felt so good, but they weren't enough.

James was always eager to please. In bed, he acted like Sebastian lit his world and he'd do anything to keep him shining, like he'd do anything Sebastian asked of him. Having that power should have made Sebastian arrogant, but instead, it made him feel loved. Which was absurd in itself. There was no way James loved him. It only felt like it because Sebastian had never had a truly attentive sexual partner before. And James always knew just what to do to drive him wild.

James aligned his dick with Sebastian's needy hole and Sebastian spread his legs wide. They hadn't fucked in this position before, with Sebastian on his back. As James bore down, pushing in and filling Sebastian with that pleasurable burn and stretch, Sebastian didn't think anything had ever felt this good.

He wrapped his legs around James, pulling him in until

James's dick sat fully inside him. James brushed Sebastian's hair back and kissed him, the gesture almost unbearably tender. Sebastian gripped the back of James's neck with his uninjured hand, holding him close, and moaned as James began to rock his hips at a slow, steady pace.

Sebastian had initially intended on demanding a hard fuck. James excelled at taking him apart with punishing thrusts and firm hands, but as James kissed him, his tongue in Sebastian's mouth, and rolled his hips in the most sensual rhythm, Sebastian realized hard wasn't what he needed.

James stroked Sebastian's hair as he worked his hips, looking down at Sebastian with so much emotion in his eyes. He pressed their foreheads together and let their breath mingle, their moans unmuffled.

Sebastian lost himself in James's tender touches. The slow build of pleasure opened his heart and laid him bare. It felt like they were making love. This wasn't fucking but a promise of more, a pledge from James to give Sebastian all his delicate feelings, all his secrets, his futures, his pleasure, and his joy.

It felt like a shift in their relationship, an acknowledgment that there could be something lasting between them. They weren't just two men trapped together burning off steam and giving in to sexual tension to get off.

Sebastian loved it. It was everything the clingy, lonely part of him needed. Sebastian held nothing back. How could he when James seemed to be pouring his heart out with every touch?

"I need you, James." Sebastian tightened a hand in James's hair.

"Oh, Sebastian, sweetheart, I need you too," James crooned in his ear.

Sebastian's heart skipped. He'd never been anyone's sweetheart before, and there was no one he wanted that with more than James. He tried to reply, but words failed him. He only managed a strangled moan.

James looked into Sebastian's eyes. Sebastian released another exposing sound, and James seemed to soak it up. He took Sebastian's straining cock in his hand and let out a deep, satisfied groan.

It only took a few strokes before Sebastian came all over James's fist. He held James tight as pleasure took him, forgetting his injury and feeling nothing but good things as he clung to everything James offered.

James moaned, his thrusts becoming more desperate as he chased his release. He came saying Sebastian's name, the sound so sweet and sexy Sebastian almost couldn't take it. He wanted to keep James forever. He needed more of this, wanted nothing between them, nothing hidden, not even their most embarrassing thoughts or desires.

Sebastian knew he was in trouble. He couldn't have that without telling James the truths that risked destroying all their newfound closeness. Really, Sebastian shouldn't have let James fuck him so sweetly with such a big secret hanging between them.

But James was the good one, not Sebastian.

He held James close, not ready to let him go or move on to what came next. James seemed happy to stay where he was, nuzzling Sebastian's neck. If only they could stay in bed forever, things would be perfect.

CHAPTER THREE

EVENTUALLY, they got up and dressed. Eli was due home soon, and Sebastian didn't think it would make the best impression if Eli found him and James lounging around naked.

They went downstairs to the compact kitchen at the back of the house. A good portion of the house's decor was dated, but not in the way things at Storm House were. Sebastian's family's manor had collected relics marking each of the eight decades since the place was built because the Storms never threw anything away. James's home seemed more like a family residence that he hadn't wanted to completely make his own. The decorative plates mounted on the kitchen wall didn't scream a James Gray aesthetic.

"They were my grandmother's," James explained in response to Sebastian's staring.

Sebastian leaned awkwardly against the counter, pulling the leather jacket close. "This was her house?"

"Yeah." James filled an electric kettle with water and flipped it on, then grabbed a couple of mugs and a box of tea bags. "She and Grandpa sold our parents' house. Eli and I both preferred living here after. It was easier than being home, so there was no real reason to keep it."

James meant after his parents died. There was no need to specify for clarity, but Sebastian wondered if avoiding saying it was born out of the grief James still felt. Sebastian's heart sank at the reminder. The last of his post-sex happiness was gone. It wasn't fair James had lost loving parents. Even if it was fourteen years ago, it wasn't the kind of experience that ever left you.

"Chamomile?" James asked, holding up a tea bag.

"Sure." Sebastian turned away and watched the kettle come to a boil. Now was the time to tell James what he'd been holding back. The longer he put it off, the worse it would be when he finally opened up.

"Do you think there's any risk in getting Eli and Parker to break the secret-binding spell so we can tell them what happened?" James poured the hot water as he spoke, his frown unrelenting and brow deeply furrowed.

"No." Sebastian was glad for the change in topic. He could tell James his secrets tomorrow. They had more pressing things to worry about tonight. "Breaking the binding trapped you, but we aren't at Storm House. I don't think the curse can consume anyone outside the property when the magic is tied to the land. I don't see how it could get to Eli or Parker from here, even if we break the binding and spill the secret."

"It makes sense for the curse's reach to have limits," James agreed before blowing on his tea. "You can't be trapped there if you're already outside the walls."

Sebastian picked up his warm mug. "We can tell them not to go onto the Storm House grounds in case the curse tries to grab them if they get too close. But worst-case scenario, we know how to free anyone who gets trapped."

"True." James sipped his tea. "But it's not like I expect to get trapped again if I walk back onto the property. I doubt the curse can grab anyone new if they're out of range when they learn the secret, even if they go to Storm House later."

Sebastian put down his mug with a *thunk*. "Why would you go back to Storm House?"

James gave him a confused look. "We'll have to at some point."

"Why?" Dread pooled in Sebastian's gut.

"We've got to feed the chickens," James said reasonably. "And we can't abandon Miss Moo. Plus, you probably want to get some clothes and things." James didn't remind him that they would have to address the curse and look for a more permanent solution to the imbalance. They'd have to go onto the property to achieve that.

Logically, Sebastian knew he had to go back. He knew he wouldn't be trapped again, not after the successful transfer. But returning to Storm House felt like certain doom.

James shifted closer to Sebastian until their shoulders touched. "I can feed the chickens for you."

"You shouldn't have to do favors for me," Sebastian muttered. He already felt guilty, and every kind thing James did for him made it worse.

James took Sebastian's hand. "If going back to Storm House is triggering for you, then it's a favor I insist on."

Fuck, James was going to kill Sebastian with all this unconditional kindness and support. It only made what Sebastian was hiding feel worse. He shouldn't accept. He needed to tell James what he knew about his parents' deaths. He never should have hidden what he'd learned, but that day in the sitting room, staring down at that old newspaper, Sebastian had wanted to protect James from the truth.

He'd wanted to protect himself too and had needed to get a handle on his feelings before opening himself up to James. Now, those excuses had worn thin. Nothing but fear and guilt held him back.

"Let's worry about the chickens in the morning." Sebastian pushed his other thoughts away.

Before James could answer, the front door opened, and Eli called out, "James?"

"In here," he called back.

A moment later, Parker and Eli joined them in the kitchen.

"I can't believe you came to the diner and didn't say hi." Parker crossed his arms. He was built like a brick wall, thicker than James and taller than Sebastian, who'd always found him intimidating.

"We didn't stay long," James explained, leaving it at that and not revealing the reason they'd left so abruptly. Sebastian's insides twisted, constricted by the pain of more undeserved kindness.

"Never mind not saying hi." Eli pushed in front of Parker with a dismissive wave, coming to stand in the middle of the small room. "What's been going on?"

"There's a reason I can't tell you." Exasperation laced James's words, then he clamped his mouth shut and turned to Sebastian, his eyes wide. Neither of them would have been able to say that before transferring the cruse.

"What's that look?" Eli pointed at his brother. "Why are you being weird?"

Sebastian considered how best to test the weakened secret-binding. "We can't tell you why we're being weird, but there is a reason. We just can't explain it. Why do you think that is?"

Eli glared. "Because you're hiding something."

"Or?" Sebastian waved his hand encouragingly, making a significant face that relied heavily on eyebrow motion.

Eli scrunched his nose. "Or you're playing some sort of a game."

"This is serious," James scolded, bringing out his most severe frown. "None of us is playing games."

"Well, excuse me," Eli sneered like he had reached the end of his patience. "I don't see why I have to *guess* the reason behind you suddenly having a different personality. You don't keep secrets, James. I have no idea why you'd be like this."

Sebastian leaned closer to James. They had to try something else. "Please tell me you have the books."

"I think so. Otherwise, I might go break into the library." James stalked out of the room.

Eli and Parker glared at Sebastian.

"What did you do to him?" Eli asked.

"Nothing." Sebastian's face went red with shame. "I just needed him to help me."

The comment confused Eli while Parker looked unmoved.

James returned carrying a pile of books. He began dropping them on the floor one by one. As he reached the second to last book, his movements became jerky, like he was fighting with himself. After a moment of struggle, he threw the book at Parker.

"The fuck?" Parker caught the book before it hit him in the face. He didn't look at it as he went to set it on the counter beside him.

"No!" James and Sebastian called out in unison, both of them lunging forward.

Parker froze. He looked sideways at Eli. The younger man grabbed the book from Parker's hand and began flipping through it.

After a few minutes, he looked up in horror. "No way. It can't — Your tongues are bound?"

James dropped the remaining book to the floor and smiled.

Sebastian reached out and patted Eli's shoulder. "See, when James asked me that, I kissed him because I was so happy. Don't think I'll make that offer this time though."

Eli shook his head, maybe trying to dislodge thoughts of his brother kissing. He set the book aside. "So that's the reason you can't explain?"

Sebastian and James couldn't confirm verbally, but Sebastian did his best to look agreeable.

There was a flurry of questions from Eli, most of which received no answers. In the end, Parker looked up an unbinding spell in one of Eli's old magical theory books and wasted no time performing the ritual on James and Sebastian. Parker had a strong enough magical ability to do the spell without linking to anyone. After moving to the living room and shifting the coffee table out of the way, the spell went quickly, the magic binding James and Sebastian to secrecy no longer strong enough to force them to flee as it had done to Sebastian.

He tried not to think too hard about that night in the ballroom. He didn't need to be fantasizing about James and those handcuffs with others in the room. It really had been way too much fun for such serious magic.

James wiped the blood from his and Sebastian's bodies after the spell was done and told his brother and Parker everything. Eli looked more horrified the longer the explanation went on. Parker just looked pissed off.

"Oh my god, James." Eli flung himself at his brother and hugged him.

Sebastian had the uncomfortable sensation of watching from the outside, knowing he'd never be let in. He'd never have a family bond like the Gray brothers. His own mother had sacrificed him to save her firstborn, and his sister had always been unconcerned with the vast difference in how the two of them were treated.

Eli released James and turned to Sebastian. Before Sebastian knew what was happening, Eli was wrapped around him, squeezing the air out of him. "I can't believe you were stuck out there all this time." He gave Sebastian one final squeeze and stepped back like he was reluctant to let go.

"Oh." Sebastian had no idea how to respond.

Eli's eyes shone with unshed tears. "I'm so sorry."

"Why? You didn't trap me?"

"No," Parker cut in, putting an arm around Eli. "But we never questioned you being out there. I knew your uncle used to get stuff delivered from the diner and never came into town. I should have thought it was unusual that you were exactly the same. I should have questioned it."

Sebastian squirmed. He shot a helpless look at James, not knowing what to say. He knew most people in Moonlight Falls wrote him off as a loner. He'd been angsty as a kid and had acted out to get attention. It was typical behavior, given he'd experienced a lot of neglect growing up. But people didn't necessarily know that. They'd never liked him, and his childhood antics had obviously fed into the belief he was someone who'd shut himself away.

He didn't know how to take Parker's apology. There was nothing to apologize for. Even the few people who'd known what had been behind his childhood behavior hadn't seen past the curse.

"The secret was more tightly bound before now," he explained. "Even if you'd questioned me, asked why I didn't come into town, or asked why my uncle was the same, I would have lied. James asked, and I acted exactly like a recluse would and pushed him away. There was no way anyone would have been able to guess I didn't want to be at Storm House when I was forced to say I wanted to be there."

"But James did guess," Parker pointed out.

Even though Parker didn't know it, his words were a painful reminder of how much of a miracle it was that James had figured any of this out. Sebastian couldn't stop from reaching for James, who reflexively pulled him close.

Sebastian was positive no one but James would have figured out what was happening at Storm House. No one cared like James. Nobody else would have looked past Sebastian's confusing

—secret-binding induced—behavior and been patient with him or tried to understand him.

Without James, Sebastian would have nothing. He owned him more than he could ever repay, but he needed to start trying.

34

CHAPTER FOUR

The next morning, Sebastian woke up feeling groggy.

"I should get ready for work," James said from beside him in bed.

Sebastian forced his eyes to remain open. "Hmm?"

"You know, work." James stretched and stood with a sigh before opening the curtains, letting in the meager sunlight. "I'll go feed the chickens first. Then, I need to talk to Hazel and explain everything. I'll bring *The Magical Tales*."

Sebastian rubbed his eyes, trying to get his brain to absorb what James was talking about. "You shouldn't need the books."

James stopped on the way to the bathroom. "You think? Even after last time?"

Sebastian shook off his haziness. "The curse and the secret-binding are linked. That's how you got trapped, but now that we've escaped and the curse can't reach us, I doubt the secret can rebind itself. We've broken the feedback loop as well as the silencing spell this time."

"True." James rubbed his chin. He seemed satisfied with the logic. "Will you be all right here today? While I'm gone."

James asked the question without any judgment. Sebastian

had no doubt he would rearrange his day if Sebastian admitted he didn't want to be alone. "I'll be fine," he lied, giving his best exasperated look.

"Great. And hey, feel free to go back to sleep. Have a relaxing day. You deserve it." James gave him an affectionate grin before disappearing into the bathroom.

Sebastian sank back into bed. He hadn't considered what he'd do while James was at work. It's not like he thought he'd go to the electrical shop with James. It wasn't normal for them to spend every second together, and feeling abandoned because he had to spend the day alone wasn't healthy, but it was exactly how he felt.

What was he supposed to do with himself? He didn't have a job. He had no friends. Reflexively, Sebastian's mind started running through all the chores he had to do at Storm House. He'd put off the laundry and needed to make the last batch of apricot jam. It was time to bake more bread. The garden always needed weeding, and he hadn't been clipping the newspapers while James was there.

He shook himself. He didn't have to do any of that anymore. He could throw his clothes in a washing machine and buy bread at the General Store in town. Hell, he could buy pumpkins and tomatoes and not have to grow his own. He never had to weed anything ever again if he didn't want, and he'd probably never look at a physical newspaper again.

Sebastian thought it would be a relief. Living at Storm House took so much work, and he'd begrudged almost all of it. But having nothing meaningful to do left him empty. He didn't know if he wanted to buy bread. What if it wasn't as good as his? He loved that first fresh slice when the loaf was still warm. It was more than worth the effort.

Tears prickled Sebastian's eyes. He wiped them away in frustration. Was he missing Storm House? That was fucking ridiculous. He never wanted to see the cursed place again.

He'd bake bread here, and everything would be fine.

Sebastian showered after James and dressed in the same clothes he'd worn yesterday. He went downstairs to find James in the kitchen eating cereal.

"Coffee's in the pot." James pointed with his spoon to the coffee maker.

"Thanks." Sebastian helped himself.

"I should run." James rinsed his empty bowl and checked the time on his phone. "Don't want the chickens to make me late. I'm not worried, but I'll text you after I'm done at Storm House to confirm I got off the property okay. If you don't hear from me, assume I got stuck somehow."

"Wait." Sebastian's heart rate picked up. He didn't want James to go. He wasn't ready to be left yet. Not that he was going to say any of that aloud. "Um." He paused. "I don't have a phone."

"Oh." James laughed. "Of course not. Why don't we drive down to Apple Valley and get you one later? I'll see if I can leave work early, but it might be best not to ask after I've left Hazel on her own for weeks."

Sebastian nodded, trying not to feel like a sad puppy facing a whole day without his only companion. He didn't want James to know how much this was bothering him. "Good luck with Hazel," was all he said as he handed over the key to Storm House's gate.

"I'll need it. Think she might be madder at me than Eli was." James leaned in and kissed Sebastian on the cheek. "See you back here at five, okay? Four if I'm lucky."

"Uh-huh. Yep." Sebastian tried to sound normal. Like he wasn't dreading the day.

And then James was gone. His absence settled in Sebastian's chest.

He poured some cereal and got the milk out of the fridge. His first bite was good. He hadn't had cereal in years. The second bite made him wrinkle his nose.

He set the bowl down. *"Ugh."*

"Not a fan?"

Sebastian whirled around to see Eli standing in the doorway. "I forgot you were here."

Eli gravitated toward the coffee. "Yeah, well, I don't spend every night with Parker."

Sebastian frowned. He probably shouldn't spend every night with James either. Now that they weren't fellow prisoners, there was no reason for them to live together. It was too soon to move in with James. Sebastian needed his own place.

He didn't *want* his own place. The idea of living alone again made him faintly sick. Though maybe that was the milk. He wasn't used to having it, and the cereal didn't do enough to disguise the flavor he was no longer accustomed to. It was just another thing he'd thought he missed but had apparently moved on from.

It was like he wasn't even the same person anymore. And that was fine. People changed, but he didn't know who he was outside Storm House.

"You can have some toast if the cereal is upsetting you."

"What?" Sebastian felt like he'd forgotten how to carry on a conversation. Why hadn't he been this thrown off with James? Everything between them was so easy.

Eli bit back a smile. "You're looking at that bowl like it wronged you."

Sebastian tried not to glare at the cereal. "I shouldn't waste it."

"Here." Eli picked up the bowl. "I was gonna have some anyway." He grabbed a new spoon and dug into Sebastian's abandoned breakfast.

Sebastian busied himself making toast with the store-bought bread sitting on the counter. How had he missed this? So what if it was pre-sliced? His bread looked way better.

"So, I was thinking," Eli said when the cereal was gone. "I want to check out those veins of power you told us about."

Sebastian tensed. "Why?"

"I study them." Eli raised his brows like Sebastian should have known this. "I'm doing my master's thesis on the fixed vein in town. But now that you said there are two *intersecting*, fixed veins, I might need to change my project."

Sebastian nibbled his toast. It tasted okay, not great. "What's the mess on my property got to do with your research?"

"I have a theory." Eli bounced excitedly on the balls of his feet. "Last night, I was thinking—the reason I'm studying the vein running through Moonlight Falls is because it behaves unlike other fixed veins. There's no record of a second vein here. Its presence could be the reason the magic is different. Fixed intersections are the rarest of rare, as far as vein formations go. Hardly any studies have been done on them, and surely one of the veins on your property is connected to the one in town. I could probably do a whole PhD on this."

"Wow, okay." Sebastian tried to sound enthusiastic, even if the idea of PhD-level research on anything to do with magic made his head ache. "The only issue is my long-dead relatives already messed with the veins. The instability is really dangerous."

"But the fuel cell is holding it all together."

"Yes and no." Sebastian took a fortifying sip of coffee. "Messing with the veins, even stabilized, has consequences. The magic responds, and don't get me started on how it riles up the shades."

Eli gave him a funny look. "I'm not going to go out there at night."

Sebastian ran a hand through his hair. This was too risky. The transfer spell had caused the veins to explode with power. There was no way Sebastian could predict what Eli poking around might trigger.

"The magic could be dangerous regardless of the shades. It knocked James and me around pretty badly."

"But you handled it." Eli crossed his arms like he was gearing up to argue. "Getting blasted off my feet won't be the end of the world. Not when the research potential is this extraordinary. I can handle myself."

Eli was right. Getting knocked over wasn't the end of the world, but far worse could happen. Except Sebastian couldn't explain how dangerous the veins were to Eli when he was still hiding it from James.

"Let's talk to the others tonight and see what they think," Sebastian said to put Eli off. "Just don't go out to Storm House without telling me."

"Of course not. I'm not going to trespass. If I'm doing research, I need permits and permission." Eli's expression turned dreamy. "This is going to be great. A more complex research project is exactly what I was looking for to kick off my career. And you and I can hang out more if you want to see what I'm doing. I promise it'll be fun. Veins are so interesting."

"Sure." Sebastian was knocked for a loop by Eli's desire to include him. It was like he assumed the two of them would become friends.

Seeming happy with their discussion, Eli left to shower and get ready for his day.

Sebastian couldn't help wondering what Eli would think of him when he learned the truth about his parents' deaths. He might not be so keen on friendship then.

James and Eli's parents died in a car accident out on North Road. Sebastian had had no idea how close the crash site had been to Storm House until he'd found that old newspaper tucked away in his upstairs sitting room. The article he'd read had mentioned the mile marker where the car had been found the morning after the crash: September 23, 2009. Meaning the crash happened late at night on the twenty-second, the same night Uncle Stephen and his mom had transferred the curse from his sister Kira to him.

Sebastian had found the notes on the curse transfer spell tucked next to the article about the Grays' deaths. He could imagine Stephen reading the paper and putting it all together. The blast that had emanated from the veins that night, knocking them all down. The loud noise Sebastian had sworn he'd heard off in the woods. At the time, he hadn't known what it was and had wondered if he'd imagined it or if it had just been the energy exploding, but the article cleared that right up.

They'd heard the car crash, but with all the chaotic magic, no one had realized the noise had come from the road beyond.

The blast had knocked the Grays' car off the road, smashing it into a tree. The speed at which the vehicle had been traveling, combined with the impact of the blast, would have created a much more forceful impact than anything the Storms had experienced in the clearing. The car hadn't lost control, as the article stated. The crash was their fault. Sebastian's fault. His family's fault. They had killed two innocent people that night, all so Kira could be saved from Storm House. They'd been so reckless with magic that they hadn't even noticed its consequences.

After realizing what they'd done, Stephen must have tucked the instructions inside the paper. Sebastian remembered his uncle acting unlike himself a few days after they'd done the spell, when the article would have appeared. Stephen had been upset and angry at Sebastian's mom when they'd left to go back to Phoenix. This had to be why. No wonder Stephen hadn't gone back for the instructions or clipped the article and archived it. He'd probably wanted to forget it ever happened.

But it had happened, and Sebastian knew. He should have told James that day in the dusty sitting room, let James piece it together as he had. Instead, he'd hidden the truth and stopped James from looking at the paper. He'd let James be excited they'd found the instructions. But he couldn't keep this from James forever. Especially not if Eli wanted to go messing with the veins. Sebastian wouldn't let Storm House kill any more of James's family.

The curse had ruined both their lives, taken their childhoods, and twisted them in different but equally traumatizing directions. James should never have had to bear the burden of his parents' deaths, and he had a right to know that the man he wanted a relationship with was at the root of all his heartache, the reason he had to grieve his parents at fourteen, the cause of his anxiety and fear over losing people. He had a right to know all of it and decide for himself how much more of Sebastian and this curse he really wanted in his life.

Sebastian cleaned up the breakfast dishes, his mood the lowest it had been since James had started coming to Storm House. He hadn't expected to feel like this so soon after finding freedom. He needed to do something to keep his mind occupied so he didn't get stuck in a downward spiral.

Before going out for the day, Eli had let Sebastian know he'd gotten a text from James saying he was at work and hadn't had trouble feeding the chickens and leaving Storm House. This should have comforted Sebastian, but the idea of returning to the house still made his chest pinch.

He decided to make some bread. Baking soothed him. He enjoyed it, and there was no reason to give up the hobby just because he could go to the store and buy things. He dug around in the cupboards, looking for everything he needed, wondering when exactly baking had turned from a chore to a hobby.

He'd learned to cook with his uncle and had been uninterested at the time. But he'd gone along with it because there hadn't been a lot of other distractions at a house with no TV, video games, or internet. Then, when he'd first been trapped on his own, he'd resented having to do everything by hand and had grumbled about every meal he made. He knew then that his uncle had used all those cooking lessons to secretly prepare him to survive being isolated in the outdated house.

Now, he was choosing to bake, hoping it would make him feel better. It made no sense.

After a thorough search of the kitchen, Sebastian's fresh bread plan was thwarted. James and Eli didn't have any yeast. Sebastian could bake something else, like sugar cookies, peanut butter cookies, banana bread, the list went on, but he'd been set on plain old bread.

He supposed he could walk to the General Store and buy dried yeast. How often had he wished he could easily go grab something he'd run out of? Sebastian kept Storm House well stocked with essentials, but he'd often run out of his treats. He'd be dying for a potato chip and would have to wait weeks for his next bulk order to arrive.

James had left Sebastian a spare key and his laptop in case Sebastian wanted to go online. He placed the key in his pocket before slipping James's jacket on. He had no idea what to even do on the internet anymore. He had no one to message. So he was going out instead.

Sebastian walked to the front door. Nerves fluttered uncomfortably inside him. He didn't understand why. Walking the few blocks to the town center was no big deal. He didn't particularly want to be alone in James's house all day, so why was it equally hard to go out?

He opened the door, annoyed with himself. Pushing away his discomfort, he locked up behind him, shoved his hands in his pockets, and stalked down the street.

Wandering Moonlight Falls didn't exactly bring back good memories after being banished here during summers growing up. Sebastian briefly wondered if he should call his mom. What would she think of his escape? It was doubtful she'd be happy about it. She'd probably fear the curse coming back on Kira. That was all she'd ever cared about.

Fallen leaves coated the sidewalks. If Sebastian didn't look at Moonlight Falls through a personal lens, he could acknowledge its charm. The town was quaint and well looked after. It was the kind of place tourists like for its character. The shades and spookiness were a big part of Moonlight Falls, but that didn't mean the place had to look uninviting or rundown. Cute with a hint of creepy was the general aesthetic.

Sebastian passed the small elementary school and the bed and breakfast. The ice cream shop on the corner wasn't open yet. The diner was open on the other side of the street, but it didn't seem busy.

There weren't too many people out walking. Sebastian didn't come across anyone in his direct path, just a few dog walkers ahead of him. He spotted a couple of touristy types entering Beth's souvenir shop on the other side of the circle, but the post office, library, and town hall were all quiet. It was a weekday morning, so most people would be at work and the kids in school. It made Sebastian glad he'd chosen this time to go out.

He entered the little grocery store next to Moonlight Diner. The place hadn't changed since the last time Sebastian had been in, and he found the yeast without any trouble. Sebastian was the only shopper, so he should have been relaxed.

He wasn't. Something about being here made him distinctly uncomfortable. He was on edge, and it wasn't a feeling he was used to. Was he just worried people would come in and startle him?

The cashier was reading a book at the register. As he approached, she put it down with a smile. "Morning."

Sebastian didn't recognize her. She was young, probably in her early twenties, if he had to guess. "Hi." He set the yeast down.

"Just this?" She picked it up, her glittery nails catching the light.

Sebastian nodded, and she rang him up. He wasn't panicked like he'd been in the diner, but this interaction didn't feel typical.

He was beginning to suspect that nothing would feel like he remembered. This anxious, unsure state was starting to look like his new normal.

"Cash or credit?" the woman asked.

Sebastian froze. His whole body flashed hot in panicky embarrassment. He didn't have any fucking money. What a ridiculous thing to slip his mind. It was like he'd never functioned in human society before.

"I just realized I forgot my wallet," he muttered. For some reason, failing at this task made him want to cry. The reaction was extreme, and he knew it wasn't just about forgetting you needed money at the store. It was everything. Sebastian wished he'd never been stuck at Storm House and that none of these changes had happened to him. It wasn't fair.

"Oh." The woman gave a friendly chuckle. "I'd start you a tab, but I don't recognize you."

"That's okay. Sorry." Sebastian glanced over his shoulder toward the exit. "Maybe I'll be back later. Should I put this away for you?"

"No, it's fine," she waved his offer away. "I'm Carla, by the way."

"Sebastian," he said, trying not to squirm. He hurried out of the shop before she could say anything else.

CHAPTER FIVE

Sebastian found himself standing outside Gray Electrical. He couldn't face going back to James's house alone and was going to use checking how things went with Hazel as an excuse to pop in on James at work.

It wasn't like he would cling to James all day. He wanted to, but he'd drawn the line at that kind of codependence. He'd leave James and Hazel in peace after a quick hello and go to the library. He just couldn't make himself go to the library yet.

Sebastian was hoping to steal a hug from James. He needed a positive moment. Yes, he was being hopelessly needy and becoming addicted to James caring for him, but he didn't want to push what he could deal with after the store incident.

He probably needed to look into some therapy sooner rather than later if this was how everything was going to feel. But again, he couldn't quite find the energy to face doing it immediately.

The electrical shop's bell jingled as he opened the door.

James jumped up from a desk at the far end of the open-plan room. "Sebastian!" He beamed as if nothing pleased him more than seeing the man he'd barely had space from for weeks on end.

Hazel sat at a desk next to James. She got up more cautiously. "Hey, Sebastian, nice to see you."

James came around the counter to greet him. Sebastian got his hug and melted into James like he never wanted to part from him. Damn, it felt good.

Hazel leaned against the counter, watching them. She wore a flannel long-sleeve top over a T-shirt and well-worn jeans, her brown hair in a ponytail.

Sebastian pulled back from his hug reluctantly, glancing between Hazel and James. "Did you two talk already?"

Hazel raised a brow. "About the curse and you being a prisoner of that creepy-ass house? Yeah, we talked."

"Eventually." Concern stole the smile from James's lips. "My tongue was rebound."

Sebastian's heart sank. "But Parker broke the binding last night, and you haven't been trapped again. You went to the house and left."

James gave a grim laugh. "I still couldn't tell Hazel anything without flapping around, doing charades, and forcing *The Magical Tales* on her after looking them up on my phone. We had to do the ritual again."

"How is it possible the secret-binding is still in place?" Sebastian didn't actually expect either of them to have an answer. "You shouldn't have to break it for each person you tell."

James shook his head.

"Yeah, no idea." Hazel crossed her arms. "This all sounds like bad news."

Sebastian didn't know what it meant that they couldn't truly break the secret-binding spell. Away from the curse, he didn't see how it could keep retriggering.

"What happened there?" Hazel pointed to the bandage on Sebastian's wrist.

"Oh, um—" Sebastian's words failed as all the issues going to the diner had caused filled his mind. The mouthy shade seemed like the least of his worries. If he returned to the diner, would he be able to manage better, or would he still want to run away?

"A shade attacked in the park last night," James explained, detailing the unusual incident and how the shades resisted the light.

"Nope, I don't like any of this." Hazel scowled, her expression identical to the one Sebastian had often seen on James. "Night before last, a group of shades attacked a family in their car. They were fine. No one left the vehicle and the shades couldn't get in, but they could have crashed. And I heard there was some trouble on the east side of town last night."

"Were those shades unaffected by light?" Sebastian asked.

Hazel shrugged. "I'm not sure. But whatever's going on, it seems to be getting worse."

Sebastian glanced at James. He knew the veins riled up the shades on his property. Was it possible they affected the beasts in town? Maybe, maybe not. The shade that attacked him had been different. He'd never seen such a large, aggressive one at Storm House. Maybe it wasn't related to the veins. No amount of riling up could change a shade's nature or make it immune to light.

"We should report what happened last night," James said. "And I was thinking we should report the power imbalance at Storm House too, but that's going to be hard to do if the secret-binding keeps retying my tongue."

Sebastian rubbed his eyes. "You're right. We can't break the binding with someone over the phone. And it's going to be impossible to get an official to come out here and take a look at the property otherwise."

"I can call and report it," Hazel offered. "I shouldn't be prevented from telling people about Storm House. The curse couldn't have spread to me. Not when you two already broke free and can come and go from Storm House. So I don't see how it could bind my tongue if the two are connected like you said."

Relief loosened James's posture. "You're right. That would be great."

"Consider it done." Hazel patted her pockets like she was looking for her phone. "Why don't you guys take off?"

"What?" James scowled. "No. I've already left you alone too long."

Hazel made an exasperated noise. "But now I understand why. You were trapped, so it's not like you have to feel bad for abandoning the shop."

"But, Hazel—"

She cut him off. "It's fine. You should take a few days to recoup. There's no need to get straight back to work after what you went through. I'll see you back here on Monday at the earliest, James."

"Fine," he grumbled. "Let me know how reporting the curse goes."

"Will do." She headed back to her desk, finding her phone among some papers. "You guys want to go out for dinner tonight? I've been meeting Eli on Fridays while you were away, but he's working tonight." She sat down and looked between them expectantly.

"Not tonight," James replied without hesitation.

Sebastian's face heated. "You can go to dinner, James."

He turned to Sebastian, his expression soft. "Let's do something quieter than Friday night at the diner. We can go out to dinner with everyone another time or go to Parker's on Sunday if you feel like it."

Sebastian wanted to argue, but Hazel was watching. "Only if you want."

"All right, see you guys later," Hazel said in a clear dismissal.

With a wave to Hazel, James led the way outside. "You doing okay, Sebastian?" he asked once they were alone.

Sebastian stared blankly at the pumps containing Gray Electrical's fuel cells. "Is it obvious that I'm not?" He couldn't stop his gaze from darting back to James, checking his reaction.

James gave him a small smile. "You haven't teased me about anything in almost a day. It's not like you."

Sebastian startled himself with a laugh, his chest warming. "Noted. James likes the teasing." He shot James a sly smile before turning serious and briefly explaining his trip to the store. "I hate this. Everything different catches me off guard, and I don't know what to do. I know I shouldn't expect things to be the same as before, but I can't help it."

James put an arm around Sebastian's shoulders. "Your time at Storm House affected you. That's normal. It had to be a traumatic experience, and of course, you're going to be upset with how being isolated changed you."

Sebastian bit his lip. "I know. I just wish I wasn't affected and that I wasn't upset about it. I want everything to do with Storm House to be over. I want to forget it ever happened." But that wasn't how life worked and wishing wouldn't help anything. "I think it'll be better when I get used to how I've changed. When it's not surprising me, maybe it'll be okay."

James hugged him close. "I think you're right. Not wanting your anxiety to exist doesn't usually help."

"No." Sebastian leaned in. He had to stop comparing himself to how he used to be and focus on his new reality. A task he didn't mind so much when his present included James.

James gave him a gentle kiss. "Anxiety can be managed. You'll get there. You'll figure out what works for you and what your new boundaries are. Just be patient. It's only been one day."

Sebastian appreciated the confidence and tried to let go of some of his frustration.

"Do you still want to go to Apple Valley to buy a phone?" James asked.

Sebastian gave the question the consideration it deserved, not just agreeing to do what he thought he should. "Yeah, let's go. I want to have a way of contacting people. I've missed technology. But if it's busy when we get there, I might stay in the truck."

James gave him another quick squeeze. "Sounds good. I can pop into the store while you wait."

Sebastian wiggled out of James's embrace and opened the truck door. "I'll get my lawyer to reimburse you for the phone, and I should probably arrange for some money to be put in an account so I can get a debit card. You know, rejoin typical modern life."

James walked around to the other side of the truck. "Don't worry about the phone. I owe you for all the new clothes."

Sebastian didn't need to be paid back for the clothing he'd bought James. He liked getting him things. But maybe it was for the best. Sebastian had to stop leaning on this relationship so heavily. It was too easy to let James be supportive and kind. Sebastian craved it but knew James might act differently if he knew what Sebastian was hiding.

Sebastian feared James blaming him for the Grays' deaths, even though part of him knew James was too understanding to blame the Storms completely. The deaths were still an accident, and without ill intent, Sebastian imagined James would be forgiving. That was the kind of guy James was. And while Sebastian could see him reacting that way, he struggled to believe it.

James seemed like he would understand, but what if he didn't? Most of the time Sebastian felt silly for thinking James could move past something like this.

The car accident never would have happened if the curse hadn't been transferred to Sebastian. He'd never be able to make up for that, and someone as kind as James deserved a partner who was just as good. Someone he didn't need to forgive. Someone he didn't have to choose despite the past.

No one ever picked Sebastian. Not even his own mother. How could he expect James to choose him when he had every reason not to?

THEY STOPPED by town hall before heading out.

The mayor of Moonlight Falls had always taken on the responsibility of dealing with shade issues and was tasked with keeping them from negatively impacting residents. The problem at Storm House would need to be reported to the official body of practitioners who helped citizens deal with magic state-wide. It wasn't the mayor's job to solve all magical problems, but keeping the shades a local matter worked best for everyone.

Outsiders had never understood Moonlight Falls, and bringing them in for things locals could deal with was always more trouble than it was worth.

Sebastian had never been inside town hall. James led the way like he knew exactly where to go. The place was quiet, and the administrator at the front desk waved James through without asking why he needed to see the mayor.

They walked down a narrow hall lined with offices. A door stood open at the back.

James knocked on the doorframe. "Eleanor?"

"Come in," called the woman within. She didn't look up from her computer.

Sebastian followed James, keeping a step behind. He hadn't wanted to wait in the truck and was more curious than anxious about being here. This was a side of Moonlight Falls he'd never seen before. Growing up, he'd avoided getting involved in the community as much as possible.

"Oh, James." Eleanor sagged in relief when she glanced up. "And—" She eyed Sebastian.

"This is Sebastian Storm." James put a hand on Sebastian's shoulder as he stepped forward. "Meet Eleanor Ashley."

"Storm?" The mayor's eyebrows rose. "How are things north of town?"

"They could be better," Sebastian admitted. Even if it wasn't the mayor's responsibility to address the imbalance at Storm House, he should probably tell her about it, given the potential for a deadly explosion.

Eleanor frowned like she wasn't pleased to hear Sebastian's complaint. "Why's that?"

Sebastian hesitated, his tongue rebound just as James's had been. They hadn't brought *The Magical Tales*, and even with the weakened secret-binding, he wouldn't be able to communicate anything useful without breaking the spell again.

"It's complicated," James supplied. He shared a significant glance with Sebastian. It seemed like James was still tongue-tied, even after having the spell broken twice. It really wasn't a good sign.

Eleanor sat up straighter. "Is trouble out at Storm House why you've come to see me?"

"No," James admitted, and together, he and Sebastian recounted the incident with the shade the night before.

The mayor's face hardened as the story went on. "Smart using fire," she said when they'd finished, nodding approvingly to Sebastian. "Glad to know that still works. There've been more than a few incidents lately. The last few nights have been a shit-show, and it's not like it was calm before that. The smashed lights. What happened to Eli not long ago."

Eleanor looked grim. Sebastian had no idea what had happened to Eli, but the scowl on James's face didn't bode well.

"I'm glad you came by, James," Eleanor continued. "I'm calling a meeting tonight to discuss the recent disturbances. I caught up with Hazel this morning, but if you could ask Parker to come along, I'd appreciate it if you were all there."

"Of course." James's agreement was quick. "Anything we can do."

The mayor nodded before turning her attention back to Sebastian. "Are the problems north of town shade related?"

Sebastian shifted under her sharp gaze. "No. But there have been a whole lot more of the beasts at the house than usual."

Eleanor didn't look pleased to hear it. "In that case, you'd better come to the meeting too. I want as much information about shade activity in the area as possible. It's a closed group, not a public session at this stage. I'm hoping we can figure out what the hell is going on before I address everyone. Too many people have been getting hurt to act like this is business as usual. We need a plan of attack."

Sebastian agreed to come to the meeting. He and James left Eleanor looking stressed, but hopefully, they'd be able to figure out something useful.

"All right, let's get me a phone." Sebastian jumped in a show of overdone excitement when they were outside. The interaction with the mayor pleased him, even though the situation was a downer. His mood had brightened more than he understood.

James's lips twitched. "There's a good burrito place I wouldn't mind stopping at for lunch too."

"Yes, definitely." Sebastian was more excited about the food than the cell phone. He remembered the place James was talking about. Their food was great, maybe not as good as the places he'd gone while living in San Diego for the year and a half of college he'd managed to attend before getting trapped, but he'd take it.

James drove them through town, heading south. Sebastian's mood continued to lift. Things felt more manageable now that he wasn't brooding by himself. He was apprehensive about the mayor's meeting, but he wanted to be there to see just how involved James was in Moonlight Falls. It sounded like James, Hazel, and Parker worked with the mayor often. Sebastian wasn't surprised. They were all typical Moonlighters.

For the first time, Sebastian wondered what it would be like to join them rather than shy away. Before James came to Storm House, Sebastian would have said he'd run far away from Moonlight Falls the second he escaped. That idea no longer had any appeal. The world was too big, and unknown things didn't excite Sebastian like they used to. He wanted a sense of familiarity with the places he went and the people he interacted with. He hoped it'd make his new anxiety easier to manage.

And he liked that the mayor had invited him to the meeting, including him in something important to the town.

He'd always wanted to be part of something bigger than himself, not just sitting on the outside watching. He'd spent his life on the fringes, alone while in Moonlight Falls and set apart from his mom and sister when he was at home. Knowing that he hadn't imagined being pushed away, that his mother had given him life and tolerated him only so he could take on the family curse, made him want to find his own place. With people who wanted him.

He'd never have thought that would happen for him in Moonlight Falls. He'd been so lonely there for so long, but understanding why his childhood had taken the shape it had might allow him to let go of his misplaced hate for the town.

For the first time, he could see potential in Moonlight Falls. Wouldn't it be great to take something he'd associated with pain and sadness and turn it into something good? Being happy here would be more satisfying than running away. He suspected nowhere else would feel quite right or give him a sense of completion and healing. Maybe he did understand what people meant when they said this place called to them.

Could Moonlight Falls turn into something good for Sebastian? Would it last, or would it come to an unfortunate end like everything else? It was a question he didn't want to dwell on. Instead, he chose to hold on to this hopeful feeling he'd found and pretend he didn't know better.

Within minutes, they were past the bulk of the town. The houses grew sparse, replaced by trees.

James drummed his fingers against the steering wheel. "Want to listen to the radio?"

"Are you going to start singing?" Sebastian teased.

"What? No." James took his eyes from the road briefly, glaring in a way that said he would *never*.

Sebastian laughed. Damn it, he really liked this man. Meaning he needed to get his shit together and talk to him and stop stealing all these sweet moments he hadn't earned.

If he could be hopeful about Moonlight Falls, could he be hopeful about James? He wasn't sure. It felt like pushing his luck, but he wanted to believe he wasn't doomed to be alone, that he wasn't cursed and wouldn't always be cast out.

"Let's get you caught up on the latest hits." James switched on the radio and selected a station.

"Once I learn the lyrics, I'm going to make you sing with me," Sebastian warned.

James pretended not to hear the threat, and Sebastian smiled at his feigned grumpiness.

Taller trees loomed ahead. The road was less windy down this way than up near Storm House, but once you got past the neighborhoods, the forest took over. Sebastian frowned at the music. He couldn't say he liked the song playing and wondered if he was destined to be an old man at heart after living in isolation. People enjoyed listening to this? What had happened while he was away?

A loud bang and the scream of crunching metal drowned out the music. Sebastian lurched forward in his seat, his seatbelt catching him, digging painfully into his neck and chest. His breath whooshed out of his lungs. The airbags deployed, and Sebastian smashed into them.

CHAPTER SIX

THEY'D STOPPED MOVING. Sebastian had no idea what had happened.

"James?" he called, pulling himself up and pushing the deflating airbag away.

"Yeah. I'm okay." James looked around in confusion, eyes darting from Sebastian to the steering wheel to the road. "We crashed? How did we crash? What's happening?" He sucked in a breath, then another, like he wasn't getting enough air.

"We're all right. Look at me." Sebastian grabbed his arm.

James focused on him, eyes wild.

Sebastian pushed the power button on the dash, turning off the truck and stopping the annoying music. "Are you hurt anywhere?"

James looked down at himself. "No. I don't think so." His breathing came in increasingly short, rapid breaths. "I could have killed us. Are you hurt? Did I hurt you?"

"No." Sebastian took James's unsteady hand. "I'm fine, just confused. I didn't see that coming. It definitely wasn't your fault."

James didn't look convinced. "*Sebastian.*" He sounded terrified.

"I'm okay. *You're* okay." He smiled at James, not breaking eye contact, trying to project a calm energy.

James took a deep breath and nodded. He kept his attention locked on Sebastian until he was breathing normally. "You're okay," he agreed at last, almost like he didn't believe it. "We're okay." His fear of losing Sebastian was written all over his face. He repeated his own words again with a little more confidence. "We're okay."

"We are," Sebastian murmured in reassurance as his pounding heart slowed to a normal rhythm. He was impressed with how well James was handling himself. A car accident had to be a worst-case scenario for his anxiety. Sebastian wanted to wrap him up and save him from all the world's uncertainties but settled for gripping his hand.

Once he was settled, James looked around. Sebastian followed suit, sensing James's need for support waning as the desire to figure out what happened intensified. There wasn't anything out the window. No other cars, nothing on the road. He unbuckled himself and jumped out, quickly circling around the back of the truck to James's side and opening his door.

"Here." He helped James out.

James shook and didn't seem as settled as he'd been a moment ago. Sebastian checked him over. At least he found no injuries.

James looked desperately at Sebastian. "I've never been in an accident before."

Sebastian hugged him. "Me either. But hey, we weren't going fast. We're fine."

James buried his face against Sebastian's neck. Any sort of accident would be traumatizing for him after what had happened to his parents, and having someone in the car with him would trigger all his fears about losing people. The poor man didn't need the added stress right now. He'd been through more than enough.

Sebastian held him close, trying not to think about being the cause of James's distress or that his family and their curse had done this to him.

After a long moment, James pulled back. He ran a hand through his short hair, expression hard and unsmiling. "What the hell happened?"

Sebastian looked around helplessly. They'd hit something, but what? The front of the truck was smashed, only there was nothing around. No deer or other animal, nothing fallen in the road.

James examined the damage to his truck. Given they had no idea what the hell they'd hit, it was wild that the whole front bumper was smashed, along with the headlights. Even the hood was crunched. "The truck looks like I drove straight into a wall."

"Like an invisible wall?" Sebastian tried to joke. His delivery failed and ice ran down his spine. Could it have been an invisible wall? No. What was he thinking? They were done with all that, and it wasn't funny.

James's brows shot up. "It looks exactly like I crashed into an invisible wall. And the impact felt like hitting something head-on."

"But—" Sebastian couldn't move. That didn't make any sense.

James stuck out his hands and inched forward. Just a few steps past the smashed front end of the truck, he hit an invisible barrier.

James surged forward, feeling the solid air. He followed the invisible barrier, running his hands over it. They were standing in the road at the edge of town, not too far past the last houses. The invisible wall spanned the road in both directions and continued off the shoulder and into the trees beyond.

Before James was out of sight, he turned back. Sebastian hadn't moved from next to the truck.

"What the fuck?" James gestured at the invisible wall in disbelief.

"I don't know," Sebastian whined. He kicked the barrier, and pain shot through his foot.

This. Wasn't. Happening. Had the universe heard his hope for things to go well and laughed in his face? He kicked the barrier again.

"Careful. Kicking it is only going to hurt you." James grabbed Sebastian's hand and pulled him off the road, leading him away from the barrier. They stopped in a patch of grass and looked at each other. James swallowed. "What if we didn't actually escape the curse?"

Sebastian shook his head. That wasn't a reality he was willing to accept. "But we did."

"Then where did this barrier come from?" James gestured at the wreck in the street. "It would explain why breaking the secret-binding isn't working. The curse still has us, but the area it's trapping us in has grown. That's why it's been able to rebind our tongues." He stopped talking abruptly, face paling.

"Meaning we've trapped Eli, Parker, and Hazel by letting them break the binding and telling them the secret," Sebastian finished, his stomach dropping.

There went his hope for Moonlight Falls being where he found his people. They were all going to hate him.

"Shit." James ran his hand through his hair again. "Maybe we're wrong," he added desperately. "Why would the area expand? And the secret-binding is definitely weakened. That must mean something. Maybe the others aren't trapped."

Sebastian hoped not, but things never went his way. This was only proof he couldn't have anything good in his life without it turning to shit.

He pushed his self-pity to the side. It wasn't helping. "We need to find out if the others are trapped. It might help us figure out what the fuck's going on."

James pulled out his phone and called Eli. "Have you left Moonlight Falls today?" After waiting for a reply, he shook his head, indicating Eli had stayed in town. "No, never mind. It's just — Can you meet us at the south end of Willow Road? Right before the highway." A pause. "No, now. Um. Don't worry. I'm okay, but I crashed my truck."

James winced at Eli's reaction. After James assured Eli that he and Sebastian didn't need an ambulance or even a first-aid kit, he hung up, eyes traveling to Sebastian's. Their shared gaze was one of mutual hopelessness.

They waited in silence for Eli to arrive.

Sebastian mentally ran through the transfer spell they'd performed. The fuel cell was definitely feeding the imbalance on his property. His magical ability returning to normal proved that. He'd never have been able to summon fire while the curse was allowing the veins to feed on him. But standing next to a new barrier, there was no doubt they hadn't been released from the curse like they'd thought.

Eli's compact car pulled up behind James's truck with its hazards on. He jumped out, wearing a frantic expression. "Are you guys all right?" He rushed over.

After assuring Eli they were uninjured, minus some bruising that was bound to appear where the seatbelts had caught them, they explained what happened.

Eli's eyes got wider and wider until it looked like they were about to pop out of his head. "So if you're still trapped, am I?"

Sebastian tried to be hopeful but couldn't manage it. That flicker of light had died. "We don't know."

James showed Eli where the barrier went off the side of the road and into the trees. Eli came forward and pressed his hand to it. He pushed against it but was unable to get through.

"Fuck." James looked at Sebastian in horror.

"And you think this barrier goes all the way around town?" Eli asked, much more calmly than Sebastian would have expected, almost like he couldn't help being fascinated.

"I have no idea where it goes. I guess we can check, though

we'll have to be careful if we're driving." Sebastian gave the barrier another kick. "It will probably encircle us in some fashion. I doubt it's just a wall stopping us from going south that we could get around if we found the end."

They all gazed into the trees off to the west.

"We have to talk to Parker and Hazel," James said, his mouth disappearing into a tight line. Sebastian's stomach twisted with a fresh wave of guilt.

"Yeah, I'm not going to lie. This isn't ideal." Eli shook his head. "I may have changed my mind about Moonlight Falls, but I wasn't planning on *never* leaving."

"We'll fix this," Sebastian promised, the horrible feeling inside him growing exponentially.

Eli grimaced like he wasn't confident in that. Sebastian couldn't blame him. He'd been screwing this up from the start, and now his curse had spread to *more* people. Yes, being trapped in Moonlight Falls was nowhere near as bad as being trapped at Storm House, but they were still prisoners, even if the cage was larger.

How had Sebastian messed up this badly? No wonder no one chose to keep him in their lives. He was a disaster. Everyone was better off without him. That much was clear. It was one thing wondering if James would want him forever when he thought they were free, now there was no hope. James wouldn't want someone who was not only the source of his past trauma but all his present problems.

Sebastian was a liability, a curse that spread to everything he touched.

"I just don't get it," he pleaded to no one in particular.

James shrugged. Was he annoyed? Of course he was. Sebastian was lucky James wasn't furious and yelling like he had been when he realized he couldn't leave Storm House.

Eli seemed deep in thought, chewing on his bottom lip. After a moment, he turned to Sebastian. "What if the transfer spell was never able to release you? What if it can only spread the curse to someone new, as it's intended to do in case the Storm bloodline dies out, and it can't release the current holder of the curse."

Sebastian frowned. "But what about Kira? They transferred it to me, freeing her."

"She was never trapped," Eli said, like Sebastian had just proven his point. "The curse never had her. She was just next in line. It would make sense for the transfer in that scenario to be complete, but not in yours or James's case."

"Then how do we fix it?" Panic gripped Sebastian's chest. This was his responsibility to solve, but he desperately wanted someone to come in and rescue him.

Instead of telling Sebastian there was no *we* and he should clean up his own damn mess, Eli considered the question seriously. "Maybe the only way to escape, now that we've all been caught, is to correct the power imbalance. The curse's purpose is to feed the imbalance. If the imbalance no longer exists, the curse can't tie us to anything. Because we're tied to the veins, not the Storm property. Surely, that's what the expanded barrier means. You must have been tied more tightly to the intersection before now, and the fuel cell loosened the leash, so to speak."

"Okay." James nodded encouragingly as if this was somehow good news. "Do you know anything about imbalances in veins of power?"

Eli scrunched his nose. "No," he admitted. "But that doesn't mean I can't figure it out. I need to take a look at what we're dealing with. See exactly what's happening at the vein intersection. Then, I can use my remote access to the university library to research the problem. I can look up practically any study published on this sort of thing through our online archive. Even if the secret-binding prevents me from asking anyone for advice, I'm sure we'll be able to figure something out."

"Damn, we are lucky to have you, Eli." James clapped his brother on the shoulder, shining with pride.

Eli went pink. "Library access isn't that impressive."

"It's not just that. You're smart," James insisted. Eli seemed pleased with the praise and didn't argue further. James turned his attention back toward town. "Should we head out to Storm House before meeting the mayor? I don't get why linking the fuel cell to the curse expanded the area we're trapped in. We need to figure out how that happened."

"No," Sebastian blurted out in alarm. "We can't look at the veins now."

Eli and James stared at him.

He swallowed audibly, trying to calm down. "I mean, we need to stop and think. Make sure we aren't going to do anything to make this worse. If there's one thing we know, it's that we have no fucking clue how this curse works."

"Isn't this us stopping and thinking?" James asked.

"What?" Sebastian's insides twisted. "No. We need to make sure it's not dangerous poking around the veins."

James didn't look concerned. "Dangerous, how? As long as we aren't messing around at night when the shades are there to get riled up, I don't think we have to worry."

James thought hordes of shades were the worst-case scenario. Sebastian needed to tell him the truth. James and Eli deserved to know, but he couldn't find the words.

He ran a hand through his hair. "I don't see why we have to rush out there now. What if we get caught up investigating and miss the meeting? Besides, we have to warn Parker and Hazel that they're trapped. We can't risk anyone else trying to drive through the barrier."

James scowled. "True. We should tell the others before we do anything else."

Sebastian was overcome with relief.

"All right," Eli agreed reluctantly. "Let's call a tow truck, and I'll drive you two back to town."

James made the call while Eli retreated to his car to sit and look at his phone as they waited. A car drove past, only to pull over and ask if they were okay. James assured the driver that they were fine, and they continued on, heading to Apple Valley to pick up their teenager from the high school. Watching the car disappear proved the barrier wasn't something that affected everyone, not that any of them had expected it to.

James put his arm around Sebastian. "You don't have to come to Storm House with us."

Sebastian cringed. James seemed to think his hesitation about looking at the veins was anxiety-based and was trying to protect him. Sebastian wondered if his guilt would eat him alive until there was nothing left. "I know I don't have to come, but I want to be there." He *had* to be there. He couldn't let everyone else deal with this while he hid. The fact that they were still willing to help was already more than he deserved.

James's brow creased in concern like he didn't believe Sebastian. "Are you sure?"

"Yeah." Sebastian tried to sound confident. "What's there to be afraid of in going to the house? We're still trapped. It's not like I can get doubly stuck."

James made a humming sound of agreement, kindly not pointing out that Sebastian's reluctance to return to Storm House was about more than the fear that he'd never leave again.

CHAPTER SEVEN

THAT EVENING, Eli left for his shift at Moonlight Diner, and Sebastian and James headed to town hall. Hazel and Parker were waiting for them on the steps outside.

James launched into explaining the accident at the edge of town. Sebastian's stomach roiled. He was comfortable with Hazel and Parker, so this wasn't social anxiety. It was more guilt. He winced when James got to the part about Eli being stuck along with them.

"Hold on." Hazel grabbed James's arm. "So that's why I couldn't report the curse?"

"What?" Parker looked at her in confusion.

"My tongue is definitely tied." She explained her failed attempt to report what was happening at Storm House when she'd called the official hotline that afternoon. "I wasn't expecting to be tongue-tied and knew it wasn't a good sign, but I had no idea it could mean we're trapped."

"I'm so sorry." Sebastian looked hopelessly between her and Parker.

Parker gave him a stern look. "It's not your fault."

"Yeah, Sebastian. You're a victim of this curse too. Way more so than the rest of us," Hazel assured him.

Great, James's friends were just as supportive and understanding as he was.

Sebastian wanted to be grateful. They had every right to yell at him and he appreciated that they weren't, but he knew their understanding would sour with time. It was easy to forgive him for trapping them now, but what about in a year? Or five? Ten? The way this was going, he might never find a solution to the imbalance or the curse, and Sebastian didn't expect anyone, not even James, to forgive him for permanent imprisonment.

And he'd thought he could build something lasting here. What a joke. These people wouldn't want him any more than anyone else, and if the rest of the town found out they were at risk of a deadly magical explosion because of the Storms, they wouldn't want him either.

"We can't tell anyone else," Sebastian said unnecessarily, but he didn't know what else to do.

"No, we definitely can't," James agreed. He put an arm around Sebastian. "At least not being stuck at Storm House will make it a lot easier to figure out a solution. We have access to resources."

"Not to mention smarter people on the case." Hazel gave James an evil grin.

"Yeah," he agreed without emotion. "Eli is way smarter than the rest of us."

Hazel rolled her eyes.

The group walked into the meeting like their lives weren't ruined, and Sebastian marveled at how light the mood remained between them all. Maybe none of them cared much about being stuck in Moonlight Falls. Was it possible to love the town that much? Sebastian doubted it. Reality just hadn't hit them yet, and like him, James was probably still comparing this to their last situation. They were better off than before, but that comfort would only last so long.

The mayor was waiting in a small auditorium inside town hall. "Hello, welcome." She greeted them with a serious air.

Hazel made her way over to Eleanor. "How are you doing?"

"Fine." Eleanor gave Hazel a small smile, a hand reflexively reaching to smooth her silver-flecked hair, which seemed unnecessary since she had a tidy pixy cut and not a strand was out of place.

As the two women talked quietly, Sebastian looked around. Chairs had been arranged in a circle like the meeting was a support group. Parker and James claimed seats, and Sebastian hurried to follow. A man in heavy work boots, who was already seated, nodded to them.

"How's the logging going?" Parker asked him.

"We'll be getting to that," the man said ominously.

Eleanor's attention returned to the group. She checked her watch. "Yes, let's wait until everyone arrives before we start swapping stories."

Hazel took a seat next to Sebastian. He was nervous. It wasn't as bad as the diner, but he didn't know who would be there or how the meeting would go.

Before they'd left the house, James had looked up some social anxiety management techniques online and shared them with Sebastian, who'd been hopelessly touched James had thought to look. He tried to focus on some of the grounding exercises now, but the ache in his chest made it hard.

Sebastian concentrated on the fact that Eleanor had asked him to be there and that he knew what they were going to talk about. He hoped no one asked him why they hadn't seen him in town for years. The secret-binding probably wasn't strong enough to make him lie convincingly. He might be able to imply he hadn't wanted to avoid the town, but that would only invite more questions Sebastian couldn't answer. Now that the anxiety people had always assumed he had was real, he didn't think he'd be able to use it as an excuse.

For the first time in years, Sebastian worried about what the people of Moonlight Falls thought about him. He didn't want to be the reclusive guy people whispered about. He wanted people to like him but didn't see why they would. They never had before.

James leaned in close and murmured, "Is there anything you want to say about the shades that I wasn't there for?"

Sebastian shook his head. James had offered to help him explain in case he got overwhelmed during the meeting and didn't want to talk to the group. Sebastian would have never thought to ask for something like that, but sitting there, becoming increasingly nervous, he was grateful for the option.

The city councilors all walked in together. Eleanor introduced Sebastian to a middle-aged woman named Melinda, who'd apparently known James's late mother. She gave James a big hug and claimed the free seat next to him.

The other two city councilors were introduced as William and Nora. They sat over by Eleanor, though neither struck up a conversation with anyone. Nora was younger than Sebastian expected someone in a government position to be. She had to be about Parker's age.

Mila Lopez was the next to bustle into the auditorium. At the sight of Sebastian, she gasped and rushed up to him. He automatically stood from his chair.

"Sebastian." The woman engulfed him in a hug. "It's wonderful to see you."

He hadn't expected her to be there. It made sense because Mila had always been involved in town affairs, but Sebastian hadn't thought about her in ages. He hadn't let himself, but the tight hug she gave him made it impossible to ignore how much he'd missed her.

Shit. Sebastian was going to cry. He was overwhelmed, and it had nothing to do with anxiety. Mila had been so much more than the woman who'd given him rides into town and looked after him when he wasn't at Storm House. She'd been the only person in Moonlight Falls he'd felt truly comfortable with. He'd spent a lot of time in the library with her throughout his childhood. He wished he'd been able to see her over the last six years and had no idea what to say when he couldn't explain what had happened to him.

"Oh, dear, it's all right." Mila cupped his cheek, looking up at him with tender eyes.

Sebastian sniffed and blinked, tears clinging to his lashes. "Sorry, it's been so long."

"Don't even worry about it." Mila smiled and released Sebastian, stopping to adjust the collar of his jacket. She glanced briefly at James, maybe recognizing the jacket as his, but she didn't comment. She shooed Hazel out of her seat so she could sit beside Sebastian. "We have to catch up sometime soon."

"Mm-hmm." Sebastian nodded as he plopped into his chair, still too full of emotion for words.

Hazel settled on the other side of the guy with the boots. Two other men had entered while Sebastian had been occupied with Mila, and with all the seats filled, it looked like they were ready to start.

"Welcome, everyone," the mayor said without getting up, keeping things more casual. "As you all know, we've had some serious problems around town and in the forest." She glanced at boots-man. "I think we can all agree something is changing with the shades around here."

"It's the first time I've ever heard the kids at school talk about being frightened of the beasts," said a middle-aged man in a blazer whom Sebastian hadn't been introduced to. "I don't think we can keep telling them there's nothing to fear, but I don't want to cause a panic either."

"No, you're right, Tony. And parents need to be made aware that it's getting less and less safe after dark." Eleanor looked around the group. "But before we go making announcements, we need a better picture of what's happening. Parker, why don't you start?"

Parker explained how Eli had been violently attacked by a shade about a month and a half ago. The incident was completely unprovoked and seemed like the start of whatever was going on. Before then, people had noticed shades getting more aggressive, but they hadn't acted completely outside the realm of their typical behavior, so no one had been worried. Even after what happened to Eli, most people seemed to assume the attack was a fluke or an outlier.

Then, in the last few weeks, things had taken a sharp turn for the worse. Unprovoked shade attacks involving physical contact had been almost unheard of before. Now, more people around town were reporting being grabbed and scratched, and there had been several attempted shade bites thwarted by light. The group was counting James being ambushed under Storm House as one of these incidents, and when that came up, Sebastian was asked to tell the group how many shades he had around his property.

He looked at the floor in the middle of the circle, glad he'd gone over what he wanted to say beforehand. "There've always been a lot of shades hanging around and peering in my windows. A group of them even live under the house, but recently, there seems to be hundreds of shades lurking in the trees on the south end of my property. They watch me when I go down there. It seems territorial." He wanted to explain how they responded to the magic in the veins, but there was no way for him to other than to say, "They react badly to magic."

No one questioned him, and he sat back in relief as Eleanor thanked him for the information. Though she looked less than pleased to hear there were hundreds of shades just outside of town.

"While all of that is concerning," Eleanor said, pulling the group's focus back to her. "Attacks and increased numbers aren't our most pressing problem. I've had one report of a shade immune to light. And not just immune to artificial shade-lights like we saw when they smashed out the streetlights in town, but immune to sunlight summoned by magic. And then there was the bear." She glanced at the man in the work boots.

"Yeah." He scowled and introduced himself as Carson Lee. "We deal with shades pretty often when we're logging, but we're never out at night, so it's no drama. Until yesterday when a possessed bear attacked my team."

"Really?" A man, who Sebastian was pretty sure was the local museum curator, leaned forward, shocked. "That was kept quiet."

Parker looked between them, scowling as deeply as Carson and the mayor. "What happened?"

"It came charging in at us and went for one of my guys. He had to go to the hospital for the bite on his arm, but he'll be okay. The bear definitely wasn't acting normal. It came in like it was on a mission to rip us apart. I saw its blackened eyes and onyx teeth myself, and it took an awful lot of shots to take down."

"Did the shade leave the body?" Parker asked.

Carson nodded. "Floated right out of its fur. My son banished it with summoned light, sent the beam directly into the shade's chest, and it dissipated."

Fear made the hairs on the back of Sebastian's neck stand up. Shades could possess animals, but it rarely happened. They rarely did it because they lost the ability to use their shadow magic while inside a living being. They couldn't dematerialize, fly, or shapeshift, but they could withstand full sunlight while inside an animal's body.

"At least it doesn't sound like that shade was resistant to light," Parker said, perhaps in an attempt to look on the bright side.

"True." James leaned forward, elbows on his knees, peering around Melinda to Parker. "But I wonder if that means we have two separate problems. The light-resistant shade that attacked Sebastian seemed different, and I remember Eli saying the same thing back when he was attacked. At the time, we thought the differences were insignificant, but what if those differences mean we're dealing with a new kind of shade, as well as shades willing to possess animals."

"We can't rule it out," Eleanor admitted, though her tone implied she wished she could.

"I'll search the archives for anything on light-resistant shades," Mila offered, to which Eleanor nodded. "At least possessions have been known to happen and dealing with them isn't unprecedented. The other problem seems more concerning."

"I agree," said the man in the blazer. "But even if it is two problems, it's hard to imagine they aren't related."

William, the city councilor, looked down his nose at the other man. "Why would you assume that?"

Blazer-man sat up straighter, apparently not put off by the condescending look. "We've seen no real change in the shades visiting Moonlight Falls for as long as I've been alive. Then, suddenly, we have a possession and this light resistance all happening at once. If they aren't related, the timing is unbelievably coincidental."

"While we're trying to figure out why any of this is happening," Nora cut in before William could argue, "we should make announcements informing people extra caution is needed."

"Yes," Eleanor agreed. "The town needs to know that light might not be enough and that going out at night without the ability to summon fire could be risky."

William crossed his arms. "But what about tourism? We can't scare away the city folk coming for the supernatural tours."

"It'll be a liability if we do nothing. People need to know the risks." Eleanor pulled out her phone. "I'll talk to the tour company. It's ultimately up to them to decide what to do about the tours they run. If their guides are comfortable swapping shade-lights for fire, that's their call."

William looked displeased. "But tourists might be too skittish to come and book a tour if they think there's a real risk."

Eleanor gave him a dismissive one-shoulder shrug before turning to the rest of the group. "Why don't we have Nora and Tony draft up some statements. One for the school and one for the general public. We have to let everyone know about the bear in the least alarming way possible."

"I'll leave that for the parents to deal with." Tony brushed off the sleeves of his blazer and made a face. "The only things I'll be saying to the kids as principal will be about safety procedures and to remind them to ask an adult about anything they're unsure of."

"We'll have to let them know shade-lights might not be enough," Nora reminded him.

Tony grimaced. "That's going to scare them. But I suppose there's no way around it. If we can have something written up and distributed around town tomorrow, we'll have until Monday to worry about the school announcement, and hopefully, the kids will have heard what's going on from their parents by then, so they won't be caught off guard."

Parker said he was happy to have notices put up at the diner, and Melinda offered to help distribute flyers into mailboxes.

The meeting wrapped up after that. Sebastian promised Mila he'd stop by the library soon, and she hugged him again before leaving.

Sebastian didn't talk to anyone other than Mila as people milled around the auditorium and he was relieved to get outside, even though it was dark and they had no real idea what would happen next with the shades. As long as a possessed bear didn't stroll into town, they'd probably be fine. People would need to readjust. The immunity to light wasn't ideal, but it was manageable.

Still, Sebastian wondered what would happen if things didn't return to normal. What if things got worse? Light immunity wouldn't be so manageable if a whole horde of shades required fire to banish. Would things get bad enough that they'd find out how many people in Moonlight Falls truly believed this place called to them and was a comfort like no other? How many would leave it all behind for a place without violent beasts from Beyond?

Sebastian hoped James, Eli, Hazel, and Parker didn't change their minds about loving life in this town, especially since none of them had any choice about staying.

CHAPTER EIGHT

JAMES PULLED Eli's car into the garage. It would be a little while before his truck was repaired, so the brothers would have to share. Parker planned to pick Eli up from work later because walking home at night didn't seem like a great idea. He'd take Eli back to his house, which meant Sebastian and James were on their own.

James faced Sebastian as he turned off the car. "The meeting went well."

Sebastian shrugged. He'd cried in front of a group of people and hadn't been able to make eye contact while talking, but it hadn't gone terribly. "Guess so."

They climbed out of the car, and James popped the trunk. "Here, I grabbed some stuff at Storm House this morning." James had transferred a couple of boxes from his truck before it was towed. They each grabbed one. "Let's take them upstairs."

Sebastian followed James through the house and up to James's bedroom. Sebastian set his box on the floor, the top flaps falling open to reveal the clothes he'd ordered for James. He smiled.

James set the other box on a chair in the corner. "This one is yours."

Sebastian maneuvered around the bed. "Thanks." He opened the box to find an assortment of his clothing.

James began putting the things from his box away in the closet. "I can make space in a drawer for you if you want."

Sebastian unearthed a book from beneath his clothes. It had been on the nightstand in his bedroom. James grabbing it for him was sweet, and so was his offer of a permanent drawer in his room, but Sebastian didn't need to be any more attached to James than he already was. "No need to clear out a drawer for me," he made himself say.

James paused. "Oh, okay."

Sebastian turned away and continued to riffle through his box. He shouldn't be unpacking when he needed to be looking for his own place to live. Something pink caught his eye and he bit back a laugh. Thoughts of getting some space from James fled his mind. "James, what are these?" He spun to face James, the fuzzy handcuffs dangling from a finger.

James went bright red. "You know what they are."

"Yes." Sebastian smiled wickedly. He loved flustering James. "But I gave them to you. Why are they in my box?"

James scowled, but his cheeks didn't lose any of their color. "I'm giving them back." He turned to face the closet and hung up the shirt he was holding. James made it so easy to tease him. He was way too bashful for a guy who fucked like a stud.

Sebastian stalked closer, and James avoided looking at him. The poor guy was having trouble getting his next shirt on its hanger.

Seeing the effect he had on James gave Sebastian a rush of confidence. It reminded him that he was still playful and deviant and not defined by his new insecurities. Not everything about him had changed since leaving Storm House. He could still be the same man who took pleasure in seeing James squirm, the guy who took what he wanted and said to hell with the risks.

"Why'd you pack the handcuffs, James?" he taunted.

A muscle in James's jaw ticked. "I don't know. They were in my room with the clothes, and I threw them in a box."

"Uh-huh." Sebastian dangled them in front of James's face. James glared at him. "You're sure you didn't pack them because you want to cuff me to your bed?"

James went even redder, the color tinging his ears. "Seems like you're the one who wants that."

Sebastian gave a careless shrug like he wasn't interested. He swore disappointment flashed across James's face. He lowered the cuffs and stepped closer, whispering in James's ear, "You can tell me what you actually want. It's okay."

James swallowed. There was such a long pause that Sebastian wondered if James wouldn't say anything, but then he whispered, "Maybe it isn't you I want cuffed to the bed."

Sebastian sucked in a breath. He'd assumed James would keep grumbling and deflecting. The fact that he hadn't meant he trusted Sebastian a great deal, and Sebastian loved that. He liked shocking James out of his shell and giving him room to indulge his desires.

"Do you want me to restrain you, James? Do you want to lie there and take what I give you?"

James dropped the shirt in his hands. "Yes," he said, voice hoarse. "Please, Sebastian."

Sebastian pulled him into a kiss. He took James's mouth roughly, stealing his gasping breaths, and felt like himself again. Sebastian wasn't lost when he was in James's arms. He knew who he was.

He was a survivor, someone who seized good things without hesitation and found things to live for even when he had nothing. The sexual relationship he'd had with James at Storm House had been mind-blowing. Sebastian had had nothing to lose and nothing to offer a man like James while he'd been imprisoned, yet he'd still been confident in what he wanted. He'd taken it without considering the risks or the possibility of rejection.

James was his dream partner, and he finally had him. He couldn't let fear get him now. Sebastian was the kind of man who could reach for things even when on the edge of despair. He could still be that man. He could still drive James wild and enjoy everything they gave each other, even if he felt on the cusp of losing it all. Even if he felt lost sometimes. His life wasn't out of his control in the way it had been before, so why couldn't he take more of the things he wanted and make them his?

Sebastian needed to take charge. He needed to sort out his life and be honest with James. While kissing the man, he felt like he could. He could stop keeping secrets. There was a sliver of hope that he could keep one good thing in his life.

He wouldn't be himself if he didn't at least try to make this last.

"Strip and get on the bed," Sebastian ordered once he was able to pry his lips from James.

James whimpered but complied. His eagerness was on full display as he shoved his clothes carelessly off his body. Being wanted that much made Sebastian's head spin. He watched, not touching his own clothes, and couldn't help thinking how lucky he was in so many ways, even when so much was still going wrong.

When James was lying on the bed, completely naked and erect, Sebastian approached. He trailed the handcuffs up James's stomach and across his chest. James panted, lying still and waiting.

"You're really into this," Sebastian observed, his mischievous grin on full display.

"Isn't that a good thing?" James tried to huff like he wanted Sebastian to think he was annoyed, but the sound was desperate.

"Of course." Sebastian set the cuffs on James's chest and began taking off his clothes. "I'm just wondering why you spent so much energy pretending you weren't instead of asking for what you wanted."

James's gaze tracked Sebastian's movements as he undressed. "I'm not as bold as you."

Sebastian liked that James thought he was bold, especially after all his recent displays to the contrary. "I think you are." Sebastian climbed onto the bed, naked. "When you remember you don't have to be afraid of what you want."

James pulled Sebastian down on top of him, the cuffs crushed between them. "I don't know if I'll ever not be afraid. But I'll always risk facing those fears for you."

If that wasn't the boldest thing Sebastian had ever heard, then he didn't know what was. But Sebastian loved to push. He loved the extreme reactions he got from James because it reminded him that this thing between them was real. "Then risk it and tell me exactly what you want. I promise it'll be worth it."

James closed his eyes. Sebastian let him take the moment he needed. "I want you to cuff me to the headboard and use me. Get yourself off on me. Do what you want with me. You decide. Anything that makes you feel good. I want to be whatever you need."

Sebastian forgot to breathe for a second. His dick was hard and leaking against James's stomach.

Maybe the reason James held back was because when he didn't, he was soul-baringly honest. His words didn't just sound dirty. They sounded like a deep, exposing need. His request didn't seem like a whim or mindless dirty talk. He wasn't saying it to provoke a reaction in Sebastian, as Sebastian often did to him. It was real and meaningful, and Sebastian wanted desperately to fulfill all of James's fantasies.

"You want me to use you?" Sebastian stroked James's cheek, and he opened his eyes. "I think I can do that."

James huffed. "Fuck, you're hot when you're smug."

Sebastian preened. "You always think I'm hot."

James shrugged beneath him. "Sounds about right."

Sebastian kissed him, then sat up, settling on James's lap. He rolled his hips, rubbing James's hard cock between his ass cheeks. James groaned, his hands finding Sebastian's hips. "No, none of that." Sebastian grabbed James's hands and stretched them above his head. He arranged the pillows beneath James, then looped the cuffs around a rung in the headboard.

He secured James's wrists, and James gave them a little tug. His breathing picked up, his face red and eyes bright with excitement. Sebastian went back to rolling his hips. He ran his hands up James's chest, tracing his muscles. This was way too fun. He felt spoiled and was already addicted to the needy way James was looking at him, tracking all his movements.

"You want this to be about me getting myself off?" Sebastian asked as he worked James's cock, feeling the tantalizing slide up and down his crease and over his hole.

"Yes." James's arms jerked like he was trying to reach for Sebastian.

"You sure you don't want me to spoil you? I could lick you all over so perfectly with you laid out like this."

James groaned. "I don't need to be spoiled. But if licking me is what you want, then please."

If James didn't want to be spoiled, he had to know Sebastian would choose to tease him. And maybe that was the other reason James held back and grumbled when Sebastian purposely scandalized him. James liked being teased, maybe even enjoyed the thrill of being shocked and scandalized.

Sebastian climbed off James, and he whimpered, the cuffs clinking as he tried to follow.

"Where are you going?" he asked, his eyes wide.

Sebastian opened the bedside table drawer. "Nowhere. I'm just getting what I need." He grabbed the lube and a condom. Back on the bed, Sebastian straddled James's lap, facing his feet. The only bad thing about this plan was he wouldn't be able to see James's reaction.

"What are you doing?" James panted, breathless.

"If I'm going to get myself off on you, I need to prep." Sebastian lubed his fingers and reached behind himself. He leaned forward, bracing himself, and canted his hips back to give James a good view as he massaged his rim.

"Fuck." There was the sound of James trying to move his arms again.

Sebastian pushed a finger inside his hole. Displaying himself like this made his face hot with a burning blush, but the way James moaned as he watched Sebastian finger himself made Sebastian feel invincible. He felt sexy and confident. Like he could do anything.

Sebastian made a desperate sound as he added a second finger. Knowing James was watching made playing with himself so much hotter than when he'd been on his own. He looked down between his legs to see James's hard cock pressed against his inner thigh, the tip slick with precum. Sebastian's own cock leaked, begging for attention, but he refused to touch himself just yet.

Sebastian withdrew his fingers to get more lube.

"No, don't stop," James pleaded from behind him.

"Don't worry," Sebastian said in what was supposed to be a teasing tone but came out more comforting than anything. He slipped two fingers back inside himself and rocked back as he stretched his hole.

James's hips twitched beneath Sebastian as he tried to find friction. Sebastian wasn't giving it to him. James let out a frustrated noise. Sebastian wondered if he'd had enough of the show, but James moaned, "Fuck yourself, Sebastian. Yeah, just like that. Add another finger."

Sebastian whined as his cock leaked. He buried three fingers deep in his ass.

"You've got such a pretty little hole."

James saying things like that was almost enough to make Sebastian come without touching his dick. He withdrew his fingers and spun around. James had his bottom lip trapped between his teeth, sweat lining his brow. He looked flushed and a bit wild-eyed. He was perfect.

"I think you liked that more than I did," Sebastian said, even though he wasn't sure it was true. He'd liked making a spectacle of himself for James.

"Maybe," James responded, more coy than Sebastian thought the guy was capable of. "But you really need to fuck me now."

"Do I?" Sebastian swept back his hair and grinned. "I thought this was about me?"

James blinked in shock. "Please?"

Sebastian leaned forward and kissed James, who accepted his mouth hungrily. Just as the kiss turned fevered and desperate, Sebastian pulled back. He soaked up the pleading moan of protest James made like it was a drug. Sebastian was just as desperate, so he wasted no time rolling the condom onto James's straining erection and slathering it with lube.

He lined himself up and sank down.

"Oh fuck." James bucked his hips, his cock hitting Sebastian's prostate as he surged upward.

Sebastian gave a shout of pleasure that turned into a moan as he settled firmly onto James's lap. He braced his hands against James's chest and rolled his hips, losing himself in the feeling of fullness. "You feel so good inside me, James."

Something about not being able to return Sebastian's touch seemed to make James feral. His gaze was laser-focused on Sebastian rather than hazy with lust. His mouth dropped open in a low moan and his biceps flexed as he gripped the rails of the headboard.

Sebastian rode James hard, bouncing on his cock, hitting that perfect angle that made his eyes flutter closed with pleasure. His own dick bounced between them, slapping against James's abs.

"Don't stop, Sebastian." James bucked his hips as Sebastian

bore down, burying himself deep. "You're so fucking gorgeous riding me."

Sebastian whimpered. He felt gorgeous and spoiled rotten. He couldn't believe he had James to do whatever he wanted with and wondered if anything could be better than this. How had he gotten so lucky that this stoic man had chosen to shower him with his emotions, to give him affection and praise?

Sebastian took his cock in his hand and stroked it. James's attention zeroed in on the rough way Sebastian handled himself. "Do you like this, James?" Sebastian continued riding him hard and jerking himself. "Do you like watching me fuck myself on you, pleasuring myself?"

"Yes." James's answer was strangled. "Yes, Sebastian. Fuck."

Their eyes locked, and Sebastian almost came, but he wasn't ready. He abandoned his cock and released the safety latches on the handcuffs.

The instant James was free, he surged forward, sitting up but not dislodging Sebastian from his lap. James's arms wrapped around Sebastian, one hand snaking up the back of his neck to bury itself in his hair. Their mouths crashed together as James thrust up, fucking Sebastian, who met every movement with one of his own. Sebastian clung to James's shoulders. Nothing felt better than their bodies pressed together, except maybe the way James's whole body shuddered as he came.

"Sebastian, Sebastian, fuck me, sweetheart," he murmured as he thrust through his release.

Sebastian sobbed with how good it felt to be back in James's arms. As hot as using him was, Sebastian always wanted to be touched. He needed to be held. It was a desperate desire he wasn't sure he'd ever overcome. He loved to tease and play, but he needed delicate things too. He needed softness, to feel cared for, to be called sweetheart, and James seemed to know that. It was something Sebastian couldn't take for himself, so James gave it to him.

Without breaking their kiss, James took hold of Sebastian's dick, slick with precum and lube, and stroked in firm, unfaltering motions. Sebastian moaned into James's mouth as his orgasm crashed through him, his arms tight around James's neck.

James pulled Sebastian down onto the bed and held him. They were sweaty and smeared with Sebastian's release, but Sebastian had never been so content or comfortable.

"I hope that gave you what you needed," James whispered in his ear.

"It did." Sebastian hugged James tighter. "You always take care of me, James."

"And you take care of me," he murmured back. "That was even better than the fantasies I had."

Sebastian smiled against James's neck. He had this man, had seduced him, and seemed to have won his heart. Sebastian hoped like hell he could keep James. But if that's what he wanted, he had a lot of work to do.

CHAPTER NINE

Later, after they'd showered, Sebastian rummaged in his box for some clean underwear.

"You sure you don't want a drawer?" James asked as he climbed back into bed.

"Yeah, it's fine." Sebastian extracted a pair of black boxer briefs and pulled them on. "I should probably get my own place in town."

"Oh." James's brow furrowed. "True. That makes sense."

Sebastian couldn't help thinking James sounded disappointed. He had a strong urge to take his words back, to tell James he needed a drawer and some space in the closet because he was never leaving James's side, let alone his house. But he couldn't. He didn't want to be that clingy, even if James would be accepting of such behavior after the isolation Sebastian had gone through. Sebastian needed to be independent. He needed to pull back from James enough to prove he'd be okay on his own, regardless of their relationship and whether it lasted. James couldn't be his whole world.

And Sebastian knew he could do it. He'd been heartachingly independent until now, but he knew standing on his own and being alone weren't the same thing, and to have a chance at keeping James in his life he probably needed a little space. At least enough so he could tell James the truth and deal with whatever happened afterward because as much hope as he had that their relationship would last, he harbored an equal amount of doubt.

Sebastian was always prepared for the worst. It was how he'd survived this long.

"I saw one of the town duplexes for rent when I was walking around today." Sebastian climbed into bed. "I'll call the landlord in the morning." Hazel had given him an old phone of hers after the town meeting. All he needed was a pre-paid SIM card from the General Store, and he would be back in the modern world.

James nodded. "That's a great idea." He almost sounded convinced. "It will be nice for you to live in town after the last six years."

Sebastian hated the idea of living alone, whether it was in town or not. "Totally," he agreed anyway.

THE NEXT MORNING, Sebastian woke up alone in bed. The sink was running in the bathroom, and after a minute, James appeared in the doorway.

He frowned at Sebastian. "Sorry I woke you."

"That's okay." Sebastian stretched.

"I was going to have a quick breakfast, then go for a swim at the rec center." James scratched the back of his neck like he was suddenly unsure of his plan. "I mean, it's been way too long since I was in the water. I usually go a few times a week."

There was an awkwardness in the air. James sounded strained, but Sebastian wasn't entirely sure why. James going for a swim was normal. Of course he'd want to get back in the pool after being stuck at Storm House.

Sebastian had the random thought that if they'd never escaped the house, he'd have built James a pool. He pushed the idea away and got up to pull on pants and a wrinkled T-shirt. "I'll join you for breakfast before you go."

James grabbed an athletic bag from the closet. "Yeah, of course."

Downstairs, Sebastian wondered if he should talk to James now. Would it be better to do it before or after he moved out? He had the feeling sooner was better, but he also didn't know if bringing up his parents' deaths right before James went swimming was the right move. It might ruin his workout.

James got the coffee started and tossed a protein bar in his bag. Sebastian knew there would never be a good time for this conversation. He'd always find a reason not to say anything. But he had to do it. James deserved the truth. He deserved so fucking much, and Sebastian wanted to be as good for him as he could, even if he doubted it would be enough.

Maybe this would end like every other good thing in Sebastian's life, but before it did, Sebastian had to try to do what was right.

"James." Sebastian gripped the counter as his stomach twisted.

"Yeah?" James turned to face him, mug in hand.

Fuck this was hard. Sebastian had about a million reasons to change his mind running through his head. He didn't *have* to tell James. It's not like anyone else knew the truth. He wouldn't get caught out. His selfishness might even be best. It would spare James unnecessary pain.

James set the mug down. "Are you all right?"

"No." Sebastian tried to dig his fingers into the counter. He couldn't lie or keep omitting the truth. If he did, he wouldn't deserve James.

"What's wrong?" James was at his side, a soothing hand snaking around his waist.

Sebastian pulled away. He couldn't do this from the comfort of James's arms. "You know how we're going out to Storm House later? With Eli?"

"Yeah," James said slowly, clearly not sure where this was going.

Sebastian swallowed. "It could be dangerous, and I have to tell you why."

"Okay." James's brow crinkled. "But I don't think Eli has to do much to examine the veins. It's nothing like the magic we were doing. I'm sure it will be way less dramatic than when we were messing with the fuel cell."

James needed to stop trying to comfort him.

"I didn't tell you everything about the night they transferred the curse to me."

James blinked in surprise. "Okay." He waited.

"I mean, I did at the time. When I gave you my notebook," Sebastian rambled, his heart rate picking up. "But when we found the instructions, I found something else and hid it." This would have been so much easier if Sebastian had the article. He wouldn't have to spell it out, but he figured his discomfort was punishment for the deception. If he'd done nothing wrong, he wouldn't feel so guilty.

James started to look worried. "What did you find?"

Sebastian couldn't maintain eye contact. He looked at the mug on the counter. "It was an article about your parents' accident. I had no idea until I picked up that old newspaper, but the accident happened the same night my mom and uncle transferred the curse to me."

Even though Sebastian wasn't looking, he could tell James had gone unnaturally still.

"I think we caused the accident. The blast. I swear we had no idea. But there was a sound during all the confusion, and when I found the instructions next to the article and realized it all happened the same night, I put it together. It was our fault, James, and I'm so, so sorry." He looked up and took in the shock on James's face.

"My parents' car crashed because of the transfer spell?" he asked like he didn't believe it.

Sebastian nodded. He wanted to hug James, comfort him, but he wasn't sure it would be welcome.

James rubbed his eyes for a long time before saying, surprisingly calm, "This is why you keep saying messing with the veins is dangerous?"

"Yes." Sebastian hunched forward, his arms tight around himself. "The magic the transfer released from the veins must have thrown the car off the road. We have to be really careful and can't risk anything like that happening again."

James mouthed the words *thrown the car*. He frowned like none of this made sense. "Why didn't you tell me before?"

Sebastian didn't have an answer. All his reasons felt too insecure and self-centered.

James crossed his arms. "Sebastian, did you think I'd blame you? You never had to feel like this was your fault."

Sebastian bit his lip. "I knew you wouldn't blame me. You're too good for that, but—"

"What does that mean?"

"Nothing." Sebastian ran his hand through his hair. "I knew you wouldn't blame me for something I didn't mean to do—"

"Something you *didn't* do," James interrupted again, harsher this time. "This was something your family did *to* you."

Sebastian waved that unimportant distinction away. "Okay, but they also did this to you, James. We're the reason you lost your parents. What we did in the clearing that night killed them. It's okay for you to be mad about that. Mad at them, mad at the veins. You can be upset."

"Upset with you, you mean?" James asked, sounding hurt now. "I said I'm not."

"But are you not upset at all?" Sebastian's thoughts swirled unhelpfully. He wasn't sure why he was pushing.

"It was still an accident," James said quietly. "I've always been upset that an accident could take so much away from me, but I've tried to move past that anger. Knowing the accident was unintentionally caused by your family—I don't know what that changes. Being mad at them doesn't help. My parents are still gone."

"I'm sorry."

James rubbed his temple. "You don't have to be sorry. Not for what happened fourteen years ago. But, Sebastian, you've known about this for weeks and didn't tell me. If you didn't think I'd blame you, why hide it?"

"I don't know," Sebastian whispered. He couldn't admit any of the reasons he'd held back, that he was scared of it changing things between them, of James waking up to the fact that Sebastian wasn't who he wanted.

Sebastian had told himself over and over that James wouldn't blame him, but he'd never truly believed it. He hadn't been able to. He'd braced for James's anger, ready for the worst because the worst always happened. Sebastian already blamed himself, and that spoke louder than anything he thought he knew about James.

Nothing lasted. Everyone left him. This would be no different.

James gave Sebastian an unreadable look. "Have you been worrying about telling me this the whole time? Since you found the paper?"

"There's been a lot to worry about," he replied, purposefully vague.

"I thought we had more trust in each other than this." James turned abruptly toward the coffee maker as if he needed to watch it percolate. "I thought we were done with secrets after I broke the spell on you in the ballroom. I assumed. But it's okay. I'm sure it was a hard thing to learn, and I can imagine why you didn't tell me. We were trapped, and nothing about the situation was easy. I can't expect you to share everything with me immediately. We've only just started dating. Really, it's only been a day."

"It's been longer than that." To Sebastian, it felt like they'd been together since he'd first gotten on his knees for James. When they'd been at Storm House, separate from the world, intimacy had seemed to count more than labels. They'd been together in all the most important ways.

James adjusted the coffee mug. "In a way, it's been longer, but maybe it's best if we don't count what happened at Storm House. Or we do, but it's still only been a few weeks. There's a lot we don't know about each other, and I shouldn't expect you to automatically be comfortable confiding something this big. Even if I had a right to know since it was about my family."

James was disappointed in him. It seemed like Sebastian had proven James wrong about their relationship, as if James had already trusted him with everything and was learning Sebastian hadn't done the same.

"It's okay," James said again, abandoning the coffee to face Sebastian. "I hope we can trust each other more the longer we're together. You can always talk to me."

"I know I can talk to you, James. I'm sorry." Sebastian felt helpless. He didn't want to lose James's trust or admit he hadn't trusted James the way James trusted him, but he knew keeping big secrets like this wasn't the way to build a good relationship.

Sebastian hadn't realized his self-preservation had come at the expense of trusting James. But it had. He'd believed in the worst-case scenario more than he'd believed in James or what the two of them had together.

James rubbed his eyes again. "We should tell Eli."

"I can talk to him," Sebastian offered, hoping that doing that for James would help.

"No, it's okay. I'll do it." James grabbed a sports drink out of the fridge. "You get that phone working and see about the duplex. I'll go meet Eli at Parker's now and talk to him, then go for my swim. Meet you back here after."

"Only if you're sure."

James gave him a kind smile. "I'm sure. And don't worry, Eli won't blame you either, Sebastian. He and I will never blame you for something you didn't do. You never had to be afraid of that." He gripped Sebastian firmly on the shoulder and left the kitchen, grabbing his swim bag on the way out.

Sebastian swallowed. His throat constricted and tears filled his eyes. He was a mess of guilt and regret. He'd been preparing for the end of everything good, but instead of helping him survive, it had made everything worse.

CHAPTER TEN

With some borrowed cash from James, Sebastian walked to the General Store to sort out his phone.

Carla smiled as Sebastian approached the register. "Got your wallet?"

His stomach was tight with a combination of anxiety due to the crowded store and worry about his conversation with James. He nodded at Carla and set the SIM card on the counter. Someone came to stand in line behind him.

"You here visiting?" Carla asked as she rang up the purchase and took his cash.

"No." Sebastian glanced at the middle-aged woman behind him in line, hoping she wouldn't get impatient as Carla talked to him. He'd never liked annoying people.

"New in town then?" Carla pressed, not yet counting out his change.

"No. I've lived just outside of town for a while." Sebastian fidgeted with the hem of James's leather jacket. He hadn't been able to leave its comfort behind, even after disappointing James. "I wanted to move closer."

"Outside of town?" Carla looked confused. Which was fair.

There wasn't anything outside of Moonlight Falls other than trees.

"You're not the one at Storm House, are you?" the woman behind him cut in, blatant curiosity lighting her face.

"Maybe," Sebastian muttered.

"Probably best to get out of that festering old place," she advised. "My mother said the Storms used to have parties out there when she was a little girl. No matter how lively they were, she said they couldn't disguise the creepiness of the place, and those were the good old days."

Sebastian didn't respond. Sullivan and his son, Simon, had lived at Storm House with their families. They'd had guests out to the house and hosted regular events. It would have been much less obvious to people in town that the two men never left the property when their wives and children came and went, and Storm House wasn't some foreboding place no one visited.

People in town seemed to believe things at Storm House had gone steadily downhill, gotten undeniably creepier and more haunted as the decades passed and guests were no longer invited out. But that was mainly because Simon had wanted peace and quiet in his final years, and Stephen hadn't had the kind of family support his predecessors had when he'd been trapped there alone.

"Well, it'll be good to have you in town," Carla said, breaking the strained silence as Sebastian and the other woman stared at each other. Carla offered his change, smiling brightly at Sebastian as he took it and fled.

The duplex was around the corner, across the street from Gray Electrical. Sebastian called the number listed on the For Rent sign in the window. When the landlord realized Sebastian was standing in the front yard, he rushed over to meet him.

"Might as well show you through now." The man seemed eager to accommodate Sebastian as he walked him through the small home. It was partially furnished, with a bed in the room upstairs and a couch and dining table downstairs.

Sebastian didn't like anything about it. "I'll take it," he said after spending five minutes in the place.

The landlord seemed delighted. He'd bemoaned how hard it was to find tenants in such a small town, especially when most residents wanted a larger property and didn't want to share a wall with their next-door neighbor.

"The man living here before took great care of everything," the landlord assured Sebastian. "He was here for ten years before moving to be closer to his grandkids, and the woman next door is lovely."

Sebastian nodded. He wasn't a fan of small talk. Never had been. He'd been quiet as a kid, and maybe the roots of his new anxiety had always been there, though there was no denying he didn't handle unpredictable situations as well as he used to.

Sebastian was given a key on the spot and a lease to sign. He sat at the dining table and looked up his lawyer's number online, then made another call.

Once the lawyer got over the shock of his famously reclusive client calling him for the first time, he was happy to arrange everything Sebastian needed. A deposit and the first month's rent were sent to the landlord and an account with debit card access was opened for Sebastian.

It should have felt good to accomplish all these things. Sebastian's life outside Storm House was more tangible now. It was working out smoothly. He had everything he needed to rebuild except the ability to leave Moonlight Falls. But even that didn't seem like much of a loss at the moment. The idea of going to unfamiliar places still made Sebastian's insides squirm.

However, instead of feeling good, he was melancholy. He didn't know what to do next. What did he want from his life now that he had it back?

Luckily, he didn't have to dwell on the big picture for long. He walked through the town back to James's house to meet the others.

Sebastian was a mess of nervous guilt as James pulled up in Eli's car. Even if James and Eli didn't blame him for their parents' accident, he was still the cause of their past trauma, and Sebastian didn't know how he was supposed to ignore that. If Sebastian had never been born and the curse never transferred, James and Eli would still have their parents. If Sebastian had never tried to escape Storm House, James, Eli, Parker, and Hazel wouldn't be trapped by the curse. These were just facts, and Sebastian couldn't ignore them.

He told himself he believed James when he said he didn't blame Sebastian for the accident fourteen years ago. James wasn't mad at him. He wouldn't lie about his feelings. But Sebastian didn't understand how James could be so reasonable, so doubt kept creeping in. No one else in Sebastian's life took his side or looked past his flaws. Maybe James did blame him just a bit. He couldn't get rid of the idea, even after how wrong he'd been this morning when assuming the worst.

The worst could still happen, a scared little voice inside him whispered.

But Sebastian had resolved to try with James, to hold on to the hope they could last. He hadn't given up when he was trapped at Storm House. If he could manage that, he could try to make this work. He could believe what James had told him despite his doubts. He could try to solve the problems he'd created, absolve his guilt, and make a place for himself in Moonlight Falls.

Sebastian wanted to be chosen for once. He wanted to be kept. He wanted friends and James, and he'd do anything to earn them. He could prove he was worth keeping. Maybe then the worst wouldn't happen.

"I got myself a place to live." Sebastian stood from where he'd been seated on the front steps as James, Eli, and Parker got out of the car. He had his box next to him, ready to go.

James looked at him for a long moment before speaking. "Glad it worked out."

Sebastian glanced between James and Eli. "How did it go?"

James approached, his hair wet from the pool. He reached out and clasped Sebastian's shoulder. "It went fine, Sebastian. It's disorienting learning something new about our parents' accident after so long, but neither of us wants to let old anger about the event back into our lives. And like I told Eli, I was already mad about what your family did to you with the transfer spell. Finding out they also hurt my family is hard to hear, but it doesn't change that much for me. I was already mad at your mother. She has a lot to answer for."

"My mother?" Sebastian asked dumbly.

James gave him a confused, almost pitying look, his eyes scrunched and lips thin.

Eli and Parker came up behind them. Eli pushed past James and captured Sebastian in another unexpected hug. "I'll be careful with the veins, okay? But we need to go take a look at them. And not just because my curiosity is killing me."

"It's not going to be hard for you to be there?" Sebastian glanced between the brothers. "Knowing what part the veins played in everything?"

Eli crossed his arms. "I spent a lot of time being mad at the section of North Road where Mom and Dad's car was found, but in the end, it's just a place. I don't need to be angry at the veins as well. I'd rather study them and see if we can fix them so nothing bad like this ever happens again."

"I agree," James added. "The best thing we can do is try and correct this whole mess."

They piled into the car. Sebastian placed his box in the trunk so he could drop it at his new place later. He should probably grab some bedding and other things while at Storm House, but he spent the ride being grateful Eli still wanted to help after learning the whole story rather than compiling a to-do list for moving into his new home.

Hazel met them at Storm House, her van already waiting outside the gate when they pulled up.

Right, it was time to do this. Sebastian climbed out of the car and marched up to the gate. "You won't feel the haunting effects of the property anymore now that the curse has you. So at least being here won't make you feel like shit." He unlocked the chain and swung the gate open. "Don't bring anything onto the property with a battery, or it will get drained."

Everyone left their phones in the cars. It took Sebastian a second to remember he had a phone in the pocket of James's leather jacket.

Eli pulled a pile of books out of his trunk and handed them to Parker, then grabbed a leather case. "I did some research on how to measure the power flowing through the veins. All my usual tools are electronic, but luckily people have been quantifying magical power since before electricity. Parker and I did some crafting this morning to recreate some old instruments."

"See, this is exactly why we need you." Sebastian smiled at Eli, and the younger man smiled back. They hadn't known each other growing up any better than Sebastian had known James, but of course, they'd seen each other around. Eli was pretty friendly, and Sebastian wished they'd been in the same grade in school. Maybe they'd have been friends.

Sebastian led everyone onto the property. His eyes kept snagging on little things. Today's newspaper on the gravel driveway. The weeds popping up near the front steps. All the apples weighing down the trees.

They were heading toward the forest when Miss Moo came charging over to them. The cow stopped in front of Sebastian and snorted before letting out a long moo.

"Hey, girl." Sebastian patted her head. "I don't think I've ever seen this cow run."

James joined Sebastian in petting the cow. "Seems like she missed you."

Sebastian hugged her neck. He felt bad for leaving her here, but he couldn't exactly bring a cow to his duplex. "Oh no." He looked at James in alarm. "We didn't feed the chickens this morning."

"I can go do it now." James gestured to the barn where the feed was kept.

"No." Sebastian glanced over at the chicken run. "I'll do it after I show everyone the veins."

As he led the group through the trees, Sebastian realized his dread of returning to Storm House had been forgotten. The sight of the house hadn't triggered him like he'd expected. He'd been too distracted by all the little things around the property that needed doing and too focused on taking charge of the vein problem. His need to show the others he was more than a hopeless mess and the cause of their problems had eclipsed everything else.

Why hadn't returning here filled him with loathing? Why hadn't it triggered his fear? Was it because he'd acknowledged to himself that he'd been strong here? That he'd done everything he could to survive the curse and had succeeded and was hoping that confidence would find him again so he could sort out the rest of his life?

He wasn't sure.

They reached the clearing and stopped at the edge of the trees. The fuel cell hummed faintly in the center. The dried blood from the ritual looked sinister on the shiny metal. A chill went down Sebastian's spine. His fear wasn't totally banished.

James caught his eye. He looked up and Sebastian followed his gaze. No shades lurked in the trees, so that was a bonus. But on a sunny day like today, he hadn't expected them.

Hazel went to inspect the fuel cell. "This is kind of amazing."

She narrowed her eyes at James. "I can't believe you pulled this off."

James shrugged. "It was pretty straightforward in the end." He joined her next to the fuel cell. "Doesn't look like much energy has been used, so that's good."

Eli set his case on the ground. "But the veins are draining its energy. This is such an interesting combination of magical principles. I'd never have thought blood magic would work on a non-living source."

Sebastian came closer so he could see what was in the case when it opened. "What are you planning to do exactly?"

Parker handed Eli the books. Eli sat cross-legged and began flipping through them. "I need to see what the veins are doing. If we don't know exactly what's happening, we can't fix it."

"The old methods of measuring power flowing through the earth are all magic-based," Parker explained when it was clear Eli had gotten too wrapped up in the books to explain *how* he would see what the veins were doing. "I'll cast the spells once Eli has everything set up."

"I don't have any magical ability," Eli explained.

"No, you've just got an incredible knowledge of how this all works." Parker looked affectionately down at Eli, who bit back a smile, still focused on the book.

Eli and Parker were sweet together, but Sebastian had other things on his mind. "What kind of spells?" He clenched and unclenched his fists. "How do they interact with the magic in the veins?"

"It's all passive," Eli replied without looking up. "Nothing like the magic you were doing with transferring the curse. That magic had a direct effect on the veins, linking you or the fuel cell to them to correct the imbalance. All I'm doing is reading what's going on beneath the surface. Observing."

"But the observational magic will still interact with the veins to some extent," Sebastian argued.

Eli finally looked up, studying him. "You're really worried."

Sebastian gave Eli a helpless look. How could he not be?

"We'll be casting spells on the instruments, not the veins themselves." Eli opened the case to reveal several wire-framed contraptions and a pencil case.

"The spells will detect what's going on around them, and the mechanism will record it." Parker pointed at the wire frames. "There's no reason the veins should react to either. That's kind of the point."

"Yeah, it'd be impossible to observe what magic is here naturally if measuring it affects the magic we're looking at. Data integrity is key. Everything I'm doing is scientific, even if the methods are dated." Eli gave Sebastian a reassuring smile. "I'm confident the observational spells won't cause an explosion of power or anything like that. I researched the theory this morning."

"Okay." Sebastian finally relented. He had to trust Eli, and now that everyone knew the risks, there was no reason to think they'd disregard them.

Hazel and Parker helped Eli set everything up. Spindly-looking structures were placed at four points around the clearing and one next to the fuel cell. They would ward the mechanisms once they were ready to go to stop any shades from messing with them. Apparently, shades liked to ruin Eli's experiments, though Sebastian had no idea why.

Sebastian turned to James. "I might go feed the chickens since I'm not really contributing."

"Want me to come?" he offered without hesitation.

"You don't have to."

James gave him a stern look. "I know that. But I'm not contributing either, and I'd like to come with you. Unless you want the time alone."

Sebastian grabbed James's hand reflexively. "I don't want to be alone." He wondered if James could tell how deeply he meant the words. He didn't look at his face to check.

"Come on then." James tugged Sebastian along, pulling him toward the path. They walked in silence for a few beats until James said softly, "How's being back here?"

Sebastian looked at him sideways. "Weirdly, not as bad as I thought."

James draped an arm over his shoulders and squeezed, filling Sebastian with affection and longing. Not being there alone must be what stopped Storm House from being triggering. The idea of spending the night here by himself still inspired a familiar dread. Sebastian was glad he'd never have to stay here overnight again. He had a feeling it would break him. But in the daylight, with James, things seemed all right.

They fed the chickens and collected the eggs. Sebastian got distracted by the state of his vegetable garden. Weeds were popping up everywhere. He set to work, James joining wordlessly.

It felt good to take care of his plants. Knowing he'd be living at the duplex, away from all the little things he'd built at Storm House, made Sebastian feel empty, but at the same time, he didn't ever want to live here again. It was a confusing mess of emotions that was starting to hurt.

"How are you doing, Sebastian?" James asked from across the small pumpkin patch.

"Huh?" Sebastian looked up from the clump of weeds in his hand. "I'm fine."

James eyed him, his face neutral. "Okay, good." He looked down at the dirt, slowly pulling more weeds.

Sebastian regretted brushing him off. He wasn't fine. Why was he acting like he needed to be? James would understand. Sebastian knew he could be open with him, but he was trying to put some space between them and not rely on James so much.

However, this kind of emotional support was okay to look for in a relationship. This wasn't the kind of distance Sebastian needed. He needed his own place to live, his independence, but he didn't have to shut everyone out.

He figured James would want to hear how he was really doing, and maybe sharing would help repair some of the trust Sebastian had broken by keeping secrets from James.

Sebastian dropped the weeds he was holding and brushed the dirt off his hands. "I'm not fine, actually."

James looked up. "Do you want to talk about it?"

Sebastian nodded. James stood and rounded the pumpkins to sit next to him. Sebastian looked at his dirty hands and leaned until his shoulder connected with James's.

"Ever since we left, I've been thinking about Storm House, but not in the way you might expect. I hated living here. Hated having to do everything by hand. Didn't want to live like this and be stuck gardening and baking because I had nothing else to do and no other way to get fresh food. But now that I don't have to do it, I feel lost. I miss being out here with my plants and planning what to do with my harvests. It felt weird not doing any of my usual stuff yesterday. But I also feel like it's kind of fucked up that I miss it."

James was silent for a moment, seeming to mull over Sebastian's words. "Your garden and routines were all you had for so long. It makes sense that you found ways to enjoy them. Maybe you'd have liked gardening and baking even if you were never trapped here. They are pretty common hobbies."

"I know." Sebastian rolled his eyes even though James couldn't see it from the way they were sitting side by side. "It's just that not being here has left me feeling so lost. But at the same time, coming back in any sort of permanent way scares the shit out of me. I can't, and I won't. I just don't want to leave my garden or Miss Moo."

"You don't have to."

Sebastian shifted to look at James.

He shrugged. "You can come here and work outside. See your cow. Bring the vegetables and fruit back to town."

Sebastian cringed. "Wouldn't that be weird?"

"Who cares? If it's what you need."

Sebastian smiled at James's bluntness. "I don't know. Escaping only to willingly come back sounds ridiculous. And I don't know if I'd be okay here alone, even in the garden. It'd be too easy to forget I was free."

"I can come out here with you," James offered. "Or, while I'm at work, you and Eli could work something out. He'll have to check on the results in the clearing. I bet you could get him to help with the plants too."

Sebastian looked down at his hands. It sounded perfect. So easy. Like he and Eli were already friends. "Maybe."

Would something like that work, and if it did, would it last? Would he and Eli stay friends? If he didn't solve the problem of their imprisonment in Moonlight Falls, wouldn't everyone resent him eventually? Sebastian couldn't help his fatal thoughts, but he was tired of preparing for the worst.

It really seemed like James harbored no blame for him in regard to his parents' deaths. He wouldn't be this caring otherwise and wouldn't seem relieved Sebastian had opened up and trusted him with his worries. It made Sebastian wonder if he could stop blaming himself or at least stop worrying James would change his mind.

James acted like Sebastian was worthy of his care and concern, and Sebastian was going to go ahead and accept it. Soak it up like a needy sponge, even if he didn't always feel he deserved it. James was giving him good things and he wanted to accept them, not worry they'd be taken away.

"I'll talk to Eli," Sebastian said eventually. "But I should probably focus more on the veins than the garden."

"If looking after your garden helps, then do it. Like you told me, we have to take care of ourselves and not let the problems with the veins consume us."

It was true, but that mentality had only been necessary when the problem didn't seem to have a solution.

CHAPTER ELEVEN

JAMES HELPED Sebastian gather some things he'd need for his new house in town. They packed a box full of cookware and utensils and another one of food from the pantry before taking them to Eli's car.

They returned to the house, this time to get some items from Sebastian's room. James opened the front door, and Sebastian stopped, frozen in the middle of the porch.

"I don't want to go in." Goosebumps erupted on his skin. "I didn't mind the kitchen, but I always liked spending time in there." He peered through the open door from where he stood several feet away. They'd gone in and out through the mudroom before, and Sebastian hadn't ventured past the kitchen. "I fucking hate this house."

James gripped his shoulders. "Of course you do."

"But I was just saying how I want to come here and garden. I'm a goddamn mess. Do I hate this place or not? It doesn't make sense to feel panicked by one thing and long for another."

"It makes sense to me," James said plainly. "The house was a prison, especially at night. You escaped outside, where you could do things you enjoyed and shape your life as much as you were able to. Your garden and the rest of the property are beautiful. The house is dreary and full of old shit that reminds you of everyone else who was trapped here before you. Even I don't like the idea of going back through this door, and I wasn't here long at all."

"The house did feel like more of a prison than the grounds." Sebastian sagged as some of his tension disappeared with James's understanding. "Even though I was trapped on the property, at least being outside, I could breath."

"I'll go get some things from your room for you." James squeezed his shoulders. "Go grab Hazel and send her in here to find me. She can help me pack."

Sebastian met James's stare. "Thank you."

His serious features tugged up in a smile. "Of course, Sebastian. It's nothing when doing this doesn't cost me anything."

But it wasn't nothing. Kindness might not always cost, but that didn't make it meaningless.

Sebastian returned to the clearing, relieved he'd never have to set foot in the main part of the house again if he didn't want to. He still thought it was ridiculous that he couldn't let go of the garden, but he wasn't going to obsess about it. He had to take what felt good and run with it. That way, he could keep going.

In the clearing, Hazel seemed excited to go find James in the house. "I'm not pretending I haven't wondered what it's like inside." She was off down the path without any more prompting.

"Feel free to poke around," Sebastian called as she headed toward the house. "And if there's anything you want, grab it. James will help you steer clear of the creepy shit."

She let out a snort of surprise. "Okay."

"Come check this out." Eli waved Sebastian over from the other end of the clearing. He and Parker were crowded around one of the mechanisms.

Sebastian approached and looked down at the thing.

Eli was practically vibrating where he sat in the dirt, a wide smile on his face. "It's working."

"Of course it's working." Parker huffed with good-natured exasperation. "I don't do shoddy spellwork."

"Definitely not," Eli beamed up at him. "But look, Sebastian, it's recording the amount of magic flowing through the vein below us."

The spindly structure held a pen suspended by a string. Beneath the pen was a roll of what looked like receipt paper. Numbers were being recorded on it in a neat line, the pen twitching as the paper slowly unrolled itself.

It was an impressive bit of magic, but Sebastian could see why modern technology had some advantages over this older method. "What if it rains?"

Eli didn't miss a beat. "We've cast moisture-repelling spells. As long as things don't get left out too long, it'll be fine. But if it starts pouring, I might need to rush out here."

"We'll rush out here together," Parker corrected.

"Right, right. That's what I meant." Eli laughed. "But that's not all." He pulled a map out of his back pocket and unfolded it so he could spread it out on the ground.

Sebastian knelt. "It's a map of Moonlight Falls."

"And the surrounding area." Eli pointed to a hand-drawn line going through town. "This is the vein I was studying for my master's thesis. It's in a straight formation, which is rare." He pointed to a section of the map north of town. "This is your property, see the lines marking it? And this is where the clearing is. My vein in town is going northeast, and so is the one here. At exactly the same angle *and* they align. Meaning, this vein going through your property connects to the one running through Moonlight Falls. In a perfectly straight line."

"Oh. Huh. I had no idea." Sebastian scratched his head. This information seemed significant to Eli, but Sebastian wasn't sure if it was relevant to the problem they were trying to solve.

"It's fascinating. I wonder how far past the clearing it stays straight. I wish I knew where the other vein went and if it's straight or not." Eli looked wistfully off through the trees.

"Feel free to explore." Sebastian stood as Eli folded the map. "I don't have a diagram of the veins. If there's one in the house, I haven't come across it."

Parker brushed a stray leaf off Eli's sweater as he stood. "Did your relatives record much about the veins?"

"Nothing technical like this. They wrote about them, vaguely, in journals and stuff. But I don't have anything detailing exactly what Sullivan and Nelson did to fuck everything up."

"That's too bad." Eli frowned. "It would make my job easier to know how the imbalance was created."

"My ancestors really did not want to make anything easy," Sebastian said bitterly.

"Hm." Eli scowled, an expression that made him look a lot like James.

With everything set up, they walked back to the cars, where they found Hazel and James loading a trunk into Hazel's van.

Eli and Parker were heading back to town since Parker was working the dinner shift at the diner. Before they left, Eli plugged Sebastian's new number into his phone.

"I want to check on things tomorrow," Eli said as he climbed into the driver's seat. "I'll text you if you want to come?"

Sebastian shoved his hands in his pockets. "Sounds good."

Eli smiled like it was the answer he'd hoped for.

As the car drove away, Sebastian turned to the others. "Thanks for grabbing my stuff." James and Hazel had already transferred his boxes from Eli's car to the van.

"No worries." Hazel closed up the back. "If you want any furniture, we'll have to come back. It's too bad we don't have James's truck when we need it." She elbowed James, and he narrowed his eyes at her.

"There's some furniture at the place already." Sebastian didn't want to ask too much of them. Not to mention, he had mixed feelings about moving into the duplex and wasn't itching to fill it with things. "I'll lock up, and we can go."

He didn't have much of a reaction to driving away from Storm House this time. Hazel had music playing from her phone through her van's speakers, and Sebastian closed his eyes to listen.

Back in town, James and Hazel helped Sebastian bring the boxes and trunk into his new home. James used magic for the trunk since it was horribly heavy and no one wanted to drag it up the stairs.

Once everything was inside, the remaining boxes sitting by the front door, there was an awkward pause.

Hazel gestured over her shoulder to the van. "I'm off to my sister's tonight. So—I'm gonna head out."

"Thanks for helping," Sebastian said again. He wasn't sure if he'd conveyed his gratitude enough.

"Any time." She smiled, and it seemed like she meant it.

James glanced between them, a contemplative frown in place. "Want me to leave you to settle in, Sebastian?"

He hesitated. "I don't know." Sebastian figured he should do this on his own, but he didn't want to. He didn't think he'd ever choose to be alone again, which was somewhat at odds with his social anxiety when there were situations that he needed to escape and would rather be alone than deal with.

James turned to Hazel. "Why don't you head out. I'll walk home if I need to."

"All right. Keep me updated on Eli's progress, and I'll see you tomorrow night." She closed the front door behind her with a quiet click.

"What's tomorrow night?"

James cracked a grin. "Parker does Sunday dinner at his place. We barbecue when the weather is nice enough."

"Cool." Sebastian wondered what they barbecued, probably some sort of meat. He'd been vegetarian most of his life.

"You're invited." James nudged Sebastian's arm with his.

Sebastian was surprised and not surprised. They were all so welcoming. It was like his childhood wish for friends in Moonlight Falls had been granted. "I don't really eat meat."

James seemed to bite back a smile. "I'm sure Parker can accommodate that. He makes great veggie burgers."

Sebastian's cheeks heated at the idea of Parker considering him enough to make him something specific. "In that case, I'll have to bring him some jam."

For some reason, the statement prompted James to kiss him on the cheek. "He'll like that. Now, come on. I'll help you unpack."

They went upstairs and made the bed with sheets and pillows from the trunk. Towels and all Sebastian's toiletries were in the trunk as well, and of course, James had added the books Sebastian had kept in his bedroom.

James pulled a first-aid kit out from under more of Sebastian's clothes. "How's your wrist doing?"

"Okay." Sebastian flexed it. "Doesn't hurt at all."

James set the kit on the bed. "Should I take a look at it for you?"

It was probably unnecessary. Sebastian had been keeping it clean and changing the bandage, but James's need to take care of him was probably about more than the wound. "Yeah, if you don't mind." He offered his arm.

James took it gingerly and did a thorough inspection of the bite.

Sebastian suspected James took care of people, in part, to express his affection for them, but that he also needed to look after the people he loved to remind himself he wasn't losing them. Giving James the reassurance he needed made Sebastian feel like they were taking care of each other. It reminded him he had the potential to be who James needed, and it was almost like he belonged to the group of people James loved.

After James deemed Sebastian fine and healing well, Sebastian hugged him.

"What's that for?" James asked, lips brushing Sebastian's ear.

"No reason." Sebastian gave him a kiss on the cheek before pulling away. He didn't actually think James loved him, not even in the way he loved Hazel or Parker, but James seemed to have a whole lot of feelings for Sebastian, and Sebastian had just as many for him.

James had shown Sebastian how much he'd cared today, even in the face of something hard. Maybe things would turn out okay if Sebastian could trust James without his fears getting in the way. Sebastian didn't know what it would take for him to truly stop believing everything good was temporary, but he wanted to figure it out so the two of them could have the chance to fall in love.

James leaned in and kissed Sebastian on the lips. Stubble scratched his cheeks. James's five o'clock shadow appeared much quicker than Sebastian's. He liked that, especially when he felt that rough scrape in intimate places. Sebastian felt so good when they were together, and he was able to stay in the moment.

The kiss didn't turn hearted, and Sebastian got the impression James was waiting for him to decide what was coming next. Eventually, their lips parted, and they pulled back.

Sebastian decided to take a necessary but unpleasant plunge. "I think I want to stay here on my own tonight." He didn't have to explain to James why this simple thing was important to him or why he needed to do it. James would get it.

He nodded, not looking disappointed at all. "Okay. You always know where to find me."

"Yeah, I've got a phone now." Sebastian smiled.

"I'm glad." James looked disproportionately relieved by the reminder for some reason.

Shaking his head, Sebastian walked him out. Then he was alone.

It wasn't as bad as his first day alone in James's house, but it was unsettling. Sebastian had had no life at Storm House, no future, but he'd rarely felt as aimless as he did now. He supposed it was because he didn't have to work so hard to survive anymore. He could be lazy without consequence, but he liked to be busy. He just had to figure out what to do with himself.

CHAPTER TWELVE

Sebastian went down a music rabbit hole online. He streamed song after song on his phone, catching up on what he'd missed.

His favorite pop artist had put out four albums while he was away. "Four!" he exclaimed aloud to the small kitchen. Talking to himself was a habit he'd had before James had gotten stuck at Storm House. It was making a reappearance now.

He called his lawyer and asked the man to order headphones and a few other electronics for him since he was too impatient to wait for his new debit card to arrive in the mail.

Sebastian figured he could dissolve the Storm trust and look after all his own finances now that he wasn't cut off from the world, but he wasn't going to make any big decisions yet. Keeping the lawyer felt like a security blanket. He'd been the only person Sebastian could turn to for so long.

He made himself take one more trip to the General Store before it closed that evening to grab a few things. He bought himself some reusable bags, almond milk, tofu, and vegetables for a stir fry, using the rest of James's cash. He'd packed rice and spices from the pantry at Storm House, so he had everything else he needed.

Back home, he enjoyed his dinner, especially since he hadn't had any bell peppers in his garden recently. Listening to all the new music took the edge off being by himself. The duplex didn't feel so empty when it was filled with his favorite pop songs.

So many little things would have made his life at Storm House more bearable, like music, but Sebastian couldn't dwell on the unfairness of how cut off from everything he'd been. That kind of negativity would consume him. It was better to just enjoy what he had now, and he'd always loved music.

It was too bad the piano wouldn't fit in the duplex. Sebastian didn't think wanting to play it would be enough to make him venture into that part of Storm House, so he wasn't sure when he'd be able to play again. Unless he got an electric keyboard.

After dinner, he decided to bake bread. He put one of his new favorite songs on repeat until he knew the words and could sing along.

Hours later, the loaves were finally in the oven. Sebastian could barely tell how late it was with the bright kitchen lights on. He felt like a time traveler, marveling at all the modern shit he'd been deprived of. Where was the challenge in getting the oven to the right temperature when you had buttons to do it for you and you didn't have to light and stoke a fire?

Every time he had a thought like this, he grumbled at himself in annoyance. *"Don't be such an old man."*

This kitchen felt bare compared to his old one, and the sight of the sparsely stocked pantry kept giving him a jolt of panic. Sebastian had only brought some of the food he had at Storm House, and he wondered if Eli would mind helping him pack the rest tomorrow. Would it all fit in his car? Sebastian had lived like a prepper for so long that he didn't think he'd be able to break the habit. He needed enough dried goods and preserves stocked to survive for six months minimum, or he wouldn't be able to relax.

Sebastian stayed up way too late eating bread. Eventually, he made himself retreat to the bedroom.

He couldn't sleep. The room was too dark without the warm glow of the fire he'd had in his old room.

After lying awake for what felt like forever, Sebastian got up and stared out the window. The duplex was two stories, while most of the buildings in the center of town—other than the library and town hall—were only one. He had a good view from his bedroom as a result. He was around the corner from the small bar on the opposite end of the circle from the ice cream shop and could see all the way across.

With all the new lights that had been installed, Sebastian could see the tall stone in the center of the street. It was a weird landmark, almost like a natural monument, jutting toward the sky. Supposedly, it'd been there since before the town was founded.

A shade swooped around the stone, running its hand over the smooth rock as it circled. It almost looked like it was dancing. Another joined it. Sebastian watched, mesmerized, as they wove between one another.

More shades flew into the center of the circle, and after a few minutes, there had to be about a dozen. The light was faintest where the stone stood, but Sebastian wondered why so many shades had come into such a brightly lit part of town.

Shades swooped above the stone in addition to the ones circling it. A flash of color caught Sebastian's eye. One of the shades was wearing his purple robe! It had been lost the night he and James made their first attempt at the transfer spell, but he'd never have guessed the shade that snatched it would have kept it. He'd never seen one wear human clothing before.

"That little shit," Sebastian grumbled in disbelief. He wanted his robe back. It looked ridiculous flowing off the shadowy beast.

The thief joined the shades swirling around the stone. As Sebastian watched the odd display, he noticed a dark mist gathering on the ground. Shadows seemed to be seeping out from between the surrounding buildings and spilling into the street like water, flowing over the pavement illuminated by the streetlights. Sebastian had never seen anything like it.

The shadows converged on the stone, winding up the smooth surface as the circling shades melted into it seamlessly. Was the shadow nothing but hundreds of shades in semi-solid form? They moved like a river, over the ground and up the stone into the sky.

It gave Sebastian chills.

He thought he saw a figure at the far end of the circle, and his heart skipped. No person should approach that many shades. The figure emerged from the shadows and headed from the middle of the street near the ice cream shop toward town hall.

The way it moved wasn't human. It appeared dark, more like a shadow than anything, and was hard to make out even under a streetlight. It glided, but its body didn't look wispy like the other shades. It was much more humanoid.

The human-like shade made its way completely around the street. Then, it drifted forward and joined the others at the stone. The figure dissolved into the black shadow and wrapped around the stone. Sebastian thought he could still see it amid the other shades as it moved skyward. He watched until he could see nothing but blackness above.

There weren't any stars in the sky, even though Sebastian could have sworn it had been a clear night.

THE NEXT MORNING, Sebastian woke up late to the sound of his phone. It was a text from Eli asking if he'd like to head out to Storm House in an hour. He replied with a quick *yes* and got up to get dressed.

Sebastian looked out his front window as he waited for Eli. It was a dark day. The clouds hung low, and it looked like it would rain. Sebastian's phone chimed again, the screen displaying a message from James.

JAMES

I'm going to go for a swim while Eli is out at Storm House with you unless you want the extra company?

Sebastian bit his lip. He wanted James to do the things he enjoyed like he normally would have before Sebastian entered his life.

SEBASTIAN

No. Go for a swim.

A car pulled up, and Sebastian spotted Eli in the passenger seat. He grabbed his keys and went out to meet him.

"The weather said nothing about a storm," Eli said to Parker as Sebastian climbed into the back seat. "I can't believe this."

Sebastian frowned at the sky. "They look like thunderclouds."

"That's what I said," Parker mumbled.

"I don't disagree," Eli insisted. "I just wasn't expecting it. Guess you can't trust the forecast."

As Parker pulled onto the road, Sebastian returned his attention to his phone. There was a new message from James waiting.

JAMES

Okay, cool. It felt so good to be back in the water yesterday.

Sebastian smiled as he typed his reply.

SEBASTIAN

Maybe I'll come watch you sometime.

JAMES

Why? Wouldn't that be boring?

Sebastian shook his head.

SEBASTIAN

No. I never thought it was boring before.

JAMES

You've watched me swim before?

Honestly, the man was ridiculous sometimes. He was the town athletic champion. The star of their high school swim team. Of course Sebastian had come to watch him at the team's home meets.

SEBASTIAN

Yes, I've watched you swim. You mean to tell me you never noticed the scrawny redhead at the back of the bleachers?

He'd meant it as a joke, even if it was true, but James took so long to respond that Sebastian wished he could take the message back. He wasn't supposed to reveal how long ago his crush had begun.

At last, the phone vibrated.

JAMES

You weren't scrawny. You were cute.

Sebastian stared at the message. It was silly that it made his heart flutter. Sebastian knew James liked him now. He knew their attraction was mutual. But still, it felt damn good to know James had found him cute all those years ago.

SEBASTIAN

OMG, you thought I was cute! You liked me, didn't you?

JAMES

I noticed you, that's all.

Like in that frustrating way you notice someone
you don't quite know what to do with.

I wish I'd figured it out sooner.

Sebastian was officially smiling like a fool, his heart over-
flowing with affection.

SEBASTIAN

You've definitely figured out what to do with
me now.

JAMES

Yes. I missed you in my bed last night.

SEBASTIAN

Me too. I'd tell you exactly how badly, but
sexting with your brother two feet away feels
weird.

JAMES

LOL. OK, I'm going swimming now.

SEBASTIAN

I'll be picturing it.

JAMES

What? Why?

SEBASTIAN

Oh my god, James, you're hot. Now go work out
so I can imagine you all wet and out of breath,
muscular chest heaving, etc., etc.

JAMES

You're a nightmare. Now I'm going to be
distracted.

IN THE CLEARING, Eli ripped off the sections of paper that had data recorded on them and slipped them into five separate folders. He noted the time he did this for each mechanism.

Sebastian peered over Eli's shoulder. "What's the time for?"

Eli glanced up from his notebook. "For cross-referencing. I recorded the time each device started making measurements, and a measurement was taken every minute. Noting the time I cut off the paper means I can check if the right number of measurements were recorded."

Sebastian had no idea why that might matter. "Oh." He glanced at Parker, who shrugged.

Eli smiled. "If the time that's passed since we started recording and the number of measurements don't match up, then we'll know something went wrong and the data isn't accurate. Also, it will allow us to see when any changes in magical flow happen."

That seemed to make sense. "Like if it spikes at a certain time of day or something?"

"Yeah. Or if energy spikes in the different branches of the intersection at different times." Eli closed his notebook. "I'll type these up and import them into my stats software, but we'll probably need more than a day's worth of data to see anything happening."

It didn't look like the shades had tried to mess with their setup, or if they had, Parker's wards had held strong. The sky was still dark enough that they feared a heavy rain was coming, so Sebastian led the other two to the barn to try and find something to cover the mechanisms.

The best they could do were a few old crates covered in tarps, but with the tarps secured to the ground, hopefully, they wouldn't blow away, and combined with the moisture-repelling spell, it would be enough to save the paper in case a storm hit.

Sebastian was beginning to realize how slow the process of solving the imbalance would be. Even collecting data to get started would take a while, but no one else seemed too concerned, or if they were, they were hiding it well.

Eli and Parker helped Sebastian raid his pantry and pack up as much of the kitchen as possible. It was surprisingly easy to convince them to help harvest the ripe vegetables in the garden.

"I really need to pick the apples." Sebastian gave the trees a guilty look.

"Want some help?" Eli stole a quick glance at Parker. "We could do it now."

Sebastian tried to bite back his surprise. "You sure?"

Eli nodded eagerly. "This place is actually pretty cool. Other than the creepy house."

Sebastian laughed. "Thanks. But I don't think we have room in the car for the apples along with everything else."

"I can drive your stuff to town and then come back," Parker offered.

"Oh." Sebastian squirmed. "You don't have to."

"I know." Parker shoved his hands in his jeans pockets. "But I don't have anything pressing to do today, and I'd rather do this than help Eli type up his spreadsheets."

"Hey." Eli shoved Parker playfully on the shoulder. "You know you're going to have to help. There's thousands of data points already."

"I know. But apples seem more fun. I think we deserve to

enjoy ourselves before getting into the rest of the work." He smiled adoringly at Eli before looking expectantly at Sebastian.

"Okay. You'll need the key to my place." He reached into his pocket and pulled it out. "Just dump everything in the living room."

Parker grabbed the key. "Will do."

Sebastian and Eli started picking the apples, and luckily, it didn't rain. Time flew. Eli was easy to talk to, partly because he was extremely chatty and seemed happy to carry most of the conversation. He told Sebastian all about magical veins of power and the project he'd originally been doing when he'd moved up here at the start of fall.

It was cold and dreary, but Sebastian couldn't complain. He was almost able to forget his problems. He'd never imagined spending time with people here, enjoying himself and making a new friend. It was happening anyway, and it made Sebastian think about how different being trapped at Storm House would have been if he'd had friends to visit him or people who hung around for more than a minute.

Maybe Sullivan and Simon didn't think being trapped was such a big sacrifice because they weren't alone, and that's why they were—apparently—so accepting of being the protectors of Moonlight Falls. It could also be part of why they hadn't tried to find a better solution to the imbalance.

Or maybe there had been no better solution back then, but like with the fuel cell, now there was some new magical advancement that could help them.

Sebastian hoped there was. As Eli talked, he intermittently mentioned going back to LA to finish his degree and graduate. It was almost like he'd forgotten that, at the moment, making a trip down south wasn't possible. None of the curse's three new prisoners had tried to leave Moonlight Falls since getting trapped. Parker's and Hazel's lives seemed to revolve around the town, and they must have been happy here. But Sebastian knew the day would come when the curse started to impede all their lives.

Hopefully they would have a solution before Eli needed to return to LA. However, Sebastian couldn't help thinking that four and a half months didn't feel like very long.

CHAPTER THIRTEEN

THAT EVENING, James picked Sebastian up from the duplex to head over to Parker's.

Sebastian had sent Parker home with a crate of apples as a thank-you for helping, but he didn't want to show up empty-handed tonight. He grabbed two jars of jam and a bottle of wine he'd swiped from the Storm House cellar and placed them in one of his reusable bags.

That should be enough, right? James mentioned he was bringing a side dish, but no one had asked Sebastian to make anything. He was nervous, even though he was generally comfortable with James's friends. So far, the only time he'd spent with them had to do with the curse. This was the first purely social thing he'd be joining the group for.

As he met James at his front door, Sebastian tried not to wonder how much Parker or the others really wanted him there.

James kissed Sebastian in greeting, his serious lips transforming into a gorgeous smile. "How was your day?"

"All right." Sebastian stole another kiss. He'd have liked his day more if he'd spent the whole thing with James, but he wasn't saying that aloud. He was resisting being clingy as best he could.

"How was your swim?" He gave James a mischievous grin so James knew he was imagining him in a Speedo.

James shook his head in friendly exasperation. "It was good. I still think it'll be boring for you to come and watch me. It's not like when I used to do races."

"Yeah, I didn't care about the competition aspect so much."

James snorted. "So you were just ogling me?"

Sebastian ran a hand up James's bicep. "You were beautiful. It was mesmerizing watching you move through the water. Talent like that kinda draws you in. You know?"

"I see." James's cheeks went pink. He shifted his weight uneasily. "Aren't you going to ask me why I didn't pursue it further?"

"Pursue swimming?" Sebastian cocked his head. "I guess I never thought about it."

"No?" Something about Sebastian's statement seemed to please James. He grabbed Sebastian's hand and pulled him out the door. As Sebastian locked up, James said, "I got a bit of flack for not taking a scholarship to swim in college. My coaches said I'd wasted all my potential."

Sebastian turned to face James. "But did you want to continue swimming?"

"Not really." James shrugged and led the way to Eli's car. "I loved it growing up, but I didn't want to make it my life. People assumed I would since I had a bit of talent. When I'd come back to Moonlight Falls to visit Eli and Grandma, everyone would ask how swimming was going and would be surprised to hear I'd given up the competitive stuff."

Sebastian climbed into the car. "Where did you go after high school?"

"Apple Valley." James buckled his seatbelt. "I went to the community college, then started an electrician's apprenticeship with Hazel. After a year of that, I was back here for Eli when our grandma died, and I was glad it was so easy to come home. That I hadn't gone far. If I'd taken the scholarship I'd been offered, I'd have had to move out of state and would have ended up dropping out when Grandma died. Instead, I was able to finish my apprenticeship by commuting to Apple Valley while living here."

"You didn't want to leave, did you?"

"No. The idea of a big university or traveling for swim meets wasn't appealing and had nothing to do with the career I wanted. Being an electrician was always the plan, and I may have been able to swim in college, but that didn't mean I'd make it as a career athlete." James started the car. "Besides, I didn't want to be too far from the magic here. People in town understand not leaving Moonlight Falls but then are confused about me abandoning swimming. Doesn't add up, does it?"

"No," Sebastian agreed. "I'm glad you did what you wanted."

James put his hand on the back of Sebastian's neck and squeezed gently, a soft expression on his face. "Me too. And I know people here are proud of me. They never meant to sound chiding. I guess my coaches' reactions hurt, and every time someone brought it up, it would remind me how much I'd disappointed them."

"I bet your coaches weren't Moonlighters. Or they would have understood."

James let out a grunt that almost sounded like a laugh. "No. You're right. They weren't."

They drove to Parker's house on the east side of town. Unlike James, Sebastian had been happy to leave Moonlight Falls, though he might not have bothered with college if he'd known he was going to get sucked back here and trapped before he could graduate.

He supposed he could go back to school now that he was free to enroll in something online while trapped in Moonlight Falls, but he wasn't sure if there was much point. Sebastian didn't need a degree for anything. He wasn't interested in research like Eli. He wanted to do something that had a clear purpose. He needed a direction in his life and didn't think a random bachelor's degree would help. He hadn't exactly had career plans when he was younger, just the need to escape.

They arrived, and James walked into Parker's house without knocking. Sebastian couldn't help feeling like an interloper. Yes, he'd spent the day with Parker and Eli, but he was only here tonight because he was with James.

James led the way through the small house and placed the potato salad he'd brought in the kitchen. They found everyone sitting in the backyard, drinking beer around a fire pit.

James took a seat in one of the unoccupied lawn chairs. "Being out here feels like tempting fate."

Parker glanced up at the cloud-darkened sky. "It hasn't rained yet, and burgers aren't as good without the charcoal grill."

Eli glanced between James and Sebastian. "Do you guys want drinks?"

"Oh, I brought wine." Sebastian pulled the bottle out of his bag. There was a pause. "We don't have to open it though. Um. I also brought you some jam." He turned to Parker.

"Thanks." Parker took the wine and examined the label. "Here, come in with me, and we can pop the cork." He turned toward the house.

Sebastian followed.

In the kitchen, Parker put the wine on the counter. "What kind of jam have you got?"

"Apricot." Sebastian handed over the jars.

"Between this and the apples, you're spoiling me." Parker was smiling, but Sebastian was unsure if Parker was genuinely pleased. Had he done the right thing by bringing a gift?

Sebastian scrunched up the empty bag in his hands. "I can't come to dinner empty-handed."

Parker set the jars on the counter. "Hazel does every week."

"But she's your friend." Sebastian froze as soon as the words left his mouth.

Parker gave him a stern look. "So are you."

Sebastian's stomach twisted. "Just like that?"

"Why not?" Parker crossed his arms, a single brow raised.

"I mean, we hardly know each other, and I've trapped you in Moonlight Falls. I know James is your friend, but that doesn't automatically extend to me." Sebastian needed to stop talking. He wanted Parker as a friend and shouldn't be trying to talk him out of it, but he wondered if challenging the other man's acceptance was the only way he might believe it was real.

Parker stood firm. "It can automatically extend to you. I have no reason not to like you, Sebastian. I'm a simple guy, and James liking you is enough reason for me to want to get to know you."

But it couldn't be that simple. If it was, why had Sebastian been alone for so long? Even before he was trapped, he'd never had a strong group of friends. "I just don't know how you all can act like I haven't screwed up your lives. I've given you my curse and dumped all my problems on you."

"Sebastian." Parker's serious expression turned disapproving. "You haven't screwed up anyone's lives. Being confined to Moonlight Falls isn't ideal. It's something I don't want to last for the rest of my life, but even if it does, it's a price worth paying for you to not be alone."

Sebastian blinked. "You can't mean that."

"Why not? I bet Hazel, Eli, and James would all agree. The problem of the veins isn't your responsibility. It's a town issue with the potential to affect all of us, so we should all pitch in to solve it. And the four of us having to deal with the curse is better than you suffering alone. If the situation had been presented to me and I'd had the choice to leave you at that house so I could be free or accept the curse and give all of us a bigger cage, it wouldn't have even been a choice worth thinking about."

Sebastian squeezed the bag in his hands so tight his fingers cramped. "But you didn't get a choice."

"Neither did you. You don't have to feel guilty, Sebastian.

What happened to you is horrifying, and any of us would have made sacrifices to spare you from it."

"Why?" Sebastian looked away. He was overwhelmed with feelings of unworthiness. He couldn't believe anything Parker was saying. Parker got nothing out of making sacrifices for him. Maybe if James had said it, he might have entertained the possibility it could be true. James liked him. James enjoyed sex with him and wanted to take care of him, but even then, Sebastian had trouble trusting James at his word when his fears screamed at him not to.

Parker gave Sebastian a sad smile. "Because no one should be left alone, bearing the burden of keeping the town safe. All of us confined to Moonlight Falls is nowhere near as bad as one person cut off from literally everything. I could never sacrifice someone else to make my life more comfortable."

Sebastian had never thought about it that way. He was astounded that Parker would be willing to give anything up for him. He almost didn't believe that kind of selflessness was real.

No one ever gave anything up for him.

"I just don't know why you care," he mumbled.

"You're worth caring about, Sebastian. You aren't defined by your family's curse. You're with us now, and we're not letting you go." Parker clasped him on the shoulder in a firm, reassuring gesture.

Sebastian looked up and met Parker's intimidating stare. He couldn't believe what he was hearing. He wanted to keep asking *why*. He hadn't earned this. It didn't make any sense.

Sebastian took a step back, and Parker let his hand fall. Sebastian glanced around the kitchen, his skin crawling with discomfort. He wanted to leave, get away from these feelings. The only reason he didn't scamper down the hall was because James was sitting in the backyard.

His distracted gaze landed on the crate of apples. "Should I make a pie for dessert?" Sebastian sounded as frazzled as he felt.

When Parker didn't immediately respond, he continued, "Or help cook? You helped me this afternoon, so just let me know what you need."

"You don't have to earn your keep," Parker said as if he'd read Sebastian's mind.

But he did. Otherwise, how could he be sure Parker wouldn't change his mind and decide he wasn't worth it. Sebastian was being given everything he wanted and couldn't handle it. Parker's friendship and frank acceptance were too perfect. It couldn't be real. The idea that it could be was terrifying.

"Come out and sit with us." Parker grabbed a corkscrew and opened the wine, then poured a glass for Sebastian. "Give this to James." He pulled a beer out of the fridge.

Sebastian accepted the drinks.

Parker took two covered plates out of the fridge. "We want you here, Sebastian, and that's not going to change." He led the way out to the yard, and Sebastian followed.

James glanced over at them and smiled, a simple, tender expression just for Sebastian like he made James's life better just by being there.

Why did Sebastian feel like he didn't deserve any of this and therefore, it couldn't be real? He had no reason to think Parker was lying to him. He could trust Parker, just as he could trust that James didn't blame him for his parents' accident. Sebastian had no reason not to take these honest men at their word. His skepticism and distrust came from his own self-doubt and he needed to stop giving it so much influence over how he reacted to things.

Maybe he didn't have to feel so unworthy.

If Parker could believe Sebastian was worth sacrificing some of his freedom for, surely it wasn't a foregone conclusion that everyone would resent him one day. Sebastian knew James wanted to take care of him and share a future with him. He wanted to take care of James too. He'd do just about anything for James, so why assume that sentiment didn't go both ways? Everything James had shown him said he was committed and not about to abandon him.

There wasn't a single solid thing to support Sebastian's fears except for his own feelings of unworthiness. None of his interactions with James, Parker, Eli, or Hazel said Sebastian would lose these people's support or that they found him in any way unworthy. He should be able to accept the facts in front of him and let go of the idea that the only way to get through life was to be ready for people to leave him.

He might not be doomed to lose everything. That fear wasn't actually grounded in reality. It was his past clouding his present, and he wanted to let it go.

Maybe he was worthy of friends and a happy life just as he was. James and the others accepted him as if that were that simple. As if he didn't have to earn love or prove himself to keep it, and if that were the case, maybe he didn't have to be so afraid.

SEBASTIAN SAT in the lawn chair next to James. He scooted it closer so he could rest his head on James's shoulder. It was a clingy gesture and gave away Sebastian's need to be comforted, but James's only response was to drape an arm around Sebastian's shoulders and pull him closer.

Could Sebastian be needy and imperfect and still keep James's affection? The idea was terrifying. Exposing himself to James so honestly would make rejection all the more painful. But Sebastian could trust James. He had no reason to think James would abandon him.

The fire in the pit burned bright. Sebastian watched the flames, the physical contact with James soothing him.

"Think we'll see any shades tonight?" Hazel asked as it got dark.

Parker stood over at the grill, tending to the burgers. "Who knows."

James rubbed his hand up and down Sebastian's arm. "The fire will probably keep them back." The patio light would have been enough in the past, but it wouldn't keep light-resistant shades away. Objects could be warded but open spaces couldn't since there was nothing physical to tie the spell's boundary to on all necessary sides. The fire was probably their best bet if they didn't want to avoid being out after dark.

"There were a bunch of shades in town last night." Sebastian had forgotten about the shades for most of the day. He told everyone what he'd seen from his window, not moving from his spot curled against James. He still felt raw and overwhelmed from all the thoughts talking to Parker had dragged up.

After he finished describing the shades' behavior, there was a pause as everyone digested the information.

Hazel frowned from across the firepit. "Sounds freaky."

"But who knows what it means." Eli picked at the label on his beer bottle. "Maybe shades do stuff like that all the time, but no one's ever seen it."

"Yeah, it's not like they were trying to cause trouble or break anything like they did in town before," James agreed.

Uncertainty seemed to hang in the air as if they all thought something was wrong with the spectacle Sebastian had witnessed but had no concrete reason to explain why.

Eventually, they retreated inside to eat. There were beef burgers and veggie burgers with all the fixings, as well as James's potato salad. Everyone made a plate and found a spot in the kitchen or adjoining pool room and tucked into their food.

"Anyone up for a game?" Hazel asked when she'd finished eating, pointing to the pool table.

"Sure." Sebastian wiped his hands and stepped forward.

Hazel had a positively evil grin. "Want to break?"

Sebastian hesitated as he grabbed a pool cue. "No, you can."

It felt like everyone was watching intently and Sebastian wondered if he was missing something. But if he was going to try and stop doubting these people's acceptance, he had to act like he was part of the group and not second guess everything he did around them or worry one misstep would push them away.

So he was going to play pool with his friends and not stress about it.

Once Hazel sent the balls scattering, Sebastian considered the table. He lined up a shot and sunk a solid ball. He went on to sink four more before he missed.

He straightened to find Hazel's narrow-eyed gaze fixed on him. "What?"

Parker chuckled.

No one explained what was funny. Hazel had her turn and got a couple of balls in. On Sebastian's next turn, he cleared the rest of the solids.

"How are you so good at this?" Hazel asked, incredulous, after Sebastian called out his last shot.

"There's a billiards room at Storm House." Sebastian sent the eight ball careening across the table and into the pocket he'd indicated. He grinned. "I've had lots of time to practice."

"Damn." Hazel frowned, but not like she was actually annoyed. It was an expression he'd seen on James many times. After a moment's contemplation, Hazel turned toward the others. "Eli, why don't you play me next."

Eli was back in the kitchen eating potato chips. "No thanks." He caught Parker's eye, and the two shared a charged look. Parker bit his lip, looking like he wanted to devour Eli.

"Hazel only likes to play when she can win," James explained to Sebastian, seeming to miss the moment between his brother and Parker.

Sebastian knocked Hazel's pool cue lightly with his. "Seems like you need practice now that I'm around. Then we can go again."

She laughed. "You're on."

Something slammed into the sliding glass door, and they all jumped at the sound.

"What the fuck was that?" The bag of chips lay forgotten at Eli's feet.

James's gaze found Sebastian in a seemingly reflexive move, like his first instinct was to seek him out and check he was okay. It grounded Sebastian, made him feel claimed and cared for, even while his heart pounded in response to the sudden scare.

He reluctantly tore his eyes away from James and looked out into the dark. He couldn't see anything.

"I'd say it was a shade hitting the door." Parker walked right up to the glass, his nose almost touching it. "I can't see anything out there now, and the house is warded, so we should be fine."

A bang came from the kitchen.

"Something hit the window." Eli pointed in front of him.

"What the hell?" Hazel stalked into the kitchen. "They can't smash through the glass if it's warded. What are they doing?"

More shades assaulted the house. Three hit the sliding glass door, and from the sound of it, at least one more hit the kitchen window. The shades on the other side of the glass door didn't dissipate or retreat this time. They hovered, staring back at everyone inside.

Parker flicked a switch on the wall and floodlights lit his yard, much brighter than the ones he'd had on while they were grilling.

The shades didn't retreat. They didn't even seem to notice.

"Should we ignore them?" Sebastian shifted closer to James. "The ones at Storm House were always peering in at me, but pretending I didn't notice usually prompted them to go away."

"The ones at your house weren't this aggressive," James murmured, his attention fixed on the shades behind the glass.

"I know. But unless we want to go outside and start conjuring fireballs, what can we do? They can't get in."

"Let's give it a few minutes. See if they get bored." Parker turned down the hallway toward the front of the house. "If they keep it up, we'll have to go out and get rid of them. I'm going to check the front."

Eli followed Parker down the hall.

The shades at the back door slowly drifted away from the house. Just as Sebastian hoped they were leaving, they swooped back in and smashed into the wards protecting the glass.

He, James, and Hazel all flinched.

As the shades retreated again, likely readying for another assault, a dark shadow began to tinge the edge of the glass door. Tendrils of darkness crept along like feelers searching for something.

"What is *that?*" Hazel pointed at the shadow as the shades struck again, banging loudly against the wards.

It had to be shades in non-solid form, but if that's all it was, why had the glass rattled this time? The charging shades shouldn't have been able to impact the house. Right?

Eli and Parker returned from the front of the house. Parker frowned at the shadow now covering a quarter of his sliding door. "There are shades out front too, charging the windows, but we couldn't see any lurking around the other houses on the street. I've got the bright lights on out front, not that it's done anything."

The shades struck again. The glass shook.

"If the place is warded, then why have those last two hits made an impact?" James asked.

"I don't know. It shouldn't be possible." Parker pulled Eli behind him as the glass rattled again.

Shades had limited magic. They could shape the shadow that made up their bodies and incorporate themselves into the dark, but they couldn't cast complex spells. They couldn't counter human magic, which was why warding against them was a standard, simple practice. There should have been no way for the shades to weaken Parker's protective spells.

"What if that shadow isn't what we think it is?" Sebastian gestured to the growing darkness blocking out the glass door. It seemed similar to the river of shadow he'd seen in town last night. Had he been wrong about what he'd seen? "What if it's not just more semi-solid shades?"

Hazel's eyes widened in alarm. "What else could it be?"

Sebastian had no answer.

"Get back," Parker barked as the shades struck again. There were more hitting the glass now, at least five that Sebastian could see.

Everyone retreated to the back wall of the room. Sebastian pressed his shoulder against James.

James gripped Sebastian's hand, pointing with his other. "That looks like a crack." Sure enough, there was a jagged fracture in the middle of the glass.

"Fuck." Parker ran a hand through his hair. "Okay, they're breaking in. We can figure out how later." He moved forward, reaching for the door handle. "I'm going to open it. If the wards have been broken, the shades will rush in, and we'll need to send fire at them. There's no need to wait for them to shatter the glass."

Everyone made sounds of agreement.

Parker unlatched the door and pulled it open, sending fire out in the process. Sparks flew through the air and caught on the first shade. Flames erupted and it burst into wafts of smoke, banished back to Beyond.

The other shades didn't hesitate as their fellow was taken care of. They charged the now open doorway and smashed into an invisible barrier. It seemed the wards were still mostly intact and hadn't been weakened enough for the shades to do more than a little damage to the glass.

Sebastian, James, and Hazel rushed forward, helping Parker send sparks after the beasts. Fire caught on each shade, and they exploded, leaving the physical world behind.

"Look!" Eli shouted.

The shadowy feelers were making their way into the room, creeping along the floor. It looked almost like they were squeezing through an invisible crack in the wards, seeping in and then expanding outward.

"How is that possible?" Hazel asked as she sent sparks at the invasive shadow.

"Don't light the house on fire," James growled as he stomped out a stray spark.

One of Hazel's other sparks caught on a tendril of dark shadow. It screeched and writhed, breaking off from the rest of the shadow before it exploded into nothing.

"Did it just scream?" Sebastian looked at the others in disbelief. They seemed as shocked as he felt.

"Fuck." James lurched back as some of the shadow reached his foot. Hazel shot sparks at the tendril as it wrapped around James's ankle, and it burst.

Eli appeared behind them with a fire extinguisher. "Just in case."

Parker positioned himself in front of Eli as he helped the others fight back the shadow crawling along the floor like the tentacles of some deep sea monster. The shadow's ability to break off into separate pieces made it impossible to banish completely. A new tendril replaced each one that was destroyed as more flowed in from outside.

More shades appeared. Sebastian concentrated on sending his sparks through the open door at them, but he was starting to get winded. His magical ability wasn't that strong. Definitely not as strong as James's or Hazel's, and nowhere near Parker's level.

He sent sparks at a shade, and it caught fire. Several more swooped around the yard, hissing and charging at the house. At least there weren't hordes of them. The situation was still manageable unless more were lurking just out of sight. As Sebastian searched for more shades in the distance, he realized the yard was much darker than it should have been, considering Parker had his floodlights on.

The others continued to battle the shadow twisting along the floor, but Sebastian was fixated on the yard. He could barely see the back fence when, before, every corner had been lit up. Were there more shades back there? Was that why it was so dark? He strained, trying to see if there was any movement.

Nothing moved, but he swore there was a hulking figure lurking behind the tree.

Sebastian blinked, and the thing came into focus. It was a shade but not quite. The frame of its upper body was more like that of a large man. The longer Sebastian looked, the more drained he felt. Exhaustion swelled, and his head spun.

He staggered, blinking rapidly, his gaze leaving the figure in the yard as his vision darkened around the edges. Sebastian swayed and fell.

CHAPTER FOURTEEN

"Sebastian!" James's urgent shout sounded close to Sebastian's ear. Strong arms held him steady.

"I'm all right." Sebastian braced himself against James, regaining his balance. He looked back into the yard but couldn't see anything by the back fence.

James pulled him back, away from a tendril snaking along the floor. The shadow coming into the house wasn't stopping.

"We need to find out where it's coming from. Attacking it like this isn't doing enough." Parker stepped closer to the open doorway. "I'll fix the fractured ward. Then we need to go outside and find the source of this shadowy mess and stop it that way."

Hazel swept the hair that had escaped her ponytail out of her face. "Sounds like a plan."

James kept an arm around Sebastian, like he was worried Sebastian might tip over again. Parker secured the wards around the house without trouble, stopping more shadows from seeping inside. Once the last tendril left in the pool room had been banished by a burst of fire from James, they made their way onto the back patio.

The charging shades were absent for the moment, and the

creeping shadow didn't line the ground as Sebastian had expected. Confused, he turned back toward the house, pulling James with him.

"Oh no," Sebastian breathed, and the rest of the group turned to look.

The shadow they'd seen from the doorway was covering the entire house. It rolled like a fog but clung to the building unnaturally.

"What the hell?" Eli gripped the fire extinguisher, a mixture of awe and horror on his face.

Hazel looked up in disbelief. "It's huge."

James's hand on Sebastian tightened. "Is it coming from the sky?" There was a dark haze above the house. If they were hoping to find the source, and it was in the air, that wasn't good.

"I thought I saw something by the fence. Like the figure I saw in town." Sebastian turned toward the back of the yard. "Look. That corner is almost pitch black."

The back left corner of the yard was so dark you couldn't see the fence. Whatever was shrouding the corner seemed to continue into the sky, just like the shadow attacking the house. They had to be connected, and sure enough, the longer Sebastian looked, the more sure he was that the shadow in the corner was flowing up, like a reverse waterfall, while what was covering the house was flowing downward. The source could very well be hiding in the corner.

Parker must have been thinking along the same lines as he said, "Looks like whatever's back there is our best bet. Let's go for it together." He elbowed James, who nodded.

The two men inched around the tree. A shade swooped in behind them. Sebastian sent sparks at the beast just as it reached out to grab James. As flames banished the shade at their backs, James and Parker sent sparks into the darkened corner. The first were swallowed by the blackness and didn't ignite, but James and

Parker didn't stop. They sent sparks into the dark until, finally, one caught.

The flames didn't penetrate the darkness enough for them to see what was lurking there. The only indication that the sparks had caught was the shrill scream that pierced the night. Sebastian flinched and covered his ears. The fire roared, flames crackling behind the dark curtain, and the shadow enveloping the house was slowly sucked back up into the sky.

When the last tendril left the house, the darkness in the corner burst, revealing a column of flame. The scream cut off and the fire fizzled out. The floodlights seemed to flare, like the whole yard had been darkened unnaturally and had suddenly returned to normal.

The corner was now empty.

"Shit," James panted, bracing himself against the tree.

Sebastian rushed up to him. "Are you okay?" He rubbed James's back, scanning him for injuries even though he hadn't seen anything that could have hurt him.

"Yeah." He pushed off the tree and let Sebastian wrap him in a hug. "Don't think I have much magic left in me though."

"Come on." Sebastian led him back toward the house, and the others followed, Eli at Parker's side and Hazel bringing up the rear. "I don't know about the rest of you, but I need to sit down."

THE GROUP LEFT Parker's house after a second dinner, necessary for everyone but Eli to recoup the energy they'd lost doing so much magic. No one had any idea why Parker's place was targeted out of all the houses on the street, but it was probably best to leave for the rest of the night. Eli insisted Parker come home with him, and Parker didn't argue.

Hazel offered to stop in on the mayor at home and tell her

what happened. Sebastian wondered if that was necessary, but no one else seemed to find it odd for Hazel to show up at the other woman's house like this. He supposed the news that shades had a way of getting past wards couldn't wait.

James drove Sebastian back to the duplex in silence. They arrived at Sebastian's place to find the entryway dark. He'd forgotten to leave a light on, unlike his neighbor, whose home was cheery and bright.

Sebastian wrapped James's jacket tight around himself, shooting a look at James. "Want to come in?"

James took Sebastian's hand, dislodging it from where it clung to the jacket. "Yes, I'll always want to come in."

Sebastian didn't release James's hand. James *would* always want to come in, wouldn't he? God, that felt good. Sebastian had no desire to be alone tonight. Not after thinking about everything Parker had said and not after the scare of the attack. He needed James and didn't care how clingy he came across.

James studied Sebastian silently, his eyes narrowed in confusion when Sebastian remained quiet. "That surprises you?"

Sebastian held James tight, his face obviously giving him away. "I know it shouldn't. But yes," he whispered. Admitting this insecurity gave him an uncomfortable jolt, but he wanted to be honest.

James looked thoughtful but didn't comment or tell Sebastian he was wrong for feeling that way, and Sebastian was grateful.

Sebastian only let go of James because it was necessary to get out of the car. Inside, he and James went directly up to the bedroom. Sebastian pulled James close, letting himself be comforted by the press of their bodies. He tucked James's face into the crook of his neck and held him for a long time, his nose buried in James's hair, breathing him in. The hint of chlorine mixed with James's shampoo and his musky scent was Sebastian's favorite smell.

James gripped him around the waist, seeming content to hold

the tight embrace. Neither of them said anything. Sebastian wasn't sure what he would even say. He was so grateful for James. He'd rescued Sebastian in so many ways. He was still saving him, even now, with this hug, showing Sebastian what it was like to have good things in his life, making him believe he didn't need to earn love, that he was accepted and worthy just as he was.

He could be what James needed. They could build a resilient relationship if the things they'd already faced were anything to go by. He'd been there for James at Storm House and shouldn't have discounted the significance of that. He'd had something to offer then and even more to offer now.

With a kiss to the top of his head, Sebastian released James. They stripped each other and tumbled into bed. Sebastian pulled the covers over them and nuzzled his face against James's chest like a cat, worshipping him and letting James fill all his senses.

He was exhausted emotionally from the conversation with Parker and physically from using so much magic. He and James were probably too worn out for much in the way of sex, but that was okay. Sebastian needed a different kind of comfort tonight.

He rubbed his face against James, his cheek gliding over James's left pec and nipple. He turned his head, burying his nose in James's chest hair, and breathed in. It felt so good. He wanted to crawl inside James, feel him everywhere. He gave in to his neediest desires and did what felt right, touching and pressing into James's body, rubbing every inch of his face against James's chest, smelling him, and making him his whole world.

"Hope I don't stink." James let out a tired laugh as Sebastian continued to rub.

"Love the way you smell," Sebastian murmured. "I can't get enough of being close to you."

James let out a soft sigh, close to a moan. He pulled Sebastian tighter against his side and buried his other hand in Sebastian's hair. "I'll never get enough of you, Sebastian."

The words washed over Sebastian like soothing, warm water.

Good feelings enveloped him, and he banished his doubt. He wouldn't let himself be consumed by the ungrounded fear of James changing his mind.

"I like hearing that. I like knowing you can't get enough of me," Sebastian whispered as his head came to rest, too caught up in the way James was massaging his scalp to continue nuzzling.

Sebastian felt calm with his ear resting above James's steady heartbeat. He was settled in a way he hadn't been, maybe ever. He'd been telling himself to trust James, but this was the first time he felt like he actually did, all the way to his bones.

Sebastian had never fully trusted anyone. Not his mother, uncle, or the people he'd had passing friendships with, and in most of those cases, he'd had good reason not to. Trusting had been dangerous and had left him hurt and betrayed, but in James's arms, he knew what it was like to be completely safe and secure for the first time.

James laid a kiss on his head. "I can tell you I'll never get enough of you every day. It'll always be true."

"You'll spoil me." Sebastian craned his neck to look at James.

He smiled, soft and lovely on his usually hard face. "I don't know if that's spoiling you, but if it is, you deserve it."

Sebastian tightened his hold on James. He did deserve it. If James thought so, how could he argue? If James could accept him and see the good in him, it must be there. He was more than a messy causer of problems. He was someone worth choosing, and he was going to start living his life like it.

Sebastian kissed the firm pec he was resting on, burrowing back into James's chest. "You do too. I'm going to spoil the hell out of you, James. I want all the good things for you."

"I don't know what more I could possibly want." James's hand stilled in Sebastian's hair. "Not when I've already got you. Everything I need is right here."

"Really?"

James tugged Sebastian's curls until he looked up. "Yes." He had that thoughtful expression again. "You're everything to me, and I'll keep reminding you. If that's what you need?"

Sebastian nodded. It was what he needed. Maybe it shouldn't be, but reassurance helped him push away the fears he was trying to let go of.

James gave him a tiny, delicate smile. "You've got it, sweetheart."

Sebastian settled back on James's chest. He was still astounded he was who James wanted, but not because he felt unworthy. He felt lucky.

Sebastian clung to James all night, and James didn't seem to mind.

CHAPTER FIFTEEN

Sebastian woke up to James playing with his hair. It felt so fucking good, fingers exploring in the most tender little motions, tugging his curls and sending tingles racing over his scalp. He floated on a happy, half-awake cloud as James's chest rose and fell beneath him.

Their bodies were hot against each other, the blankets mostly kicked back. Sebastian moaned as James's massaging became firmer. He stretched, arching his back and pressing his half-hard cock against James's hip.

"Hey there," James crooned in a deep, lust-laden voice.

Sebastian cracked his eyes open to the pre-dawn darkness shrouding the room. "Your hands in my hair feel so good."

"Yeah?" James turned, dislodging Sebastian from his chest. Before Sebastian could protest, James aligned their bodies, both of them on their sides, facing each other, and cupped Sebastian's ass. He brought them together, his erection pressing against Sebastian's.

"Fuck, yeah. This feels even better." Sebastian rolled his hips as his dick hardened fully. He hitched a leg over James and pulled them tighter together. Their lips met. James squeezed Sebastian's ass, his fingers delving between his cheeks. Sebastian groaned into his mouth. "I want to wake up like this every day."

"So do I." James held Sebastian firm, massaging his hole as he rolled his hips, rubbing their erections together.

Sebastian whimpered. James wanted to wake up with him every day. He was wanted, and every touch James gave him confirmed it, over and over. Sebastian was wanted, and it felt fucking amazing to accept without caveats.

James rubbed his nose over Sebastian's. He made a satisfied sound as Sebastian's hole twitched against his finger, eager for more. James pressed against the puckered flesh, tapping and rubbing but not penetrating. The teasing touch had Sebastian panting, his cock leaking, giving away just how needy he was.

James held him in place, lining them up perfectly, and rolled his hips, precum easing the slide of skin against skin. "You're so wet. Fuck, Sebastian, you feel amazing."

Sebastian's cheeks were on fire. "You like that I'm wet for you?"

"So much." James pulled back and grabbed Sebastian's dick, watching as more precum beaded at his slit and rolled down his already glistening head. "Look at you leaking, sweetheart. You want me so much."

The first time they'd hooked up, Sebastian had been embarrassed by how much of a mess he'd made of himself aching for James. His arousal had always come with an excessive amount of precum, but with James, it was unparalleled.

"I want you," Sebastian panted as James worked his leaking cock. "Can't hide how much I need you, James."

James moaned, swiping the wetness with his thumb and rubbing it around Sebastian's tip. He rolled Sebastian onto his back and aligned their dicks, taking them both in his hand. James squeezed their lengths together, tight. "Tell me you've never needed anyone like you need me."

"Fuck, James," Sebastian whimpered. "Never. I've never needed anyone but you."

"Yes, Sebastian." James stroked them hard, his face flushed, gaze fixed on their cocks. "You're mine. You know that, right? Say you're mine."

Sebastian clung to James's shoulders, digging his fingers into the taut muscle. "I'm yours. All my wetness is for you, James. Every drop."

"*Fuck*." James came on a strangled cry. Cum spilled over his hand, onto their cocks and Sebastian's stomach. James thrust into his fist. His cock slid against Sebastian's swollen, aching erection as James chased his orgasm, grunting, "Mine, *mine*."

A whine escaped Sebastian. He was so close. James was a hard, unrelenting beauty on top of him, and his words were just as potent as his touch. Sebastian was nearly sobbing it all felt so good.

James readjusted his grip around Sebastian, not even pausing to catch his breath as he smeared his cum over Sebastian's cock. His intensity didn't die. It was as if he wanted Sebastian's release more than he had his own. James jacked Sebastian off with perfect, tight strokes, his attention shooting up to study Sebastian's face.

"Come for me, sweetheart," he commanded in a low rasp. "Show me you mean it. All of this is for me. I'm the only one for you."

Sebastian moaned and came hard, James's stare searing itself into his memory. Nothing had been easier than letting James know he meant it. Nothing had felt better. No orgasm in his life as consuming as this one. All of Sebastian's arousal was for James. All his feelings. And the fact that James seemed to come alive knowing that, like Sebastian's desire burned a fire in him, was the most intoxicating thing Sebastian had ever experienced.

James worked him until he whimpered. Only then did he

relent, collapsing on top of Sebastian and kissing him deeply until neither of them could breathe.

James rested his forehead against Sebastian's shoulder, panting.

Sebastian felt almost high. He'd never been this keyed up while simultaneously spent and deeply satisfied. He wiggled beneath James. In response, James picked up his head. Sebastian grinned. "I like this possessive side of you."

James's face heated, his breathing still ragged. "I may have gotten carried away."

"Good." Sebastian rolled his hips, smearing their cum between them. "Hope it happens again soon."

James bit his lip like he was going to protest and retreat back into his bashful shell. Then his eyes flashed mischievously. "Think I can arrange that." He lowered his head and bit the crook of Sebastian's neck, not hard enough to hurt, but not too gently either. "Mine," he growled in a commanding yet playful voice that sent a shock of pleasure through Sebastian. James bit him again, groaning and sucking on the spot before picking his head up and fixing Sebastian with serious set eyes. "Now you've been claimed and can't be taken away. How's that for possessive?"

The words were tender and unfaltering, causing Sebastian's breathing to turn shallow. He threaded his fingers through James's hair and pulled him back down. "Again," he whispered.

James bit and licked and growled *mine* with more intensity. It seemed like something had unlocked within James, like he was freeing a need he'd longed to express but hadn't allowed himself to.

Sebastian wondered if James was letting this side of himself out to show Sebastian how much he meant to him, like Sebastian's need for reassurance had given James permission to express himself without worrying it would be too much.

James bit him again, letting out a guttural moan. There would most likely be an array of bruises on Sebastian's pale, freckled skin later, and he couldn't wait to see them.

He loved this, even if James's possessive side was born out of his fear of losing people, as Sebastian suspected. Chances were, James wanted to claim Sebastian so he couldn't be taken away, assert to the universe that Sebastian belonged to him so it would know not to separate them. That was a level of possession Sebastian hadn't even dreamed of.

Sebastian's neediness was the perfect match for this side of James. Their imperfections fit together like they were made for each other almost as if their traumas had been twisted together for the last fourteen years, not out of random chance, but to create their other half. A person who understood them like no one else.

It made what they had feel inevitable. Meant to be. There was no room left for doubt between them. Nothing would tear them apart now. Not when they both wanted each other with equal desperation.

Sebastian tugged on James's hair. "Let me claim you too."

James let out a low whining sound. He tilted his neck, exposing it to Sebastian.

Sebastian bit James where his neck and shoulder met. James moaned and rolled his hips in response, pressing their soft cocks together.

"Don't leave me," Sebastian warned, then bit him again. "If I'm yours, you can't leave me. I need you to stay with me. I can't survive without you. I want to be yours forever."

A day ago, Sebastian never would have let such co-dependent words out of his mouth, but James whimpered in response and crashed their mouths together, kissing Sebastian as if he'd just heard exactly what he'd been longing for.

With anyone else, Sebastian didn't doubt it would be too much, but that didn't matter. He was with James, where the imperfect parts of him were as wanted as the rest. It was acceptance like he never would have believed if he hadn't experienced it.

"I won't ever leave you." James rasped, licking Sebastian's throat. "No matter what, I'll always want you to be mine. You're so strong. You make me feel brave, and I'm fucking addicted to it. You turn dark things into light, Sebastian. You're the best thing that's ever happened to me."

Tears filled Sebastian's eyes. He was speechless. He was loved. Even if neither of them were saying that word yet. Sebastian was sure beyond doubt that James would love him one day, and he would love James back, and they would share a future no matter what. No past tragedies or curses could stand in their way.

James kissed Sebastian's cheeks as his tears fell. "Believe it," James ordered, and Sebastian nodded, smiling like everything in his life was perfect, even though it wasn't. It didn't need to be when the important things worked out.

"I believe it," he promised, blinking through tears, cheeks straining in a smile that probably had his dimples out.

James kissed him, eating up all his tears, swiping them off his cheeks with his tongue. When they were gone, he worked Sebastian's lips until they were swollen.

Sebastian had never been lavished with affection like this. He felt pampered to the point of dazed by the time James flipped him over, laying him out on his belly and spreading his legs.

James settled behind Sebastian and kissed down his spine. "I'll never get enough of these perfect little freckles." His mouth moved to Sebastian's hip. "Or these dimples." He kissed Sebastian's lower back. "Or this lovely ass."

Sebastian made a strangled sound of anticipation as James parted his cheeks to expose his hole.

"I'm going to eat you out until you come, sweetheart." James shifted, his next breath ghosting over Sebastian's pucker. "And you're going to let me because you're mine. Your pleasure is mine."

"Yes," Sebastian panted. He always begged for James's cock to fill him when James's mouth was on his hole, but it wasn't exactly a hardship to let James get him off this way, especially not if it was what James needed. "Yes, *please*, James."

He pressed his face into Sebastian, stubble scraping in all the right places, as he lapped at Sebastian's hole, groaning like he was devouring his favorite dessert.

James's tongue swiped and swirled. "You're mine to give pleasure to," he rasped. "Mine, and I need you to know it."

"I know," Sebastian whimpered. "I'm yours. I'll never doubt it again. I trust you. I trust us."

"Good." James bit each globe of Sebastian's ass, then buried his face between Sebastian's cheeks and ate him relentlessly. He didn't stop or slow down when Sebastian started rutting into the mattress. James squeezed his ass cheeks, groping as he licked and fucked Sebastian with his tongue. He groaned and made sounds so obscene Sebastian's face burned, but all Sebastian could do was press his ass back against James's face harder.

"Damn, you feel so good, James." Sebastian buried his head in the sheets. He rolled his hips, his hard cock trapped between his stomach and the bed. He couldn't take it. His body flamed. "Oh yeah, oh fuck. *James.* I'm gonna come."

James growled against Sebastian's hole, pressing his face impossibly closer.

Sebastian bucked his hips and shouted as he erupted into the mattress. He white-knuckled the sheets, his hole contracting against James's mouth. James licked and kissed him through it, only stopping when Sebastian was nothing but a limp, satisfied puddle.

After a few deep breaths, Sebastian glanced over his shoulder, propping his chin on his palm. "Wow." He wanted to say more but his thoughts weren't quite coming together.

James pushed himself to a kneeling position, his eyes heavy-lidded with lust, lips parted, swollen and glistening from eating

Sebastian's ass so fucking thoroughly. He grabbed his straining dick in a tight fist.

"I love seeing you satisfied." James spit in his hand and pumped his hard length. He grabbed Sebastian's ass and squeezed, pulling one cheek back to better expose Sebastian's hole as he continued to jerk himself off.

"Yes," Sebastian breathed, biting his lip as he watched. His cock did its best to rally.

The muscles in James's abdomen tensed. His cock jerked, and he came in long white ropes. Sebastian felt James's cum hit, covering his hole and dripping down his crack. If Sebastian could have, he would have orgasmed again, just from that. He watched James work himself until every last drop was spent and covering him.

James let go of his softening dick and massaged Sebastian's backside, rubbing his cum over Sebastian's cheeks.

"Fuck it into me," Sebastian panted.

James groaned. He didn't take his eyes off Sebastian as he rubbed cum into Sebastian's rim, then pushed it inside with a finger. He took his time filling Sebastian, swiping all his cum from the globes of Sebastian's ass and pushing it into him.

One finger became two. Sebastian arched. He wanted so badly to get hard again, for James to fuck him without a condom so he could get him deeper inside and be absolutely flooded with his cum.

"There you go, sweetheart." James crooned as he pumped his fingers. "Take it all and know you're mine."

"Yes," Sebastian whimpered as he accepted what James gave him.

When James seemed satisfied he'd stuffed Sebastian full, he flopped forward, covering Sebastian with his body. They lay there unmoving except for James's lips on Sebastian's neck.

Sebastian luxuriated in James's weight on top of him. "I'm

yours," he whispered, and he fucking believed it. Nothing had felt so good.

"And I'm yours," James whispered back.

They stayed like that for a long while until James shifted his weight slightly, saying, "I want to lie here forever, replaying this morning in my mind on repeat. Because *fuck*, that was the most amazing sex I've ever had. But we should probably shower."

"No. I can't move. I'm stuck," Sebastian whined, and James chuckled. "I'm staying in these cum-stained sheets forever. Though, instead of replaying all that mind-blowing sex, we could just keep fucking."

"Forever?" James sat up and tugged Sebastian's arm, giving him a bemused grin. "Don't be ridiculous."

"But you like it when I'm ridiculous." Sebastian rolled onto his back, feeling smug as James's attention went automatically to his soft, cum-covered cock.

James blinked and met Sebastian's eyes. "Yes, I do." He frowned and tugged Sebastian's hand again, this time with determination, like he was trying to be sensible in the face of Sebastian's silly, forever-fucking idea. "Come be ridiculous in the shower with me."

That got Sebastian up.

It was still too dark to be close to when James needed to get to work—they must have woken even earlier than Sebastian thought—so they took their time. The shower here wasn't as nice as Sebastian's at Storm House. It was a much tighter fit with two, but they made it work.

James didn't seem to be done with his claiming. He kissed Sebastian roughly and insisted on washing him with a soapy cloth, fussing and pampering him, paying extra attention to Sebastian's groin and backside.

"I can feel your cum leaking out of me," Sebastian groaned, one arm braced on the wall as water cascaded down his back.

"Think I'll need to fill you up again."

Sebastian turned around to find James red-faced. "Listen to your dirty mouth."

James stuttered, going redder. "I—yeah—I still prefer you being the scandalous one."

"I don't think it's that scandalous, James." Sebastian bopped him on the nose.

He frowned.

"I love it when you say dirty things while you're fucking me, but hearing it now is almost better. I think it's a good sign you aren't holding yourself back."

James's frowny lips twitched. "What can I say? You bring it out in me."

Sebastian smiled, overly pleased with himself.

James traced Sebastian's curved lips with a wet finger. "I'll say anything to show you how I feel."

Sebastian's breath caught, but James wasn't done.

"I know we're only at the start of us, but I'm fucking gone for you, Sebastian. I'm constantly in awe of you. Your humor, your enthusiasm, your resilience. I just need you to know you don't have to be strong alone anymore. I'm here for you. You can come to me with anything."

James's finger continued to trace Sebastian's lips as tears slid down Sebastian's already wet cheeks.

James cupped Sebastian's jaw. "You burn so bright nothing could put you out. You're amazing, and I can't believe I'm with you."

Sebastian threw himself on James and crushed him into a hug. "Holy shit, when you open up, you go all in."

"Yeah, well." James shrugged from within Sebastian's embrace.

"You're my dream, James," Sebastian murmured in his ear. "Having it come true, knowing you wanted to actually date me, scared the hell out of me. I didn't think I could have you. I didn't trust it would last, but I was wrong."

James pulled back. "Why didn't you think you could have

me?" He didn't sound accusatory or incredulous, just like he needed to understand.

Sebastian blew out an exaggerated breath. "I didn't deserve it." James opened his mouth to protest, but Sebastian held up a hand to stop him. He grabbed the washcloth and soap and began washing James. "Nothing good has ever lasted for me. No one ever wanted me. My mom conceived and raised me to sacrifice me for my sister, and even before I knew that's what was happening, I could feel it. Every little thing she did to abandon me, to not choose me, added up and left me hollow. So I tried to earn it. I tried to be worthy of her loving me." He choked on a breath, the washcloth stopping in its tracks.

"Sebastian." James covered his hand.

He cleared his throat and continued his washing. "Even my uncle, who was kind to me, who I trusted when I didn't trust my mom, even he betrayed me. I thought we had a good relationship, even though I was a moody kid and he was this seemingly out-of-touch adult. But it was all a lie. He let my mom discard me at Storm House. He trapped me and forced me to face all the worst parts of the curse blind. And alone." A sob choked out of him despite his best efforts to hold it in.

James took the cloth from Sebastian and hugged him. Water cascaded over them, rinsing the suds from James. Sebastian cried into James's shoulder, glad he could let it out. James didn't rush him or try to tell him it was okay and not to cry. He let Sebastian be, and when Sebastian was done, James turned off the water and guided Sebastian out of the shower, wrapping him in a soft towel.

Sebastian leaned into James. Talking felt good. Even crying felt good. He felt so safe in James's arms that he didn't even consider holding back. "I didn't know how to believe anyone would want me when the people who were supposed to couldn't manage it. I was afraid I'd caused too many problems for you and that, in the end, I'd be alone again. If no one could choose me when I was a kid who'd done nothing wrong, how could anyone tolerate me when I came with this curse. But I believe you aren't holding the curse against me and never will. It just took me a while."

Sebastian blinked and looked James straight in the eye. "Before you, I don't think I believed genuine trust was real. I didn't think I'd ever give it to anyone, but I trust you, James, with everything I am."

James gripped both Sebastian's hands in his. "I'll guard that trust with my life, Sebastian. I choose you." He pressed their faces together, nose to nose.

"I know, and I finally believe it." Sebastian gave him a tiny smile. "I'm yours. You've claimed me, and I'm never doubting you again."

"Good." James released Sebastian's hands. "And just so you know, biting you was actually magic in disguise, so you're stuck with me now. We're bound together. No takebacks." He almost delivered the line with a straight face, but he cracked, a laugh snorting out of his nose.

"No, it wasn't." Sebastian whipped off his towel and snapped it at James.

He jumped out of the way just in time, laughing fully now. "Might as well have been."

"Na, it's better this way." Sebastian threw a fresh towel at James, disappointed he was going to cover up his glorious Speedo tan lines. They really accentuated his toned ass. "Your promise means more than magic."

James puffed up his chest at that. He kissed the crook of Sebastian's neck, where mouth-shaped bruises were staring to appear. Sebastian sighed. Nothing had ever been more romantic.

James seemed unable to stop peppering Sebastian with kisses as they dried off. On the way back to the bedroom, James caught Sebastian's hand. "I was afraid to open up too, you know." He tugged Sebastian close like he wasn't ready to part. "I didn't let anyone in. I resisted you at first because I resist everyone. Even when I was young, I tried to push my crushes away and did my best to ignore them. I never liked dating and didn't want to connect with anyone in that way. Then, with you, I did want to, but I was still afraid to get attached to you."

Sebastian traced James's serious-lined brow. "Because you were afraid of losing me?"

"Yes. And that fear still hits me sometimes. But being trapped at Storm House with you forced me to face that fear in a way I'd avoided all my life. It also gave me a chance I never would have taken. Even though it was a crushing situation, I wouldn't change it. Not when it allowed me to reach for you and open up in a way I'd always been afraid to."

Sebastian's heart pounded. "Really?"

"Yes. There isn't anything I wouldn't sacrifice for you, and you can't throw any problem at me—no matter how big—that I'd give you up to solve. I'd choose to deal with the curse all over again to end up with you. Would not change a thing. I just wish you hadn't been left alone for so long."

"Of course not." Sebastian couldn't find it in him to be bitter about his confinement just then. It was over, and James was saying too many soul-shattering, loving things. "I wish I'd known you were back in Moonlight Falls sooner so I could have written to you years ago. You were the one I needed, James. Not anyone else."

The furrow in James's brow deepened. "But why? How did you know I would figure it out?"

"I didn't." Sebastian shrugged. "I just knew you were good. That you'd care about me. Or if you didn't care, then no one would. And—more importantly—I had a massive crush on you."

James's eyes widened, and a smile broke through his thoughtful expression. "You did?"

Sebastian grinned wickedly. He wanted James to know how deep his feelings went, how far back through history they stretched. If James liked Sebastian enough to be glad he'd been trapped, to not want to wish away any of the stress of the past weeks, then Sebastian needed him to know his feelings were just as strong.

Sebastian cupped James's face. "I've been pining for you since we were kids. It was always you, James. My first crush. My queer awakening. My light in the dark. My future."

Tears clung to James's lashes. "I wish we'd gotten together sooner."

Sebastian kissed the tears away, as James had done for him. "Doesn't sound like it would have worked out. We weren't ready when we were younger."

"You're probably right."

"Course I am." Sebastian released James and swept back his damp hair. "Besides, seducing you as an adult isn't something I'd want to give up for any teenage fumbling."

James snorted a laugh. "You would think that, you nightmare."

"Aw, don't pretend you'd want to change it. Unless you wish I was your first. Oh, you *do*, don't you?"

James went red and grumbled, "Shut up," without any real bite. He glanced down at his clothes from last night, discarded on the floor, then at the curtain-covered window. "How early did we wake up? The sun still hasn't risen."

Sebastian was distracted by James's ass as he bent to retrieve his phone. Even towel-covered, it was perfect. "We can always role-play. You know, pretend we're deflowering each other. You can wear your swimsuit and 'catch' me changing in the locker room on the way to swim practice."

James straightened and stared. "I—that's…" His words trailed off, a blush spreading down his neck as the front of his towel tented.

"Mm. You're into it. Fuck yeah." Sebastian dropped his own towel. "Come on, James, show a shy little boy like me the kind of stamina all that time in the pool gave you."

James's eyes were glued to Sebastian's rising erection. "You are not shy."

Sebastian stalked closer. "But I could be. If it's what turns swim-star James Gray on. The shy little virgin you saw around town and thought was cute. He'd have been overwhelmed by you."

James squeezed his phone, maybe in an effort to resist pulling Sebastian in and fucking him senseless—Sebastian could dream—but before James had the chance to give in to his apparently conflicted desires, the screen on his cell lit up, drawing their attention.

"It's nine o'clock!" James shoved the phone under Sebastian's nose in disbelief. "I have to be at work. Like now."

Sebastian narrowed his eyes at the phone. "No way." He marched to the window and drew back the curtains. "Look how dark it is. The sun hasn't risen. We must've started fucking at four a.m."

James checked Sebastian's phone. "No. It's really nine. Look."

It wasn't pitch black outside, but nine o'clock should be nowhere near this dark.

"Come on." James pulled him away from the window. "Let's get dressed and see what's going on."

CHAPTER SIXTEEN

Sebastian and James rushed into what felt like the pre-dawn morning and hurried over to Gray Electrical.

Hazel was already at the shop, seated at her desk in the back, glowering. "It's the fucking apocalypse." She gestured out the window unnecessarily.

James seemed to be getting more worried by the second. He'd run his hand through his hair three times since leaving the house, and they'd only walked across the street. "Did the sun just *not* rise?" he asked in a tone that suggested he was personally offended by the situation.

Sebastian followed him past the counter into the work area of the electrical shop. "That's not possible. Because of, you know, physics." He waved his hand in a circular motion. "The earth didn't stop spinning."

"Then what's happening? Even if it isn't as bad as the sun not rising, whatever is going on out there isn't good." Hazel glared at James, who returned the look with equal intensity. "Eleanor is going to let me know if she hears anything, but sitting around waiting might kill me first."

Sebastian perched on the edge of James's desk. "You talked to Eleanor already?"

"Yeah." Hazel's eyes flashed, her scowl dropping for a split second. "I wondered this morning if the darkness had to do with the magic last night, and she agreed."

James narrowed his eyes like he was trying to decipher something. "Hazel, did you—"

"Not now." She waved at him impatiently. "Focus."

James grunted, shaking his head, and went to turn on the coffee maker in the corner.

"The weird shadow thing was coming from the sky last night," Hazel continued, leaning back in her chair with her arms crossed. "So when the sky was dark today, I wondered if it could be connected."

"But James and Parker banished that thing in the yard," Sebastian argued.

"Maybe." Hazel didn't look convinced. "When we were fighting the shadow in the house, it kept breaking off. We know it retreated when the thing in the corner caught fire, but what if part of it splintered off and stayed up in the sky. It was too dark last night to see if anything like that happened."

Sebastian and James shared a look. Hazel had a frighteningly good point.

"I should call Eli." James pulled out his phone. "I wonder if Parker has gone home yet."

"Hope his house is still there." Hazel stood and grabbed a mug from under the sink next to the coffee station.

James was already talking into his cell. He hung up after a few quick words. "Parker's house is fine. He's at work, and Eli is heading over here now." James's stomach growled audibly. "Sorry, skipped breakfast."

Hazel raised an eyebrow. "Too freaked out to eat?"

"Uh…" James hesitated, a faint blush staining his cheeks.

"Why don't I go make you something?" Sebastian hopped off the desk. "Want some eggs? I'll just run home."

James's stoic expression melted. "That'd be wonderful, sweetheart."

Sebastian's heart thudded. He blushed in what had to be a much more obvious display than James's subtle coloring. His cheeks were on fire. Hearing James call him sweetheart in front of someone else was another claiming. He had to tear his eyes away from James's soft expression before he combusted. "You want anything, Hazel?"

"No, thanks." She raised her coffee mug. "This is all I need after the morning I've had."

Sebastian hurried across the street. He wished he could ignore the unnaturally dark sky. He wanted to bask in James's affection without distractions. It was a good thing that dealing with insurmountable magical problems was what he and James spent a lot of their time doing together. At least they were used to it.

He made scrambled eggs and pan-fried some of his fresh bread. He didn't have a toaster and might not bother buying one. He preferred the crispiness that a dash of olive oil in the pan provided.

With silverware tucked in the pocket of James's leather jacket, Sebastian headed back across the street carrying two plates. James beamed at the sight of Sebastian and the food. He swapped Sebastian a plate for a mug of coffee, and they ate at James's desk, Sebastian perched on the edge next to James's chair, his plate in his lap.

"Mm. This is amazing." James hummed as he chewed a large bite of eggs and bread.

"Glad you like it." Sebastian preened. He loved feeding James. It brought together all his favorite things.

"Ugh. You guys are so fucking cute." Hazel rolled her eyes, half her face hidden by her mug, but Sebastian could have sworn a smile lurked there.

James blushed but did nothing other than continue to eat like it was the best meal ever. Well, maybe not the best meal. Sebastian's ass had already claimed that title.

Sebastian squirmed. James content and eating his food after Sebastian had satisfied him with his body made Sebastian feel like he was bubbling over. Without his doubts weighing him down, he was just so happy. It should have scared him. Good things always did. But not this time. James would never take this away from him.

Eli arrived as James rinsed the plates in the sink. Eli hadn't heard more than they had about the strange darkness. Parker was working the breakfast shift that day and promised to call if anyone came into the diner with news.

The flyers about the light-resistant shades and the possessed bear had made the rounds over the weekend. Eli said the few people he'd run into were taking the darkness as another escalation of the shade problem.

"Makes sense," Hazel agreed. "If it's dark and we can't use light to fend them off, the shades will have free rein. And after what we saw last night, with the shades and the shadow working together, it's hard to think it's a coincidence."

"True, but the darkness outside looks nothing like the shadow that attacked Parker's house," Eli argued. "It's normal, except for the fact that it should be light this late in the day."

"Well, whatever it is, Eleanor reported it. So someone equipped to deal with it should be on the way." Hazel sounded reassuring, but her pinched expression gave her away. It was hard to imagine what anyone could do about this.

Eli turned to face Sebastian. "Let's head out to Storm House. I need to collect my data."

"Yeah, I've got to feed the chickens." Sebastian glanced at James. "It'd be good if you came too. It's dark enough that shades will be out and about." Sebastian was weary of dealing with them on his own, especially after the size of the horde that had attacked when they'd been transferring the curse to the fuel cell. "My magic seems back to normal, but I haven't tried to use it at the house yet. I don't want to assume it will be fine and then it not be."

"Of course I'll come." James stood from his desk. "You good here, Hazel?"

"Yeah. I'm not doing anything. I doubt we'll have customers today, with everyone panicking. I'd come with you, but I want to stay by my phone in case Eleanor has news."

"No, that's a good idea." James led Sebastian and Eli toward the door. "We'll meet you back here after we're done."

As they exited the shop, Eli turned to Sebastian. "What do you mean your magic is back to normal?"

"When the curse tied me to the veins and they started feeding off me, my magical ability diminished. I'm not that strong to start with, so I couldn't actually do much magic while I was trapped at Storm House. It tired me out too much." Sebastian pushed memories of dark, candle-lit nights away. His loneliness in the dark had been unbearable a lot of the time.

Eli's brow furrowed like he was trying to puzzle something out. "But I thought James linked to you to borrow power for the unbinding spell."

"He did." Sebastian glanced at James, who didn't seem to know what Eli was getting at either.

Eli frowned. "Just doesn't seem like you'd have enough power to lend if you couldn't do magic with the veins sucking you dry."

"Well, it definitely worked." James opened the driver's door.

Eli stopped short of the car. "Why didn't your magical ability diminish after you got trapped?"

James shrugged. He and Eli turned their attention to Sebastian.

"I don't know." Sebastian wracked his brain. "I hadn't even thought of that."

"Hm…" Eli didn't appear satisfied by the lack of answers. "It doesn't seem like Parker or Hazel have had any issues with their magic since the curse claimed them either."

Sebastian gave Eli a helpless shrug.

They all climbed in the car. Eli leaned forward from the back seat. "It must be something to do with Sebastian being in line to inherit the curse and the rest of us only getting caught up through the secret. We must not be tied to the veins the same way you are, Sebastian."

"That's good." Relief rippled through Sebastian. He may have let go of his guilt for trapping the others, but knowing they might be better off than him still eased something inside him. "Maybe it will be easier to untie you all."

Eli leaned back and buckled his seatbelt. "If we're trying to free ourselves by correcting the imbalance, I don't think it will matter. We should all be equally free when the veins are restored."

The drive north was quiet after that.

Returning to Storm House in the near-darkness gave Sebastian a spike of anxiety. As he unlocked the gate, a primal part of his brain told him he shouldn't be out on the grounds, even though he hadn't spotted any shades. The thought of going inside the house, even the kitchen, made him feel even worse. With the darkness shrouding the property, it was too much like all the nights he'd been trapped here.

James placed a hand on the small of his back. "You okay?"

"Not quite, but it'll be fine. I've got to get through this." Sebastian leaned into James, who encircled his waist with a steady arm.

"You can face anything, sweetheart," James murmured into Sebastian's hair.

Sebastian straightened. "Yeah. With you, I know I can."

James's arm tightened around him.

Eli held back under the guise of getting his backpack out of the car. Sebastian was grateful for the moment with James. His feelings for Storm House were so tumultuous. He never quite knew what coming to the property would do to him.

"Being here in the dark is freaky," Eli whispered as they walked up the driveway.

No one disagreed. They quickly fed the confused chickens and collected their eggs. Sebastian gave some attention to Miss Moo, who was munching the hay set out for her near the barn.

Now that they were deeper into the property, shades floated overhead. The beasts didn't seem to take much notice of the three of them as they made their way around, so at least there was that. Sebastian was surprised he hadn't seen any lurking around the house. They'd always been looking in the windows and waiting outside the doors. It was like they knew Sebastian wasn't home and had lost interest.

The thought gave him chills.

More shades drifted through the forest as Sebastian, James, and Eli walked along the path to the clearing. Sebastian wished he had one of his oil lamps so he could see better. The shadows were deep and dark under the trees.

As the path opened into the clearing, they all stopped. Shades lurked everywhere. Half a dozen circled the fuel cell in the middle, running their hands over it. Others sat in the trees, their onyx eyes fixed on Sebastian and his companions.

"You want to keep going, Eli?" James put his hand on his brother's shoulder, not taking his eyes off the infested clearing.

Eli chewed on his bottom lip. "We have to. I need that data, and who knows how long this darkness will last."

"If we try not to startle them, it might be okay." Sebastian took a step forward. "The shades here were never more than a nuisance unless I messed with the magic in the veins, and we aren't doing magic. Just grabbing pieces of paper."

"Exactly." Eli sounded more confident. He and James followed

Sebastian into the clearing. "Sebastian, will you write down the times as I get the papers?"

"Sure." He took the notebook and manual-wind pocket watch they'd been using to check the time on the property as Eli unearthed his folders from his backpack.

James watched the two of them as they worked, his focus on the shades. The ones preoccupied with the fuel cell didn't seem to notice them, but the ones sitting in the trees tracked their movements.

As Eli lifted the tarp-covered crate off the first mechanism, a shade drifted down from its perch in a nearby tree. Sebastian tensed, but the beast didn't come too close, staying out of arm's reach. It watched like it had been curious what lay beneath the warded crate.

Sebastian and Eli gathered the paper and recorded the time, then moved on to the next mechanism. More shades appeared in the clearing. The atmosphere was tense even though the shades kept their distance. Sebastian wasn't looking forward to getting to the mechanism in the center of the clearing. He didn't want to have to disturb the shades worshipping the fuel cell.

As they got to the fourth mechanism, the shade wearing Sebastian's purple robe drifted into the clearing from the dark forest beyond.

"Hey," Sebastian hissed at it. The shade spun around, robe swirling, almost like it was taunting him. "Little shit. I can't believe you still have my robe." The purple fabric was dirty and ripped in places, making Sebastian irrationally upset.

James pressed in close, keeping his voice low. "Why is it wearing your robe? Since when do shades care about human clothes?"

Sebastian gritted his teeth against the urge to steal the garment back. "I don't know. I saw it in town too."

"Is it the same one that stole it? Do you think it recognizes us?" James paused briefly. "It must, or else why would it be staring like that?" The shade eyed them, swaying the long sleeves of the robe back and forth. "It's weird that it stuck around. I thought shades were transitory."

"They are," Eli hissed. "But it's only been a few days since you escaped. Staying in one area that long isn't unheard of."

"Except I lost my robe two weeks ago," Sebastian muttered.

Eli didn't seem to know what to say to that. "Come on. Let's get the last set of data and get out of here. I want to come back again tonight. Collecting data twice a day works better since I have to type it all up."

The day before, Eli had gathered a second round of data with Parker while Sebastian had loaded apples in the car. Sebastian didn't doubt Eli would collect the receipts every few hours if it weren't such a pain to come all the way out here.

The three of them inched toward the mechanism next to the fuel cell. All the shades swirling around it froze.

"Shit," James grumbled.

"Maybe when they see we aren't after the fuel cell, they'll relax," Eli offered hopefully.

Sebastian thought that sounded like wishful thinking. "Why do they care about the fuel cell?"

"Fuck if I know," Eli muttered with grumpiness worthy of his brother. "Come on. Slowly."

They crept forward. The shades tracked their progress.

It wasn't guaranteed these ones were light-resistant. If the same shades had been lurking around the property for ages—as Sebastian suspected despite Eli and James's insistence that the beasts were always transitory—light would work against them just fine. Sebastian and James could fight them off. There were nowhere near as many as the night James almost drained himself to death.

Eli crouched next to the last covered crate. He gingerly lifted it off the mechanism. Sebastian held his breath. As Eli set the crate aside, the shades beside the fuel cell drifted closer. They all peered at the mechanism with unwavering intensity. One reached out a hand, but Parker's warding kept it from getting anywhere near the spindly structure.

Eli tore off the receipt paper, and the shade hissed.

Sebastian quickly scribbled down the time in the notebook. "Let's go."

Eli covered the mechanism with the crate and stood. As he went to tuck the paper into the correct folder, the closest shade lunged forward. It tried to snatch the paper, but Eli was quicker, ducking out of the way with an expression that said he would protect his data at all costs.

James sent a spark at the lunging shade, and it ignited, fire banishing the beast in a puff of black smoke. The other shades next to the fuel cell hissed. Eli hastily shoved his folder in his backpack as shades swooped in on him, trying to grab him and the bag.

Sebastian and James sent sparks flying. Some found their mark, making quick work of the shades, but others fell to the forest floor.

"Fuck." Sebastian stamped on the sparks before they could ignite the fallen leaves. It was a good thing it had been so damp recently.

James conjured a ball of light, sending it toward the shades. They retreated. Sebastian was right. These ones weren't light-resistant. It was a small relief.

They hurried back to the car, with the shades from the clearing following closely. Luckily, James's light kept them back, and they didn't try to fight it. It was almost like the shades were escorting them off the property, content to see them go.

BACK AT GRAY ELECTRICAL, Eli settled at the counter with his laptop. Sebastian offered to help enter the data they'd collected and was tasked with reading the numbers out as Eli typed. It took forever. Sebastian had never been so aware of how many minutes there were in a day and was dismayed to learn they'd have to go through every entry again, this time with Eli reading out and Sebastian checking what had been entered.

"It needs to be accurate," Eli said, not at all fazed by the monotony. "Parker will be happy I've gotten someone else to do this set with me though."

The sky didn't change as the day dragged on. James and Hazel were both restless. A few cars stopped by the pumps outside, but other than that, the shop had no customers. From periodically glancing out the window, it didn't seem like many people were moving through town.

Everyone was probably sitting tight, waiting to see what would happen, just like they were.

The ring of Hazel's phone pierced the relative silence of the shop. Sebastian stopped reciting numbers, and Eli looked up from his laptop. James migrated away from the window, where he'd been glowering at the sky.

"Eleanor." Hazel seemed to sigh into the phone. "I'm fine. Yes, really. You?" A pause. "Mm, yes, I agree— Stop it. Everyone's listening in. Uh-huh. You're kidding me?"

Eventually, Hazel hung up. She turned to face the rest of them. "The sun did rise, just not for Moonlight Falls."

"Meaning?" Eli asked impatiently.

"There's a darkness encasing the town. Eleanor's driven through it. Everything is bright as day outside of town. She's found the southern, eastern, and western limits but hasn't driven north yet. She was trying to contact Carson to see if his crew is in the dark before she heads that way."

"But where did it come from?" James crossed his arms. Sebastian wished James was wearing his leather jacket so he could see the material flex and pull over his shoulders. "Do you still think it's part of the shadow from last night? I've been watching the sky and haven't seen a single flowing tendril. Nothing like we saw at Parker's house."

"There's no word on where it's come from." Hazel plugged her phone into the charger at her desk. "Apparently, the official who drove up here won't come into town."

Eli's mouth dropped open. "You're kidding."

"No." Hazel frowned. "Eleanor is pissed. The guy said he isn't venturing into the shadow without proof it's safe."

Sebastian looked around at them all. "But we're all fine."

Hazel shrugged. "The official said that if people are concerned, they can leave, but no one is rushing in to check things out."

"We can't leave," Sebastian muttered, the ghost of his previous fear everyone would resent him rearing its head.

"We wouldn't even if we could." James rested a hand on Sebastian's shoulder.

"Of course not." Hazel looked annoyed by the very suggestion. "If no one's going to help figure this out, we'll have to do it ourselves. Probably best that way, honestly."

The question of *how* seemed to float menacingly in the air.

"I wonder if anything like this has happened before." Sebastian glanced at Eli hopefully, even though he didn't study this sort of thing.

Eli made a who-knows face.

"I tried looking it up online." Hazel made her way over to the coffee maker and scooped fresh grounds into it. "No luck."

Sebastian stood. "Maybe I should go to the library. See Mila. I bet she's already looking into it, along with the stuff about light resistance."

"That's a good idea." James took Sebastian's seat. "I'll help Eli finish."

"I wonder—" Eli hesitated, not turning back to his laptop.

"Where do you think the exact spot the darkness stops is, going south?"

Hazel looked up from the coffee. "Eleanor didn't say."

Eli tapped the counter with restless fingers. "What if it's confined by the same barrier trapping us. Maybe we should head to where you crashed your truck, James."

"We could." James's brow furrowed as he frowned at the idea. "But why would the darkness have anything to do with the curse trapping us?"

"I don't know." Eli sighed. "I'm just trying to think of *something*. The darkness probably doesn't have anything to do with the veins. It just seems odd that there's a clear boundary in both cases, but what do I know."

"Wait, hang on. Maybe the darkness *does* have to do with the veins." Sebastian reflexively tugged James's leather jacket, pulling it tight against himself. "How many different invisible barriers can be surrounding this town? It's probably the same one. The simplest solution is usually right. I must have missed something changing in the veins. Maybe the fuel cell isn't holding up as well as we thought. Maybe—"

James stood from his seat. "Slow down." Sebastian's gaze found James's. "More than one thing can happen at a time. I checked the indicator on the fuel cell this morning. The power reserves look fine."

"But the boundary." Sebastian's heart sank. He felt guilty, like he'd done this unknowingly. He knew it wasn't true, and he shouldn't feel that way, but a horrible ache consumed him anyway. What if his escaping Storm House had done this?

James pulled Sebastian into him. Sebastian hunched to rest his forehead on James's shoulder. "This is not your fault," James said in a firm but soft tone. "It's probably not connected, and even if it turns out it is, it still won't be your fault."

"You're right." Sebastian straightened. "I know. It's like I'm still waiting for everything to fall apart. I can't help it."

"Even if things fall apart, it will be okay. We'll figure it out together." James held Sebastian's gaze until he nodded in agreement. "Go see Mila. She's missed you and will be happy to see you. There are a lot of people who care about you, Sebastian, and we're all on your side. It's all of us against the curse and anything else that dares to get in our way, and I'll keep reminding you of that for as long as I have to."

Because Sebastian was James's to look after and protect, even from himself. The unsaid words burned between them. Sebastian pressed on the bite marks covered by his shirt collar. James watched, the gleam in his eyes saying *mine* as clearly as if he'd spoken the word.

They were in this together. No matter what.

CHAPTER SEVENTEEN

THE LIBRARY WAS QUIET. Not surprising given there didn't seem to be many people around the center of town.

Mila wasn't at the front desk. Rather than ring the bell, Sebastian opted to go looking for her. The shelves of neatly organized books made him smile. He hadn't enjoyed his time in Moonlight Falls when he was a kid, but a lot of his better memories had happened here. He'd participated in all the summer programs the library offered kids, and the ones he was too old for, he'd joined in as a helper to the volunteer running it.

Maybe that's what he would do with his time when it wasn't so taken up with magical crises. He could volunteer at the library.

Sebastian found Mila in the downstairs nonfiction section at a table with a stack of books. "Hi."

She glanced up, peering over the top of her glasses. "Sebastian!"

He was enveloped in a hug a half-second later, unsure how the woman had moved so fast.

"It's so good to see you in town again." She pulled back to scrutinize him, her glasses now hanging around her neck from a beaded chain.

He fidgeted. "I rented one of the duplexes in town, so you should see me more now."

Mila beamed. "That's wonderful." She clasped his hands like he might slip away if she wasn't holding on, her skin soft against his. "How are you, dear? Really."

Mila had always been someone Sebastian could confide in. He'd cried on her shoulder the first summer he was left in Moonlight Falls while his mother and sister returned to Phoenix. Things had improved after he'd become closer to his uncle and the man hadn't seemed so intimidating, but no amount of puzzles, building tree forts at Storm House, or time spent doing crafts in the library had cured his childhood loneliness.

At least in high school, once his mother had abandoned him for good, he'd been able to let go to an extent. He'd stopped hoping things would get better between them and had just been angry at her, and throughout all of it, Mila had been there. He'd needed someone outside the family, and when he hadn't had friends, he'd had her.

Sebastian met Mila's eyes. She had to be about sixty now. Time had lined her face and lightened her dark-brown hair while Sebastian had been trapped at Storm House.

He didn't want to lie to Mila. He wished he could tell her the whole truth, everything about the house and the curse. But he couldn't without trapping her, so he focused on the personal side of how he was doing, facts that would make sense with the story of him being a recluse. "I'm okay sometimes and less so the rest of the time. Life's gotten kind of overwhelming. I think I have anxiety now."

Mila nodded in understanding. "There's a lot you can do to manage that. If you need help finding resources, I'm always here."

"Thanks." Sebastian gave her a small smile. "I'm getting there."

"Just don't disappear again, Sebastian." Mila looked down at their hands. "I should have come out to the house to see you. But after Stephen died, I have to admit I was angry, and by the time I'd let go of that, I wasn't sure you'd want to see me."

Sebastian fought back a wince. "I'm sorry I didn't write to you." He'd known Mila would have wanted to hear about Stephen's passing and probably would have come to the funeral on the property, but Sebastian had been consumed by the curse, panicking and raging at his dead uncle. He hadn't been in a fit state, not even sparing a thought for Mila at the time. "I don't have a good reason for shutting you out. I wasn't in a good place, and I'm sorry I let that get in the way."

"I figured as much. I'm sorry I didn't reach out." She squeezed once more before releasing him. "Now that we've got the apologies out of the way, why don't we leave the past where it belongs?" She waited for him to nod, the tension between them lifting. She smiled. "So, has James fixed your electricity?"

Mila was one of the few who remembered that Storm House didn't have power. That particular quirk had been passed off as a choice during Sullivan's and Simon's generations to keep people from prying into the situation. Once Simon's wife passed away and visitors stopped coming to the house, things like the lack of electricity were forgotten by the general population of Moonlight Falls as Simon's generation passed on and not many people left in town had actually visited the property.

"We gave up on the rewiring," Sebastian admitted. This time he wished he could tell Mila what was going on at Storm House, not for his sake but hers. He suspected it would give her much-needed closure on what had happened between her and Stephen. Sebastian had always gotten the impression that Stephen and Mila loved each other, but Stephen hadn't wanted to pull her into the family's mess.

"Ah well." Mila raised her eyes to the ceiling. "Good riddance to that old house. I'm glad you've found somewhere else to live."

Sebastian huffed. "Me too."

Mila leaned in close like she was about to tell him a secret. "You and James are together, right?"

Sebastian's cheeks heated. "How did you know?"

Mila shook her head in exasperation. "Dear, you're walking around town in his jacket. Before you turned up wearing it at town hall the other night, I couldn't remember the last time I'd seen him without it. I'd recognize it anywhere. It's like that man's second skin."

"Oh right." Sebastian laughed, his hands reflexively going to rub the material of the jacket's sleeves.

Mila leaned in close again. "James came in here asking about you a few weeks ago. I figured something had to be going on. He seemed intrigued, and that boy never dates."

"That's because I've never tried to get his attention before." Sebastian tried not to sound too smug and failed.

Mila laughed. "You'll be keeping him on his toes, that's for sure."

Sebastian didn't deny it, just grinned like a menace. He cleared his throat. "What were you reading when I interrupted?"

Mila turned back toward the table, her expression frustrated. "I was trying to learn about light-resistant shades. There isn't much out there."

"But you found something?"

"A few mentions." Mila picked up a book. "They all suggest that typical shades can't gain strength or abilities without outside help."

"Outside help?" Sebastian inspected the other books on the table, but the titles didn't give much away.

"Like enchantments," Mila explained. "Someone could cast a spell on a shade to make it immune to light, but I doubt that's what's happening. Why would anyone in Moonlight Falls do that? The only other explanation is in this book on the classification of shades." She passed it to Sebastian. "There are different types, though only the ones we're familiar with usually come from Beyond. It's harder for more complex beings to slip between worlds. They aren't as malleable as the shades we know, that can easily shift in and out of their physical form."

There *were* different kinds of shades. It made sense that people might not know that if only one type generally visited this world. Sebastian handed the book back. "But these other beings can get through? It's not impossible?"

"Sure. The only way we'd know other types of shades exist is if they've visited our world at some point. Humans can't go to Beyond. That's why we know so little about it and don't know what else might be lurking there."

"Great." Sebastian ran a hand through his hair. "So the light-resistant shades are a more complex being. Does that mean they're smarter?"

Mila perched her glasses on her nose and opened another book. "The more complex shades are thought to be more intelligent, but that doesn't mean all the light-resistant ones we've seen in town are. They could still be regular shades that have been granted extra abilities."

Maybe, but the shade that had bitten Sebastian had seemed different. It could very well have been one of these other shades. The humanoid one he'd seen by the stone in town and possibly at Parker's was even less like the shades he was used to. It had to be some other kind of being from Beyond.

"There are records claiming some of the more intelligent beings have magical abilities much more like ours and can cast spells, but the original sources are all very old," Mila continued.

Sebastian frowned. "How old?"

"Nineteenth century."

That surprised Sebastian. "It's been that long since intelligent shades have come to our world?"

"As far as humans have noticed. Unless more recent incidents weren't recorded in the places I have access to. Not everyone who interacts with shades is part of the scientific community. I'm sure there's all kinds of information outside of scientific publications from all around the world, but finding it isn't a quick or straightforward task."

"We'll just have to go off what's been happening around town. I think I saw one of these intelligent or more complex shade-like beings." Sebastian described what he'd seen around the stone in the town center.

Concern lined Mila's face. "That sounds way too organized for regular shade behavior. To have a large group working together like that. I don't like it."

"Yeah, the groups of shades I have around Storm House have never acted anything like that." The hordes were animalistic. Whatever had happened in town wasn't.

Mila glanced toward the library entrance and where the stone stood in the circle beyond. "I wonder what they were doing?"

Maybe it was magic. Dancing and manipulating shadow wasn't how human magic worked, but Sebastian had no clue how an intelligent shade-like being harnessed power. "I don't know. But the fact that we're sitting under a cloud of darkness could have something to do with it. I need to go find the mayor."

"That's probably best." Mila patted his arm. "If I come across anything helpful, I'll let you know."

They exchanged phone numbers and Sebastian hurried toward the exit.

"Oh!" Mila called after him. "Remind James that the book on countermagic he checked out is overdue."

CHAPTER EIGHTEEN

SEBASTIAN ENTERED town hall and found the administrator much more frazzled than the last time he'd been there with James.

The man was on the phone, hold music crackling out of the speaker. He held the mouthpiece away from his face as he addressed Sebastian. "Yes?"

"I'm looking for the mayor. I might have an idea about the darkness."

The administrator looked somewhat relieved. "Go ahead, though I'm not sure if she's in her office. Everyone's been all over the place today."

Sebastian thanked him and headed down the hall. Most of the doors were closed, and when he reached the end, so was Eleanor's. He knocked, but there was no answer.

"May I help you?"

Sebastian spun around, coming face to face with William, one of the city councilors. "I was hoping to talk to Eleanor."

"She'll be running around like a headless chicken, I'd wager," William sneered, his nose wrinkling. "You won't find her here."

Sebastian glared. What a rude and condescending thing to

say. "I'm sure she's doing everything she can to deal with the darkness."

William shrugged. "You're that Storm boy, aren't you?"

"My name's Sebastian." He gritted his teeth, stomach cramping uncomfortably. "We met at the meeting the other night." He forced himself to hold William's gaze even though he yearned to look at the floor and sink into the wall behind him.

"Do you have some urgent news? I know Eleanor likes having townsfolk stopping by for no reason, but you really shouldn't be here without an appointment."

Sebastian wanted to be anywhere but here. Dealing with this guy was making his heart rate climb. He hated feeling like he didn't belong or wasn't allowed to be in a space others were permitted to occupy unchallenged.

"I saw something odd in town the other night," he muttered.

William narrowed his eyes. "What did you see?"

Sebastian reluctantly described the shade spectacle. Hazel had probably already passed it on to Eleanor when she'd gone to see the mayor after the incident at Parker's, but after what Mila had told him, the event seemed even more significant. He wanted to tell the mayor about possible shade magic.

"I wouldn't worry about it." William rolled his eyes. "Sounds like typical shade nonsense."

"Right." Sebastian looked around the man blocking his escape path. "If you'll excuse me, I'll go."

William moved, and Sebastian didn't hesitate to get out of there. He'd get Hazel to call Eleanor again and pass on what he'd learned from Mila. Hazel and the mayor seemed closer than he'd originally realized. He was sure an extra phone call wouldn't be a big deal.

On his way back down the street, he passed Beth's souvenir shop. Light spilled out the windows and onto the dark sidewalk. Sebastian hadn't ever spoken to Beth in person. He'd first written to the shop about his jam years ago, and Beth's son was the one who'd come out to Storm House to pick it up each season.

Sebastian hesitated. He could walk by and write to Beth later. Or look up the shop's phone number online and call her. But part of him wanted to go in and see if she was around.

Steeling himself, Sebastian opened the shop door. He was nervous even though the shop was clearly empty of customers. Maybe it was leftover discomfort from the run-in with William or the fact that he didn't know what to expect of Beth.

Would she like him or wish he'd kept his distance?

He inched forward. A woman, maybe a decade older than Mila, stood behind the counter, preoccupied with her cell phone.

"Hi." Sebastian cleared his throat. "Um, Beth?"

"Yes?" She looked up.

"It's Sebastian." He raised his hand in an awkward wave. "I make the apricot jam."

"Oh, hello." Beth beamed. "I hope you've got some more ready for me. I've usually heard from you by now." She glanced at a wall calendar tacked next to the register as if she'd had an appointment with Sebastian noted down.

"Yeah, sorry." Sebastian stuffed his hands in the pockets of the leather jacket. "I've got a batch I can bring by before you close."

She clapped her hands together. "Wonderful. The labels are all ready. Hopefully this weird weather—or whatever you want to call it—goes away before all the tourists get scared off. Your jam is always very popular."

"Glad to hear it, but it's probably your spooky packaging that sells it. I love the labels." He smiled, the twisting in his gut almost completely gone.

"Thank you." Beth seemed genuinely pleased he liked how she'd branded the jam. "If you start making other flavors, I'd be very interested."

Sebastian left the shop and headed around the corner to Gray Electrical. While he really liked James's friends, he was glad to have some of his own people too. It felt good to have connections in town even though he hadn't been here in so long. He liked providing jam for the souvenir shop. It made him feel useful and reminded him he had lots to offer, not just to James but to the community.

It all helped Moonlight Falls feel like home in a way it never had before. He wasn't some outsider. He belonged here as much as anyone else.

Sandwiches were waiting at the electrical shop courtesy of Parker, who seemed to have taken over helping Eli check the data he'd entered.

The rest of the day passed as more of the same. Hazel relayed Sebastian's message about potential shade magic to Eleanor, but there was no more news about the darkness and no progress on getting help from outside Moonlight Falls.

Sebastian, Eli, and Parker returned to Storm House that evening to collect the last few hours of data. The trip went as the last one had. The shades were curious but kept their distance, only getting territorial when the three of them got too close to the fuel cell.

"I'm going to try and run some analysis soon," Eli said once they were back in the car. "Hopefully, after I've typed this up, there will be enough information on the veins' energy flow to start getting a picture of what's happening."

"You're telling me we have another fun night of typing ahead of us?" Parker teased as he pulled onto the road, leaving Storm House behind.

"There's no way around it." Eli reached over to rest his hand on Parker's thigh. His voice dropped to a purr. "But I promise I'll make it worth your while."

Parker chuckled. His eyes caught Sebastian's in the rearview mirror. "I'll drop you at home then? Doesn't sound like tonight is a good night to have you over."

Sebastian snorted. No, it didn't, but he liked that Parker's comment implied he might invite Sebastian over some other time outside of the group's Sunday dinner. "Can you take me over to James's house instead?"

Parker smiled. "Sure thing."

Sebastian's heart fluttered for some reason. He shouldn't feel giddy getting to see James again. They'd been together all day and had only spent a single night apart in weeks. Still, he arrived at James's place full of silly butterflies.

Maybe this was what people felt like when they were happy. Sebastian decided not to fight it now that he was embracing good things.

James greeted him at the door, pulling him inside and kissing him like they'd been parted for months. Sebastian's heart thudded as James's tongue slid over his. He'd never been so in sync with anyone, especially not with the desperate side of himself.

The front door fell closed with a click. James pressed Sebastian against the wall, and Sebastian dug his fingers into James's hips, pulling him as close as possible.

"We need to kiss more during the day," he said when James released him.

"Agreed." James leaned forward, recapturing his mouth.

Sebastian ran his hands along the waistband of James's jeans until he came to the button. He popped it, then slid the zipper down. James groaned as Sebastian slid his hand into James's underwear. He palmed James's hardening cock, running his thumb up the underside and over the tip.

"I've changed my mind," Sebastian breathed against James's lips. "We need to have more sex during the day. Kissing isn't enough."

"You're a deviant," James huffed as he thrust into Sebastian's fist.

"And you fucking love it." Sebastian pulled James's lower lip between his teeth and squeezed his cock, eliciting a small gasp of pleasure.

James sunk his hands into Sebastian's curls, their foreheads pressed together. "Yes, I do."

Sebastian gave him one more rough kiss, then dropped to his knees. He felt so fucking good right now. He loved every second with James and wanted to show it, to seize everything being with James offered him. He could be his ridiculous, imperfect self with James. He could be sweet and doting or filthy and outrageous, *anything*, and James would accept him.

Right now, he wanted to pamper James and get lost in how much he loved having sex with him.

Sebastian pulled James's jeans and boxer briefs down, freeing his dick. Sebastian looked up as he grabbed hold of the hard length and guided it to his lips. James's mouth dropped open, letting out a low moan as Sebastian teased his cockhead, licking his slit and swirling his tongue around the tip. He loved James watching him. It made him ache to see lust and affection shaping James's usually controlled features.

"You're so good at that, sweetheart. Fuck." James ran his hands through Sebastian's hair, gathering the loose curls into a firm hold.

Sebastian glowed with the praise. He sucked James into his mouth as James tightened his grip on his hair. He loved the consuming feeling of connection he got when James's cock was in his mouth, filled and held in place, and undeniably wanted.

Sebastian bobbed on James's cock, keeping his eyes focused upward so he wouldn't miss James's reactions. He needed every shred of James's pleasure, and Sebastian knew he could have it. He believed he was worthy of it. He sucked James's cock like he had every right to all the good feelings James gave him.

Sebastian hollowed his cheeks. James made an obscene noise, and Sebastian would have given him the most devilish grin if his mouth hadn't been so full.

"Gonna make me come if you keep doing that," James warned.

Sebastian doubled down, James's cock heavy against his tongue. He wanted to take him all the way in, truly let giving head consume him. He let go of the base of James's cock and pushed forward, taking him into the back of his throat.

"Oh shit." James's grip on his hair tightened.

Sebastian groaned. His own cock throbbed, but he didn't take his eyes off James, just slid up and down James's length, taking him as far in as he could.

James moaned. "Fuck, Sebastian. Feels so good. Like you were made for it."

Yes. Sebastian needed more. He took James deeper as one of his hands dropped from James's thigh to rub his aching dick through his jeans.

"You like that? Being made for me?" James stroked Sebastian's cheek with a thumb, making Sebastian whimper.

Yes, he loved the idea of being made for James. The thought had his own orgasm crashing into him. He spilled into his pants with a few rough strokes of his hand.

"Oh shit." James thrust into Sebastian's mouth as he watched Sebastian come. It was as consuming as Sebastian wanted it to be. Pleasure soared through him as James's dick pulsed and hot cum flooded his mouth.

Sebastian swallowed, bobbing on James until he'd sucked everything he could out of him. He pulled off reluctantly, wanting to stay connected and keep the taste of James from fading.

Why couldn't James be his whole world? It felt so fucking good. Sebastian had been so lonely for so long. He wanted to fill himself with James and cling until he forgot he'd ever been alone.

James took a few unsteady breaths and pulled Sebastian up. It seemed James didn't want to let go either. Without speaking, he reached for Sebastian's jeans, undoing them and pulling them down. He peeled back Sebastian's ruined underwear to reveal his soft, sticky cock. James dragged his fingers through the cum cooling against Sebastian's skin. Sebastian shivered, moaning as James brought his fingers to his mouth.

"It's so hot seeing you make a mess of yourself for me." James licked his fingers, and Sebastian's cheeks burned. "It's like just knowing you're mine gets you off."

Sebastian made a desperate sound. "Knowing I'm yours is all I need, James."

James shook his head. "All you need, huh? Didn't I say you deserved to be spoiled?" Sebastian nodded, and James knelt before him. "That's right. Now, can I clean you up?"

Sebastian's eyes widened. He nodded again, words failing him. James leaned forward, and Sebastian had to bite back a whimper as James ran his tongue over his sensitive cock.

James licked him delicately, moving to kiss and swirl his tongue over the crease between Sebastian's groin and thigh when Sebastian's cock became too tender. He cleaned the cum from his skin before burying his nose against it and breathing in. Eventually, he made his way back to Sebastian's dick and cleaned that too, like he was worshipping it. It wasn't just sexy. It was…more.

Sebastian felt exposed, vulnerable, and so pampered as James's soft ministrations tickled and teased him, each gentle caress perfect and loving.

When he was done, James kissed the head of Sebastian's cock and righted his clothes, then stood and did up his own jeans. He ran a hand through Sebastian's hair. "You probably still want to change before dinner."

He said it so matter-of-fact, as if he hadn't just given Sebastian an unfathomable gift. Like it was normal to be so treasured.

Sebastian scratched the back of his neck. "Yeah, my boxers are a bit sticky."

James grinned. "Come on. You can borrow some of my clothes."

Sebastian followed James upstairs. He hoped he'd made James feel as treasured as he did right now.

He perched on James's bed as James dug around in his drawers and closet. Instead of handing him the pile of clothes as Sebastian expected, James set everything on the bed and pulled Sebastian's shirt over his head.

James kissed the freckles cascading over Sebastian's shoulders, lingering on the bite marks at the crook of his neck. His lips were as delicate as they'd been on his cock.

Sebastian sighed. It felt so good.

James continued to take care of him, handing Sebastian a T-shirt and helping him out of his jeans and underwear. He caressed Sebastian's skin as he went, tracing the shape of his hips, kneading his thighs and calf muscles.

Sebastian had never felt so cared for.

James watched as Sebastian pulled on the borrowed boxer briefs and a pair of sweats. His gaze didn't feel sexual. His expression wasn't lust-laden like it had been earlier. It seemed more proud, if anything. Which Sebastian didn't quite understand.

"I like seeing you in my clothes." James reached out to adjust the collar of the T-shirt Sebastian was wearing.

"Ah." Sebastian smiled, getting it now. "You like staking your claim."

James shrugged. "Yeah. I like being able to see that I'm the one you trust to take care of you. I've never been into it before, but I'm dying to cover your neck in hickeys for everyone to see."

Sebastian touched the hidden bite marks. "There's a horny animal trapped inside you, James."

He snorted. "What a romantic way to put it." He shook his head. "See, this is why I hold back. When I don't, I turn into a caveman."

"No. I think when you're in, you're *all* in. That's all. It's not a bad thing." Sebastian pulled James into a kiss. "I need to be claimed as much as you need to mark me. I promise."

James wrapped his arms around Sebastian. "Man, I like hearing that. I've never felt this strongly about anyone. It's kind of terrifying, but you get me, and that makes it so much easier. It's like you knew this *need* was inside me and pulled it out into the open. Being with you feels so right."

"I know, it really does." Sebastian wrapped his arms around James's neck. "We're basically perfect for each other. And I couldn't be happier that I'm bringing out the horny caveman in you. He's hot."

"Oh my god." James rolled his eyes, but his smile didn't dim in the slightest.

"None of that." Sebastian kissed him on the nose. "This might be my proudest moment: getting the guy who used to blush at the word dildo to say he wants to cover me in marks so everyone knows how thoroughly he's satisfied me."

James went bright red. "When you put it like that—"

"It's exactly how you put it. And I love it. I love being yours. It makes me happier than I thought possible." Sebastian released James, taking in the soft smile and affectionate shine in his eyes. Sebastian kissed his nose once more. "Now, let's go make dinner. I need to feed you."

CHAPTER NINETEEN

The next morning, it was still dark. Sebastian and James didn't comment on it. The darkness just hung over them like the worst kind of third wheel. But what could they do other than go on as usual?

Down in the kitchen, Sebastian handed James his leather jacket. "Here."

James's brow wrinkled. "You don't want to keep wearing it?"

"No, I do. But if you never wear it, it'll stop smelling like you."

James grinned. "I hadn't thought of that." He slipped the jacket on, and Sebastian took a moment to appreciate the sight. He'd missed James wrapped in leather.

Sebastian grabbed the hoodie James had been about to put on. "I'll settle for this, for now." He pulled it over his head, brought the collar to his nose, and sniffed. "It's almost like being wrapped up in you all day."

James crushed him into a hug. "I'll wrap you up whenever you want, sweetheart."

Sebastian melted.

They'd managed to stop clinging to each other and eat breakfast by the time Eli and Parker walked into the kitchen. Sebastian hadn't even heard the front door open. He'd been too caught up in James and making sure he finished his pancakes to notice anything else.

Eli plonked his laptop down on the counter without saying hello. "Analysis is not going well."

James gave his brother a concerned frown. "Why not?"

"I don't know why. That's the problem." Eli opened the computer. "If I knew why the data looked like this, everything would be fine."

"What does it look like?" Sebastian peered over Eli's shoulder at the laptop screen. It was nothing but a mess of numbers to him.

Eli opened a graph depicting a scattered mess of dots. "There's almost no pattern to the energy flowing through the vein intersection. It's chaos." He pointed at the dots. "This is nothing like what I recorded at the vein in town, which *is* connected to this mess, so you'd think they'd have some similarities."

Eli pulled up another graph with dots forming a tightly grouped, fairly steady line. "The amount of energy flowing through town hardly changes. And look how much higher the energy levels are at the intersection." He switched back to the first graph.

"Doesn't that make sense?" James scratched his chin. "We know the veins are unstable at Storm House. Maybe this is what unstable looks like."

Parker bumped Eli's shoulder with his. "That's a good point."

"Sure." Eli ran a hand through his hair with a frustrated air. "But the fuel cell is supposed to be stabilizing things. And speaking of the fuel cell, why does adding *more* energy stop the veins from exploding? After seeing this, I'd have thought less energy would help the situation, bring it back down to the levels I'm seeing in town."

"But we can't take energy out of the veins." Even Sebastian

knew what an impossible task that was. Solving that riddle made Nelson Power one of the richest companies in the world, and the answer was kept tightly locked away.

Sebastian wondered if Nelson Storm had been trying to use the veins on their property to figure out how to extract magical power from the earth all those years ago, but he had no idea how Nelson might have done that. If that's what Nelson and Sullivan had been up to in the clearing, it had clearly failed. And if sucking more energy out would have solved the problem, Nelson surely would have come home to save his brother once he'd figured out how to do it properly, not disappeared on him and never looked back.

"Of course we can't take energy out." Eli huffed at the suggestion.

"My family always framed the problem as an energy debt," Sebastian said. "So adding more makes sense."

"Only this doesn't look like a lack of energy being filled." Eli pointed at the graph accusatorily.

"Then what does it look like? Do veins *ever* behave like this?" Parker brushed back a stray lock of Eli's hair that had fallen in his face. "Have you ever read anything about this kind of chaotic energy?"

Eli chewed his lip, looking up at Parker. "Shifting veins are much more variable, maybe even a bit chaotic. But this vein is fixed. Its path doesn't change. I don't know if its energy pattern resembling a shifting vein tells us anything about how to fix it." Eli seemed overwhelmed and much less sure they'd be able to solve this problem than he had before.

Parker put a hand on Eli's shoulder. "Eli, you aren't going to have the answer instantly. We just need to do some research, like you said. We should see if the secret-binding is weak enough for you to write to your supervisor and ask for advice. Even if you can't tell him the whole story, he might have some insight on what this data means, or he might be able to give you some general information on chaotic energy patterns."

Eli took a breath. "You're right. I just wasn't expecting it to look like this. It threw me off. I need a new perspective or more data."

"What about these bits?" James pointed to three dips in the mess of dots.

"I'm worried about those." Eli frowned at the computer. "At first, I was like—yay—it seems like the veins calm down for a few minutes a day. It's some of the lowest the energy gets. But those times correspond to us collecting the recordings on the receipt paper."

"Why's that worrying?" Sebastian didn't get it.

"It means we're probably interfering somehow. Who knows if it's a real dip in energy or if it's us disrupting the magic we set up to measure the veins."

"Couldn't we be affecting the veins themselves rather than the spells on the mechanisms?" Sebastian stared at the dots. "Maybe something about us being there calms things. Maybe we can use that." As soon as he said it, he felt like he'd missed a step going down the stairs.

Parker leveled a stare at Sebastian. "You mean like trapping a person at the property to stop the imbalance from getting out of hand because their presence calms things?"

Sebastian's mouth went dry. "What? No. The fuel cell is taking care of that. Or else, how did James and I get out?" But they hadn't gotten out, not really. They were still stuck.

Maybe the fuel cell hadn't done anything they'd thought it had. Maybe it wasn't doing enough to stabilize the veins. Who knows if the energy had been this chaotic over the last six years while Sebastian had been trapped. Maybe it hadn't been. Without past measurements, there was no way to know.

But if that was the case, and not having a person at the property was causing problems, wouldn't things have exploded by now?

"The fuel cell is taking care of it. It has to be." Eli pointed to the computer. "This is chaos but doesn't look like explosive levels of chaos. The energy level needed to cause the kind of destruction you described, Sebastian, would be much higher than this. This would not blow up Moonlight Falls." Eli frowned at his graph for a minute. When he looked up, he seemed hesitant. "But if these dips aren't us interfering with the mechanisms, and it's us affecting the veins, then I wonder if it's not so much *us* but Sebastian influencing things."

Sebastian took a step back from the group. He didn't know why Eli thought that, but he didn't like it. His heart pounded like it was trying to leave his chest. He didn't want to be different. Didn't want to be set apart from everyone else. It was too close to being cast out.

This wasn't his fault.

"Hey." James gripped his shoulder. "It's okay. Even if you caused these dips, it doesn't change anything. We're still in this together."

It was like James had read his mind. Sebastian sagged in relief. James knew him, understood him, and cared about him so fiercely that he didn't mind dealing with any of this.

Sebastian wasn't going to be abandoned, no matter what they learned.

"Sorry, Sebastian. I didn't mean to imply anything bad." Eli's voice softened as he spoke. "I only think it's you, not everyone, because of what you said yesterday and because the time Parker and I collected the receipts without you, there's no dip." He pointed it out on the graph for everyone to see. "You said the veins had access to your magic and drained it before they started draining the fuel cell. What if that connection is still there? The dips could be showing us that you're still linked in a different way than the rest of us. Which we already suspected."

True, that was nothing new. Sebastian knew that James's and the others' magic had never been affected, but he'd hoped that some of the hold the curse had allowed the veins to have over him had broken now that his magic was back. "You think the veins are still taking my energy?"

"If that's the case," James cut in before Eli could answer, "why would taking energy from Sebastian cause the veins' energy to dip lower? Shouldn't it be the opposite?"

"You're right. That's what I would have thought." Eli narrowed his eyes. "So then, does this mean Sebastian is taking energy from the veins?"

"BUT we just said taking energy isn't possible." James looked at Eli like he'd lost it.

"It's not possible. Normally." Eli ran another nervous hand through his hair, making it stand on end. "At least not without the secrets of modern magical power. But what if Sebastian and the veins are so tied together that it isn't really taking per se. What if it's more like they're one unit, sharing energy. It makes sense given the nature of the curse binding people and the veins together."

"Wait. You're saying that all this time, I could have taken energy from the veins?" Sebastian looked at Eli in disbelief. "Then why didn't my uncle or his predecessors do it? They could have been super powerful, done all kinds of amazing magic, not to mention cast spells to light up the whole dark, miserable house."

Eli put up a hand, stopping Sebastian's increasingly frustrated words. "I'm not saying it would be safe to take magic from the veins to cast spells. It probably wouldn't be. It could be as near-impossible to do in a controlled way as extracting energy for electricity is. I'm just saying *in theory*, I bet the connection goes both ways. There could be a natural flow between the two, but this is all conjecture."

James made a frustrated sound. "If it's true, does it even help us?"

Eli shrugged. "I'm not sure it does. Seeing the energy levels dip could be evidence of Sebastian's continued tie to the veins. A tie the fuel cell didn't break. And a tie I bet the fuel cell now has to the veins. To know for sure, we'd have to take turns going to the clearing alone and see what each of us does to the energy compared to Sebastian. See if every time Sebastian is around, we get a dip. We'd need to try and measure any changes in Sebastian's personal magic too. But I don't think getting a conclusive answer will get us any closer to solving this."

Everyone was quiet for a long moment. Sebastian felt faintly ill. There was an undeniable ring of truth in Eli's theory. Sebastian knew he was connected to this thing more so than the others. But there was no way he could draw power from the veins or be so fundamentally linked to them that they were *one unit*. The idea horrified him. He didn't want to believe it. It made him think he'd never escape this.

However, not wanting it to be true didn't mean the theory was wrong. He thought back to Eli's questions about how James had linked to him when doing the unbinding spell. If Sebastian had so little magical energy, where had the energy James had borrowed come from? Had James taken energy from the veins *through* Sebastian? He wanted to say no way. Sebastian had never been able to access extra power when he'd been too tired to conjure light, but if it was a natural flow between him and the veins, maybe James could have drawn on it through him just as he'd normally draw on any other person.

But if Eli was right, how would they ever untie Sebastian from the veins? Would solving the imbalance break a connection like that?

James tapped the counter like he was deep in thought. "We need to figure out why adding the fuel cell expanded the boundary. It clearly changed something, and if it didn't untie Sebastian, we need to know what it did. Maybe that will help us find a solution." He glanced at Sebastian with the ghost of a smile. "Or we can try and find a way to keep expanding the boundary until it's essentially nonexistent. As long as the veins are stable enough to not cause problems, then we can consider this shit done."

Parker snorted.

Eli looked between them. "The boundary is a smart thing to look into while we continue collecting measurements from the vein intersection."

"Do you think connecting the fuel cell did anything to the veins in town?" Sebastian pointed to the laptop. "Maybe that will help us see what happened that day. If you were recording stuff then."

"I was." Eli turned back to his laptop and pulled up more graphs. "I haven't looked at any of the data from my setup in town since you two came back to town, but at least it's all imported automatically. It really is a pain that we can't use electronics at Storm House. I'm getting sick of copying off of receipt paper."

Eli studied the computer screen for a few minutes. James sipped his coffee. Sebastian had abandoned his. He still felt queasy.

"There's nothing from the night you connected the fuel cell. It all looks normal."

Sebastian's shoulders sagged. Damn.

"Wait—" Eli's brows shot up his forehead. "What night did you see that creepy shade activity in town, Sebastian?"

"Three nights ago."

"There was a huge spike of energy that night. I have a monitor set up near the stone. Holy shit. Maybe the shades *were* doing some sort of magic. This part of the vein has had a steady flow since I started studying it at the beginning of fall. No way a spike like this is a coincidence."

Parker leaned over Eli's shoulder. "Was there anything the night my house got attacked?"

"No." Eli scrolled through the information on the screen. "But if Hazel's theory is right, and the darkness surrounding the town and whatever happened at your house are the same, what if it all started with what Sebastian saw around the stone?"

"There were weird shadows that night too." Sebastian wasn't sure how well he'd explained that to everyone when first describing what he'd seen. "I thought they were just shades not in solid form, but what if it was more like the stuff that attacked Parker's house?"

"Could be." Parker nodded, frowning thoughtfully. "We need to figure out more about the darkness and what's going on with the shades. While it'd be great to solve the imbalance and free ourselves, that doesn't look like it's happening any time soon, and being stuck here is a lot more of a problem when we don't know what's going on or how dangerous it's going to get." Parker reached out and closed Eli's laptop. "If there was an energy spike in town when we think this all started, the veins must play a part in the darkness somehow."

"And not in a way that's necessarily connected to us being trapped or the curse or imbalance," Eli added. "What if that humanoid shade you saw is using the veins? We have no idea how intelligent shades do magic. They might have a better handle on vein power than humans do." Eli trailed off, looking lost in thought. "I want to look at the darkness boundary."

"Why?" Sebastian asked.

"I have a theory." Eli turned to Parker. "I'm going to get my portable meter and map. You're driving."

Parker smiled fondly. "You got it, gorgeous."

Eli rushed off down the hall toward his room.

Sebastian turned to the others. "But what's the theory?"

"Probably something to do with the veins being straight," James guessed. "But who knows."

Eli dragged Parker away with him, and James and Sebastian drove across town to Gray Electrical.

Sebastian hated that they were getting nowhere. Nothing they'd learned felt helpful. They didn't know why the veins on his property had a weird energy pattern. They didn't know what exactly the fuel cell had done when it was linked up to everything. Being trapped wasn't even their biggest problem.

CHAPTER TWENTY

"I SWEAR it's even darker today." Sebastian glanced over his shoulder as he got out of the car in front of the electrical shop. It was more like night than pre-dawn.

He caught sight of a few shades swooping around the duplex across the street. That wasn't a good sign. They hadn't seen any of the beasts in town yesterday. It seemed the prolonged darkness was making them bolder. A few had been floating in the town center when they'd driven through.

Hazel wasn't at the shop yet. James checked the time. "It's only ten past." He sounded worried but seemed to be trying to suppress it.

"Give her a call." Sebastian put a reassuring hand on James's arm. "It's probably nothing, but with what's going on, I'd say it's better to be cautious and check on her."

The tension in James's brow eased. "True." He pulled out his phone and dialed Hazel, pressing it to his ear. "Hey, you're late," he said grumpily when she picked up. "Don't huff at me. It's the apocalypse, remember? Are you coming in?" After a few more words, he hung up.

"She's alive and well?" Sebastian bit back a smile at the look of frustration on James's face.

"She's fine." He rolled his eyes, perhaps more annoyed with himself for worrying than with Hazel. Not that he was admitting it. "She's heading over now. Said she was with Eleanor."

Sebastian followed James as he crossed the shop. "What's she doing with Eleanor this early in the morning?"

James snorted. "I'm pretty sure they're sleeping together."

"*What!*" Sebastian squealed, causing James to snort another laugh.

"I've had a feeling something was brewing between them." James plopped down at his desk. "Hazel keeps deflecting every time I ask, but it's not like she's trying that hard to hide it either."

Sebastian perched on James's desk. "How old is Eleanor?"

James shrugged. "Mid-forties, I think."

Sebastian sucked in a breath, a shit-eating grin on his face. He loved gossip and hadn't had any in years. "An older woman in a position of power? Hazel doesn't mess around, does she?"

James gave him a bemused look. "You're making it sound way more scandalous than it is."

Sebastian swung his legs back and forth. "But it's more fun that way."

"Right." James captured Sebastian's legs, stilling them. He rolled his desk chair to position himself between them, hands sliding up to Sebastian's hips. "How are you doing?"

"Um?" Sebastian squirmed. "Good. But I don't think it's the best idea to get me all excited if Hazel is on her way."

James pinched Sebastian's side. "That wasn't what I was doing, you nightmare." His amused smile softened. "I meant after what Eli was saying about you and the veins being connected like a unit."

"Oh, that." Sebastian slumped. "I don't know. I'm not exactly looking forward to Eli testing his theory. The dips look pretty damning, even if it's not totally scientific proof. I just— Does it matter if he's right or not? I might not be able to do anything about it." Sebastian tried valiantly to fight a familiar hopeless feeling. "I have to believe that when we find a permanent solution to the imbalance, I'll be free of the veins, no matter how I'm connected to them now."

James pulled himself closer to Sebastian. "I just want you to know I'm here for you, no matter what we find out. No matter what it means."

"I know, James." Sebastian cupped his face. "That means so fucking much to me. It makes scary unknown magical shit easier to face. And I'm here for you too. If I can use this supposed two-way connection to help us, I will." Even if he didn't want it, and even if it meant he'd never be rid of this mess, Sebastian would do anything for James, and in the end, he believed they'd still be together. No matter what. They'd make this work.

They were inevitable. Bound together through their pasts and the choices they'd made in their present. Nothing could separate them.

James held on to Sebastian's hips and looked into his eyes. Sebastian reached out and traced his jaw. There was so much affection in James's expression, and even in the dark, surrounded by magic he didn't understand, James made Sebastian feel light.

They sat quietly for a while, but Sebastian didn't want to dwell.

"I bet Eleanor is holding Hazel up." Sebastian waggled his eyebrows at James ridiculously. Hazel still hadn't arrived.

James cracked a grin. "I'd say it's more likely Hazel is holding Eleanor up. Eleanor is too responsible to be late for work, especially in a crisis.

"Ha. You're right. I feel like Hazel and I have that penchant for misbehaving in common." Sebastian wrapped his legs tight around James, who was still sitting between them. "She seems like fun."

James shook his head. "She is. Just be careful. You mess with that woman at your own risk."

"Oh, now I can't wait to get to know her better." Sebastian beamed.

The door banged open, and Hazel rushed into the electrical shop, out of breath. Sebastian's smile disappeared as she leaned heavily against the closed door. "Shit, the shades aren't being calm today."

Sebastian and James jumped up.

"What happened?" James rounded the counter.

Hazel pushed off the door, brushing past him and beelining for the coffee maker. "A small swarm of them attacked my car as I was driving."

James crossed his arms. "Why not just run them down?" When shades were hit by a vehicle, they usually dissipated, meaning it was more like driving through smoke than colliding with something.

"Gosh, I wish I'd thought of that," Hazel snapped.

"It didn't work?" Sebastian guessed.

Hazel switched the coffee on. "They burst into shadow but didn't scatter. It was like they were expecting me to drive through them and covered my windshield in wispy darkness. I couldn't see."

James joined Hazel by the coffee. "What did you do?"

"I got out of the car and banished them." Hazel redid her ponytail. "There were more when I got to the shop. They surrounded the car, and I had to fight my way in here."

"Shit." Sebastian came over to stand next to James. "They didn't bother us at all."

"I'm going to call Eleanor." Hazel took out her phone. After a quick call, she let Sebastian and James know the mayor hadn't had any issues getting to the elementary school, where she was meeting with Tony that morning.

James made a call, checking on Eli and Parker, who were also fine. "Eli wants to know if we'll go out to Storm House and get this morning's data."

Sebastian grimaced. "I thought we decided figuring out the darkness was more important right now."

Hazel sipped her coffee. "We might as well go. Sitting around here isn't helping anything. We'll just have to be careful driving."

No one else had had trouble with shades that morning, so the beasts weren't exactly a reason to stay in and do nothing, but Sebastian wasn't thrilled to go to Storm House today. He had no real reason for it, so he didn't say anything. It would be better to get it over with and get Eli his data.

They piled into Hazel's van. As they headed north, several cars passed, going the other direction. A family that lived in one of the last houses out this way was piling in their car with a bunch of suitcases as they drove by. Sebastian wondered how many other people were leaving town.

No shades bothered them as they wound their way to Storm House. Instead of being relieved by the lack of trouble after what happened to Hazel, it made Sebastian uneasy.

At the iron gate, Hazel conjured a small ball of light so they could see. Sebastian unlocked the chain, trying to suppress a shiver that had nothing to do with the temperature. Something felt wrong, but he wasn't sure why.

The property was quiet, and something unsettling hung in the air. They all hesitated at the bottom of the driveway.

"Snuff out that light," James whispered to Hazel.

She obeyed, leaving them in darkness.

It took a minute for their eyes to adjust. Once they did, Sebastian could see the property better. The house was dark and abandoned. He inched up the driveway, feeling the others following closely behind him. As he passed the trees blocking the rest of his land from the road, he stopped.

There were shades everywhere. Hundreds, maybe close to a thousand, given it was hard to make out what lay in the distant corners of the property other than shifting shadow.

"The place is crawling with them," Hazel muttered, her voice unsteady.

"Come on." James grabbed Sebastian's hand, pulling him backward.

Sebastian was rooted to the spot. There were even more shades than there'd been the night they'd linked the fuel cell and had almost been crushed to death. "Where are they all coming from?"

"I don't know." James pulled him again, and this time, Sebastian moved. "We need to go."

They hurried back to the van. Sebastian's hands shook as he locked the gate.

"Why do they like my property so much?" he asked as they drove away.

James twisted around in the front seat to look back at him. "It was like they were gathering there. Do you think it has to do with the fuel cell?"

The fixation some of the shades had on the fuel cell was odd, but Sebastian didn't think it was what was drawing them in. "There's always been way more shades around Storm House than in town. Whatever's drawing them has been here a lot longer than the fuel cell. It has to be the veins, right?"

"But why would shades care about the intersection? And why are there so many more now than ever before?" James didn't sound like he expected Sebastian to have any answers. They all had to be wondering the same thing.

"At least they're not in town," Hazel pointed out.

James grunted his agreement before adding, "There's nothing stopping them if they decide to head into Moonlight Falls, and with so many out here, how do we know there aren't large groups of them in town too? Or in the woods? It's not a good time to be wandering around." He pulled out his phone and made a call. No one answered, and he hung up.

Sebastian could feel the tension in James growing. "Calling Eli?"

"Yeah. I don't like not knowing where he is. Not with that many shades so close and this darkness going nowhere."

Sebastian understood. James's fear of losing Eli ran deep, and while he could deal with every day worries, this situation was way higher risk. Anyone would be stressed.

Hazel drove past the electrical shop into the center of town. A few shades hovered around the stone while others swooped between the streetlights. Most of the shops were dark. The diner had its lights on, but the closed sign glowed in the window. It seemed like everyone had been happy to go on as usual yesterday, but the sun not rising a second time was too much, even for Moonlighters.

James made another phone call as they drove around the circle. "Where are you?" he barked as soon as someone picked up.

As James spoke into the phone, Hazel took them past the bed and breakfast where a couple was loading suitcases into a car and the elementary school that only had the lights on in the main office and two cars parked out front.

The whole place had a creepy, deserted vibe that even the cheerful, well-maintained building couldn't counteract. The fall leaves blowing across the road didn't give off the same cozy feeling they usually did on crisp mornings. The sight gave Sebastian a sense of dread he'd only ever felt late on winter nights at Storm House. Alone in the dark, in a world that felt deserted.

James hung up the phone. "Parker and Eli are out on Pine Steet, past the bridge."

Hazel took the next left. They drove through the east side of town, where more lights were on in the houses, making it seem like people had chosen to stay in, protected by their wards, and wait out whatever was happening.

Word must not have gotten out about the wards on Parker's house being penetrated, but since that night, Sebastian hadn't seen any more of the shadowy tendrils. Not even at Storm House. None of the houses seemed to be under attack, and it looked like there were fewer shades out this way, so at least there was that.

The houses grew thinner, giving way to larger plots of land and small paddocks. Trees loomed in the distance. Past the creek, Parker's car was pulled over next to a plot of land for sale, the car running, high beams on, and hazards flashing. He and Eli were standing in the road, Parker holding a flashlight.

As Hazel pulled over behind them, Sebastian noticed something odd about the trees in the distance. It seemed almost brighter over there, but somehow, the light wasn't reaching the cars.

"Found the boundary." Parker gestured in front of himself as they approached.

Eli stood in front of Parker, pulling on a rope tied to a skateboard.

"What are you doing?" James grumbled, hands shoved in his pockets. "I thought you were staying in the car, driving around, and measuring things? There are about a million shades at Storm House. You shouldn't be standing out here like this."

"Hold on." Eli sounded exasperated as he pulled the skateboard back to himself. A metal box sat on top of it. "We're figuring out important shit. The darkness boundary is in the exact same place as the barrier trapping us." He stepped forward and pushed on an invisible wall. "See?"

Parker handed Eli his laptop. "We've been to the spot where you crashed your truck already, James. It was the same there."

"Ha!" Eli exclaimed as he looked at his laptop screen.

James rubbed a hand over his face. "Can we go somewhere the shades can't get to us? Then you can tell me all about whatever you found."

"You said the shades were at Storm House. That's miles from here." Eli looked up from the laptop. "I know you want to wrap us all up in bubble wrap, James, but how are we going to fix anything if we do nothing but hide?"

"I'm not saying that." James's expression pinched, showing his hurt.

Sebastian put an arm around James. He couldn't help wanting to protect everyone.

Eli must have noticed James's reaction. He looked down at his feet. "Sorry, I know."

James didn't seem to know how to respond. He probably still wanted to get everyone somewhere safe, but Sebastian knew he was fighting against his sometimes-irrational anxiety of losing people and wouldn't want to seem overbearing. Though Sebastian thought he was being perfectly reasonable right now.

After a strained moment, Hazel asked, "Why would the two boundaries be the same?"

"The veins end here." Eli pushed on the invisible boundary again, like he was glad to finally get back to explaining. "I sent the skateboard with one of my meters on it past where we're trapped. I was able to record energy flow in the veins right up until here, where it disappears completely."

Sebastian eyed the boundary. "Is that normal?"

"Sure." Eli shrugged. "Veins don't go on forever. Fixed ones have set boundaries. The theory is that where the flow ends is where it leaves this world and goes back into Beyond. Whatever created the darkness has to be using the veins to do it. There was an energy surge when we think it was created, and it looks like the darkness is tied to the veins with some sort of magic, just like we are through the curse."

Sebastian turned away from the barrier and looked back down the road toward town. Knowing the darkness was another problem tied to the veins made his heart sink. If he knew anything, it was that they were terrible at untying anything from the damn veins. Even if the darkness wasn't related to his curse, dealing with it felt just as insurmountable.

Sebastian caught movement in the sky off in the distance. He grabbed James's arm, turning him around. "Look." He pointed.

"Shit." James grabbed Eli. "Come on. Time to go. That looks like a whole lot of shades heading this way."

CHAPTER TWENTY-ONE

Everyone turned, squinting off into the distance, where it looked like the darkness was moving. It was definitely shades or those shadowy tendrils moving through the dark sky.

Parker scooped up Eli's skateboard and headed to his car. Eli followed. James took half a step after him like he wanted to stop Eli from leaving and keep him close.

"We'll follow behind." Hazel hopped in the driver's seat of the van. Eli and Parker were already in the other car.

Sebastian leaned in close to James. "Go with him if you want."

James turned a piercing stare on him. "I'm not leaving you."

"Come on then." Sebastian grabbed James's wrist and pulled him into the back of the van. James's pulse fluttered under his fingers. "I know you don't want to lose any of us," Sebastian muttered. "I'm right here."

James swallowed and nodded.

Sebastian gripped his hand. He figured James's fear he couldn't keep them all safe was starting to overwhelm him. "Let's concentrate on what we can do. We're all together," Sebastian reminded him. "We'll hunker down somewhere safe like everyone else in town."

Hazel did a U-turn and followed Parker back the way they'd come.

"Okay." James held on to Sebastian's hand. He seemed to calm slowly, getting his panic under control before it could take hold of him. "I don't want any of us going off on our own again. Not with this many shades around."

"I don't think we'll argue with you on that," Hazel assured him. "This is way more shades than I've ever seen in town."

The horde in the sky was getting closer. It was definitely shades and not the tendrils. Their eyes glinted in the gloom.

Parker turned right, and Hazel followed, putting the flying shades out of sight as they drove down a street lined with tall trees. They went north for a few blocks through nothing but a quiet neighborhood, and then, after a few turns, they were headed back in the direction of the center of town.

"I wonder where those shades were going," Sebastian muttered. "I don't see why they'd head for the darkness boundary. They aren't trapped like us, but the sunlight on the other side would stop them going anywhere until nightfall."

"True." James squeezed Sebastian's hand. "Unless the light-resistant ones can stand direct sunlight."

Hazel glanced at them in the rearview mirror. "We've never seen them out in direct sunlight. When there was still daylight, that is. That kind of light resistance would be a whole other beast compared to what we've seen." She stopped behind Parker, who was paused at a four-way stop. They were the only two cars on the road.

Just as Parker's car began moving forward, something crashed from the sky, slamming into Hazel's van. All three of them shouted in alarm. A second later, Hazel's windscreen was completely backed out.

A shade's face appeared in the window next to Sebastian, and he gripped James's hand with all his strength. "Were they heading out that way, coming for us?" Sebastian was bewildered. He'd thought they'd lost the shades coming toward them when they'd turned down the street with all the trees. Unless these were completely different ones?

James looked frantically between all the windows. "Can you see Parker's car?" There was panic in his voice.

"No." Hazel grabbed a shade-light from her glove box and flicked it on, sending the bright beam out the front window.

Some of the shades scattered. She swept the beam back and forth until they could see the other car. Shades had swarmed it as well.

"Why would they be coming for us?" Hazel tossed another shade-light into the back seat. "They aren't going after any of the houses."

"Maybe they don't want us moving around," Sebastian guessed.

James turned on the other light. "There's too many to risk getting out." He seemed to be ignoring the discussion, only focusing on being unable to reach Eli and Parker.

The ear-piercing screech of claws on metal came from above their heads.

"Fuck." Sebastian held tight to James.

Parker's high beams flicked on in front of them. Shades scattered, but one that was obviously immune to the brightness stayed where it was. The car surged forward, colliding with the beast. It burst into shadow, only to resolidify once Parker's car was through it.

Hazel followed suit, smashing into the same shade, sending it back into shadow form. As she moved forward, more beasts rammed the vehicles from either side.

"We need to drive into a garage at someone's house. Get inside somewhere with stronger wards," Hazel said as she continued to follow Parker.

They didn't make it far.

Three shades blocked the road ahead, hovering shoulder to

shoulder. A pool of shadow seemed to form beneath them. Parker didn't slow down, even when his lights did nothing to scatter the shades. He drove right into them, hitting them with a loud crunch.

The shades didn't burst or abandon their solid form as the others had. They withstood the collision, stopping Parker's car in the street.

"Shit." Hazel slammed on her brakes so she wouldn't rear-end Parker.

The shades didn't move away from Parker's car. They seemed unharmed. The one in the middle leaned forward, slamming its clawed hands into the hood, denting it.

James's grip on Sebastian's hand tightened.

Parker's car shut off, lights going out. More shades surrounded both vehicles, swooping and scratching the windows, making it hard to see what was happening outside.

James surged forward in his seat. "Drive up alongside them."

Hazel didn't need to be told twice. She pulled out onto the wrong side of the road, going slow so a collision with any shades that didn't dissipate wouldn't damage the van. As she pulled up, she left enough space for Parker and Eli to get their doors open.

Sebastian could just make out Eli scrambling into the back seat so he would be on the side of the car closest to Hazel, but before he could open the door, shades flooded the space between the vehicles.

Shit. How were Parker and Eli going to get across to the van?

The shade that had dented Parker's hood slithered up to the windshield. It raised clenched fists like it meant to smash the glass.

Sebastian, James, and Hazel all yelled in useless warning.

The glass smashed at the same time James threw the van's back door open and sent sparks at the shades blocking him from his brother. Sebastian scrambled to help, sending his own sparks. Shades burst, banished to Beyond, but more filled their place.

James lunged out of the van and yanked the back door of Parker's car open. Sebastian tried his best to set the shades grabbing at them on fire, but there were too many. It was chaos.

James grabbed Eli from the backseat as Parker climbed out of the driver's door, blood running down cuts on his arms. A path cleared to Eli and James, and Sebastian seized it, pulling Eli into the van, but James didn't follow.

Shades converged on Parker like they had been ordered to strike him. In an instant, Parker disappeared, engulfed by a writhing black mass of ghostly forms.

"Parker!" James shouted.

Eli screamed. He tried to lunge around Sebastian, back out of the van, but Sebastian grabbed him in time. Hazel leaned across the front and threw the passenger door open for Parker, sending sparks flying. Sebastian did his best to send his own sparks while clinging to Eli. Getting out wouldn't help, and he had to keep Eli safe.

The sparks weren't doing enough. Every shade that burst into flame had two more to replace it.

"What are we going to do?" Eli wailed.

Before Sebastian could think of a response, James threw himself into the swirling shades, and Eli went deathly still in Sebastian's arms.

"Fuck," Hazel swore in a panicked whisper.

Fire burst out of the mass of shades, the heat hitting Sebastian in the face. Flames licked the van as shades ignited. The beasts were so packed together, and the fire so massive, that it caught from one to another, burning up into the sky, swathing the whole horde in flame.

There was nothing left but swirling smoke as the fire went out. It cleared, revealing James and Parker back to back and panting like they'd just run for miles. Parker slumped, losing his balance, and stumbled to his knees. James whirled around to catch him.

Sebastian was out of the van and helping James before he could even process it. The smell of burned cloth filled his nostrils. Parker could barely stand, and it was an effort to get him into the van even though they were right next to it.

Hazel pulled from the inside, and at last, Parker was in the passenger seat. He seemed dangerously drained and was struggling to hold on to consciousness.

Sebastian couldn't think about that now. They had to get somewhere safe. He slammed the door, closing Parker in, and herded James into the backseat. "Drive!" he shouted at Hazel once they were in the seats next to Eli.

Hazel floored it.

Eli was sobbing, trying to climb over the center console to reach Parker in the front seat.

"I'm okay. Sit down," Parker murmured, sounding exhausted. "If Hazel crashes, you're going to get yourself killed."

Eli let out a choked sound, words apparently beyond him.

James grabbed him around the waist and dragged him back into the seat, reaching across Sebastian to click Eli's seatbelt into place. "He's okay, Eli."

"No," Eli protested. "He's not. That wasn't okay."

Sebastian's heart pounded. Parker wasn't in great shape, but he hadn't lost consciousness. Sebastian clung to that faint shred of positivity as Hazel tore down the street. She turned onto northern Main Street but sped straight past Gray Electrical and into the town center.

More shades had gathered in the circle around the stone. Others drifted randomly around the road. Several streetlights had been smashed, making it much darker than the last time they'd passed through.

"Got through my wards," Parker grunted in tired outrage, clearly noticing the busted lights.

Hazel slowed as she drove by the school. It was completely

dark now, and the cars that had been there before were gone. "Damn it, where's Eleanor?" Hazel growled.

"I'll call." James had his phone out and was scrolling through his contacts.

They needed to get inside a warded building but Sebastian couldn't ask Hazel to hide before they knew if Eleanor was safe. He watched out the window anxiously as Hazel made her way to the west end of town, seemingly at random.

Sebastian gripped Eli's shoulder in comfort as James spoke hurriedly into the phone on his other side. Eli's face was red and puffy, his cheeks wet. He trembled slightly, but he'd stopped crying.

"She's at Nora's," James informed Hazel before he hung up.

Hazel made a sharp right. A car passed them, going the other direction. "We need to tell people to stay inside." Hazel gripped the wheel tight as she took another turn.

James put his phone away. "I told Eleanor to get in the house."

"She wasn't already?" Hazel sounded livid.

As they approached what had to be Nora's house, Sebastian caught sight of a figure on the sidewalk. It didn't look like Eleanor had listened to James.

Hazel slammed on the breaks as they drew level with Eleanor. "What are you doing?"

"Getting in my car." Eleanor pointed to a small vehicle parked ahead of them.

"Get in with us," Hazel shouted through her closed window.

Eleanor's confused frown turned to shock, her eyes going wide. "Hazel!"

Before Sebastian knew what was happening the world flipped upside down. Someone screamed. There was a loud crash. The dizzying motion stopped, but Sebastian was still upside down, the seatbelt biting into his neck. He looked around frantically. James and Eli were hanging on either side of him, and out the window, there was nothing but the dark asphalt.

The van had flipped, and they hadn't even been moving. How had that happened? Hazel and Eleanor were shouting. James and Eli were simultaneously trying to ask everyone if they were all right as someone wrenched the door next to them open.

"We need to get out," James said from beside Sebastian. "Unbuckle yourselves."

Sebastian scrambled, bracing an arm on the roof below him so he wouldn't fall on his head. He managed to free himself and crawl out after Eli. He didn't see Hazel or Eleanor.

What had flipped the van?

James crawled out closely behind Sebastian. As soon as he was standing, he immediately began checking Sebastian and Eli for injuries. Something rustled in the air above them, and Sebastian looked up. Two shades hovered, peering down at them.

"They flipped us?" James sounded as shocked as Sebastian felt.

"Grab his other arm." Eleanor's voice cut through Sebastian's confusion. She and Hazel were on the other side of the van, helping free Parker.

Eli rushed toward the two women just as the shades struck. One went for Sebastian and James, while the other bore down on the other side of the van.

Strong hands gripped Sebastian's throat, knocking him off his feet. He couldn't draw enough breath to form the words to summon fire.

The beast was heavy and undeniably solid. Sebastian had a second to think: *this must be one of those damn complex shades* before it burst into flames. The pressure on his neck disappeared, only to be replaced by burning. He choked on the air as he drew breath, fire in his face. Then, there was nothing but smoke and shadow.

James's face filled his vision. "Sebastian." James cupped his cheeks, anguish in his eyes. "Shit, did I hurt you?"

"I'm okay." Sebastian pushed himself up. It had been close, but the flames had only been near him for a split second before they'd gone out, and he hadn't been burned.

Fire flared on the other side of the flipped van.

Eleanor appeared beside them, grabbing their arms and dragging them to standing. "Come on." She pulled them toward the house.

Hazel and Eli were helping Parker move unsteadily. Eleanor didn't wait for any of them. She rushed forward, picked up a flowerpot next to the front door, and threw it aside, grabbing a key underneath.

As Sebastian and James rushed to help Hazel and Eli with Parker, movement caught the corner of Sebastian's vision. "Hurry."

Eleanor held the front door open. Eli pulled Parker over the threshold, and everyone stumbled inside.

James looked around the darkened hallway. "Where's Nora?"

Eleanor heaved a ragged breath. "She and her family drove off a few minutes before you got here. They're leaving town for now."

"I hope they got out—" Hazel's words were cut off by a loud hiss.

Shades converged on the doorway. The wards on Nora's house stopped them from entering, but Sebastian's skin crawled at the sight of them so close.

Eleanor slammed the door in their faces. "We need to get Parker something to eat."

"No," a deep, eerie voice echoed around them. "We must speak."

CHAPTER TWENTY-TWO

Iᴄᴇ ʀᴀᴄᴇᴅ through Sebastian's veins. He looked from James to the others.

Hazel's eyes were wide. "Who the fuck said that?"

"I did." The door behind them burst open, and a bone-chilling wind filled the entryway.

Sebastian whirled around to find the shades gone. It was so dark outside he couldn't see beyond the front steps. It was like the world ended in a pit of blackness. At first, that was all he saw. Nothing. Then, a form materialized out of the dark.

It was no wonder he hadn't noticed it at first. The thing seemed to be made of darkness itself. A broad-shouldered figure that had to be close to seven feet tall stood on the threshold. It had no discernible features, no face or details on its body. It was like a silhouette turned solid.

The eerie voice filled the space even though Sebastian saw no mouth move. "Eleanor Ashley and Parker Hayes, Moonlight Falls has been taken. It belongs to those from Beyond. Light will never reach this soil again. You and your people should leave before it is too late."

There was a stunned silence. As far as Sebastian knew, shades had no understanding of or ability to communicate using human language. Apparently, he was dead wrong.

Eleanor stepped forward. "You know our names?" She sounded stunned as she gestured to herself and the barely conscious Parker.

"You are the leaders. Communicate to the rest that they must leave." The imposing shade didn't move but seemed to loom larger. Its words filled the space and made Sebastian's ears ache. It was humanoid, like the shade Sebastian had seen in the distance at the town center by the stone. Could it be using magic to communicate? Was it the one that had created the darkness?

"Moonlight Falls will not be forfeited to Beyond," Eleanor said resolutely. She was bolder than Sebastian. He'd never challenge a being like this. It radiated power. You could feel its tie to another world in a way you couldn't with regular shades.

"It will be," the shade said, making Sebastian's head tingle. "My magic is stronger. It has already broken yours."

Eleanor said the words for fire, sending sparks at the shade, only for the sparks to be engulfed in shadow and extinguished before they could ignite.

"We need more fire." James stepped up next to Eleanor. "Together."

They all—except Eli and Parker, who was slumped against the wall—sent sparks flying. The shade drifted slowly away from them as if it wasn't concerned about their attack. The sparks fell uselessly into the darkness and disappeared. Soon, they couldn't see the shade in the opaque blackness shrouding the front yard.

Hazel swore.

"We've got other problems." James grabbed Sebastian's hand and pointed toward the floor. Black tendrils exactly like the ones at Parker's house were creeping off the porch and across the empty space of the open doorway, inching along the invisible wards keeping everything from Beyond outside.

"It's trying to break in like it did at my house," Parker said softly from behind them.

Eleanor shut the door. Even though it didn't do more than block the view of the intrusive shadow and horrible void of darkness beyond, it allowed Sebastian to relax a fraction. "You need something to eat before we do anything else." Eleanor patted Parker on the shoulder, then walked past him down the hall.

Everyone followed her into Nora's kitchen. Eli didn't hesitate to raid the pantry, shoving anything edible in front of Parker, who'd collapsed into a seat at the dining table.

"What are we going to do?" Eli's words came out high-pitched. He didn't stop moving as he frantically piled bags of chips on the table.

Eleanor crossed her arms. "You all should leave. I'll call the state and demand assistance. They can't let Beyond claim our town. Surely, the federal government would object to an invasion." Eleanor shook her head like she couldn't quite believe the turn things had taken. She rubbed her temple. "The military must have some classified way of fighting otherworldly magic, even if general magical assistance doesn't know what the hell to do about it."

Hazel rested a hand on Eleanor's shoulder. "We aren't leaving you here."

"I'm leaving too. Holy hell, Hazel. I just need to make sure everyone in town hears the evacuation notice first. There's no need to wait for me. It looks like you five have been through much worse than me."

"We aren't leaving," James said at his most stern, leather-clad arms crossed. "Let's not waste any more time arguing about it."

Eleanor looked like she wanted to argue, her mouth set in a stern line.

"Eleanor, please." Parker swiped a hand over his face. "None of us are abandoning this town. We can help."

Eleanor gave him a resigned look. "Fine. I can't tell you what to do." Though it sounded like she wished she could.

But they couldn't leave, and James was right. There was no point arguing with Eleanor about it. They couldn't tell her why without trapping her.

"They're using the veins to create the darkness somehow," Eli said as he passed a sandwich he'd quickly made to Parker. He went on to explain to Eleanor what he'd learned at the boundary.

"Could that be how that—that *thing* got here?" Eleanor pointed back toward the front of the house, her composure cracking for a second. "From the point where the vein disappears into Beyond."

"No," Eli said like this was obvious, but from the looks on everyone's faces he was the only one who thought so. "Shades need the magical space created by shifting veins to pass between worlds. The end of a vein isn't a gateway for anything but raw energy."

"Right." Eleanor scowled. "I need to pass all this on because I am not even remotely equipped to handle this." She marched out of the room, and Hazel followed.

"We can't stay here long," James warned.

Parker nodded, swallowing the last of his sandwich. "If that shadow breaks the wards here like it did at my house, I won't be able to repair them easily. I don't know how the protections on this building were constructed. It will take too much time and effort for me to work it out and fix them, and wiping out what's here for new wards will be even harder."

"Yeah, and you need to rest. Not do any of that." Eli handed him a banana.

"You're taking great care of me, gorgeous. I'll be fine." Parker smiled at Eli, but he seemed exhausted. His arms were smeared with dried blood from the shattered windshield, and his T-shirt had holes burned into it. He needed more than food and first aid to recover. Eli was right. Parker needed rest.

James paced back and forth across the small kitchen. "We have to find somewhere that giant shade-thing isn't likely to find us and hide."

Parker rubbed his brow, adding, "Somewhere I know the wards would be ideal, so I can fix them if necessary."

Sebastian couldn't help thinking that didn't leave many options. Maybe Parker's house, Parker's parents' place, or the diner. Sebastian absently chewed his nails. He pulled a finger out of his mouth. "It's going to hunt us down, isn't it? No matter where we go. I mean, the shades are targeting us, right? It knew your name, Parker. You aren't even a leader of the town. Not like Eleanor is. How does it know anything about us? Has it been watching us?"

"It can't be a coincidence that my house was attacked when no one else's was." Parker let out a grim breath. "It must be able to tell I have some of the most powerful magic in Moonlight Falls, and that's why it assumed I was a leader."

Sebastian thought about all the shades on his property. Could this have anything to do with him? Why were there so many shades hanging around his house? Was their group being targeted because of something to do with Storm House, not just because of Parker's power or Eleanor's leadership? Did it have to do with the veins?

"We need a new vehicle if we're going to get anywhere." James grabbed a set of keys off a hook by the fridge. "I hope Nora had more than one car, and this one is still here."

"I have my car." Eleanor reentered the kitchen. "Though we won't all fit."

"Any luck?" Sebastian gestured to the cell phone in her hand.

"We'll see. My message is being passed on. I don't exactly have the governor or any military officials on speed dial."

Hazel stuck her head into the kitchen. "There's a minivan in the garage."

Eli began stuffing his pockets with granola bars. "But where are we going?"

"I should try and get to my office." Eleanor led the way down the hall, and everyone followed. "I can use my work computer to send an emergency alert text to everyone in the area. Then we really should get out of here."

Sebastian and James shared a look. There was no getting out of here. Sebastian didn't particularly want to stick around and see how the government handled an invasion from Beyond, but military rescue was better than being left behind completely.

They climbed into the minivan, with Hazel driving. Sebastian leaned close to James, who reflexively wrapped an arm around him. "Mila said it was hard for more complex beings, like intelligent shades, to pass through into this world. How do you think that thing got here?"

"I have no idea." James sagged against him like he was letting himself feel an exhaustion he'd been fending off. "Who knows how long it's been here. This could have been brewing for months."

"Yeah," Eli agreed from the back seat. "The shade that attacked me was different. And that was close to two months ago."

This invasion could have easily been brewing since then or even earlier. Over the last few months, the number of shades at Storm House had increased, but Sebastian hadn't thought much of it until recently when the numbers had skyrocketed. But looking back, it made sense if this thing had started slowly, and once the darkness set in, Beyond made its move on Moonlight Falls, and all the shades came pouring in.

Hazel opened the garage door with a remote she found tucked into the sun visor. The door rolled upward, revealing black tendrils of shadow covering the doorway like a second wall. Sebastian watched one near the roof poke through into the garage. It was breaking in.

The van's high beams flooded the area, but the shadow didn't retreat.

Hazel looked around at everyone. "Think it's a bad idea to drive through it?"

"Floor it, babe." Eleanor rested her hand on the back of Hazel's neck. "We'll fight off anything that sticks to the van if we need to."

"You heard her." Hazel gave them all a devilish grin through the rearview mirror. "Buckle the fuck up."

"Oh god," Eli whined.

Tires screeched as Hazel sped out of the garage. The shadow stretched like rubber, tendrils groping the sides of the van, then burst, allowing them through as it sprang back and continued to attack the house.

The pit of darkness had disappeared from the front lawn, so at least they could see. Hazel braked in time to turn onto the street and not roll the van. She took off in the direction of town faster than you should normally drive in a neighborhood, but not so recklessly that Sebastian worried they'd die in an accident rather than a shade attack.

As they drove, shades appeared out of the darkness like they'd been waiting for them. They followed the vehicle, keeping pace and peering in the windows. None of the beasts attacked or tried to block the windshield as they had before. It was almost like they were escorting the van so they would know where it was going.

James took hold of Sebastian's hand. "We're never going to be able to hide."

He was right. With so many shades around unaffected by artificial light, there was no way to shoo all the beasts away without draining themselves. They'd never escape every single pair of onyx eyes watching them. And if the shades were watching and reporting back to the large shadow being, they were doomed.

Several other cars passed them on the road, going in the other direction, but the shades paid no attention to anyone else. Their vehicle was the only one with an otherworldly tail. When Hazel pulled in front of town hall, the shades did nothing more than hover in the street, watching the minivan from a distance.

Eleanor placed her hand on the door handle. "We should go inside."

There was an alarming number of shades gathered at the center of town. Sebastian had never seen such a big crowd around the stone. There probably hadn't even been that many humans there during the town's popular summer festival. As Sebastian watched out the window, even more shades drifted into the circle.

Eleanor opened her door and marched across the sidewalk and up the steps of town hall like there wasn't a huge swarm of shades a hundred feet away.

"I'd still rather go somewhere I know the wards," Parker mumbled.

Hazel turned off the van and climbed out. "We're not leaving here without Eleanor."

"Never said we should," Parker called after her.

Sebastian tore his eyes off the still-growing crowd of shades and got out of the minivan. James and Eli helped Parker, who still seemed worryingly weak. He'd used way too much power banishing all those shades with fire.

The four of them hurried into the empty town hall. The shades kept their distance but closed in once Sebastian and the others were over the threshold. It felt like they'd never get out again. If the shades decided to attack when they exited, they'd be overwhelmed.

Sebastian wandered past the empty reception desk and down the hall. He spotted Eleanor in her office, the door left wide open, with Hazel standing beside her. He stopped. There was no need to intrude, so he turned back to the entry where the others had stayed.

Parker sat on a bench in the reception area as Eli fed him and gave him little paper cups of water from a cooler in the corner.

James came to stand beside Sebastian and leaned against the wall. "What the fuck do we do now?"

"No idea."

James gave a tired nod.

"Hey, are you okay?" Sebastian reached out just as James slumped and slid down the wall. Sebastian caught him and lowered him to the ground. "James! What's wrong?"

"It just hit me." He blinked up at Sebastian. "I might have used a bit too much magic helping Parker with the fire."

"But you seemed fine." Sebastian gripped James's shoulders, his chest tightening.

James leaned his head back against the wall. "Must have been adrenaline keeping me going."

"Fuck." Sebastian jumped up and got James some water. Once he was sipping from the small cup, Sebastian rushed over to Eli. "How much more food do you have?"

Eli's eyes went wide. "Is James okay?"

"I don't know." Sebastian tried not to sound like he was panicking. He'd fucked up. He should have taken better care of James, but he'd been distracted.

"Here." Parker handed him a handful of granola bars.

Sebastian rushed back to James's side and passed him the food.

"Don't worry, sweetheart." James squeezed his hand.

"Impossible," Sebastian protested. "I'll only stop worrying about you when you figure out how to not worry about me. You're my whole world, James. I need you."

James tugged Sebastian against his side. "And you've got me. I just need some rest. It will all be okay."

Sebastian nodded even though things were far from okay. They were trapped in a town that was slowly turning into a nightmare.

CHAPTER TWENTY-THREE

Eleanor must have gotten the emergency alert sent because all their phones blared, cutting into the silence of the reception area. James and Parker groaned like the sound physically hurt.

Eli kissed Parker's cheek as he cleared the message from his screen. "I hope people leave."

Sebastian met Eli's solemn stare across the room. "I hope the shades let them."

"They should," Eleanor said from the hallway. "It was what that thing said it wanted. If it thinks it's winning, maybe it will let people go."

"The shades seemed to be letting other cars pass before," Hazel reminded them.

"Exactly." Eleanor gestured toward the door. "So why don't you all get going?"

No one moved.

"Please," Eleanor begged. "I'll come with you. We can all pile into the van. There's no reason to stay. This is not normal Moonlight Falls weirdness or our responsibility. We can all come home again once the National Guard or whoever-the-fuck kicks out the monsters."

"Eleanor, we can't. You go. We'll catch up." Hazel sounded pained, and Sebastian felt a familiar stab of guilt. He pushed it away as best he could, but things had gotten so out of hand.

"Can't?" Eleanor narrowed her eyes at Hazel. "What's that supposed to mean?"

The silence that followed was thick with tension. So many words were on the tip of Sebastian's tongue. He could feel how weak the secret-binding had become. It seemed even flimsier than when he and James had told Eli and Parker, almost like telling Hazel afterward had weakened it further. But it didn't matter how easy it was to spill his secret. Sebastian knew they couldn't trap Eleanor by explaining.

Eleanor fixed Hazel with a serious stare. "What do you mean *can't*, Hazel?"

A loud crash came from above. Glass rained onto the reception area carpet, tinkling where it hit the desk and tiles by the door, glittering in the artificial light. The large front window halfway up the vaulted front wall had shattered. Black tendrils reached inside, feeling down and around.

"See, we need to go!" Eleanor shouted, grabbing Hazel's elbow.

The door to town hall creaked open. "You sound properly motivated." A familiar eerie voice washed over them as the huge shade glided into the reception area. Even with the lights on, Sebastian couldn't see it any better than before. It was like a walking shadow, no hint of a face, nothing, only a menacing presence.

Shadowy tendrils flowed around the base of the shade, slithering along the floor. The wards protecting town hall must have been completely shattered. Had they even been intact when they'd walked in?

Sebastian helped James stand. He didn't want them to be on the floor as the tendrils crept closer.

"There is no point staying to fight." The shade moved closer. "Your kind don't do well in the dark."

Eleanor took a step forward. "Then let us go."

The shade moved its blank face as if looking around the room at them. Sebastian swore it lingered on him and James, but he had to be imagining it. It was just his fear making him see things. The shade didn't even have eyes.

"All but one can go."

James's grip on Sebastian's arm turned bruising. Did he suspect the shade was looking at them too? But why?

Eleanor hesitated, still clutching Hazel's arm. "We're all leaving."

No one contradicted her. Even if they couldn't escape Moonlight Falls, it was better to get away from this shade before convincing Eleanor to leave them behind.

Typical-looking shades floated in through the open door. They didn't flinch at the lights as they lined the front wall of the room like sentries waiting to strike. Now that he could see them better, Sebastian realized how translucent they were, nothing like the well of darkness that was their apparent leader.

"If you don't cooperate, we won't let the rest of the town leave." The faceless shade glided forward, and Eleanor took an unsteady step back. "All but one. You choose, or I will, but there is no negotiating. You must cede leadership to me. Prove you understand by giving me a sacrifice, and you can go."

Sebastian's heart pounded. His instincts screamed in warning.

James squeezed Sebastian twice in quick succession, like he was trying to communicate something. Sebastian was lost. He had no idea what it meant. He just wanted to get out of there and keep James safe. Keep them all safe since it was his fault they were stuck in the damn town in the first place.

Even if they didn't hate him for it, Sebastian would hate himself if his curse got them all killed.

The carpet underneath the towering shade erupted in flames.

Stinking smoke billowed as the fire roared. Eleanor and Hazel jumped in surprise, backing out of the flames' reach. Eli dragged Parker toward the hallway as the blaze spread, and Sebastian tried to do the same to James, but James was shaking, his body rigid and unmovable. At first, Sebastian thought it was fear, but then he realized James was straining with effort as he burned the room in front of them.

The shades along the wall caught fire and burst into shadow while the tendrils creeping along the front door did the same, shrieking as they disappeared from this world, but the shade in the middle of the room remained untouched.

The fire raced along the carpet, closer to where Sebastian and James were standing. "James!" Sebastian shouted in his ear as he pulled him.

James stumbled and almost fell into the growing fire. Sebastian caught him and dragged him backward toward the hallway. A burst of water sprayed in front of them, dousing some of the nearest flames. James wasn't holding his own weight. It terrified Sebastian as he dragged him closer to where everyone was cowering in the hall.

Cold air whipped through the room, and in an instant, Sebastian felt like he was freezing. The roaring fire snuffed out like it'd been nothing more than a small candle flame.

"Are we done?" The shade stood unaffected in the middle of the destroyed room, its voice as cold as the air.

Sebastian clung to James, unable to concentrate on the beast in front of him. James's eyes were hooded. He was barely conscious. All that magic for nothing. A sob tore out of Sebastian's throat. He needed to take care of James. He had to get out of there and find somewhere safe.

"Parker! Parker!" Eli shouted, but Sebastian felt like he heard it from far away. He turned to see the big man slumped on the ground. The water spell must have been his doing. Conjuring moisture was even harder than conjuring light or starting a fire.

The shade glided forward, stopping in front of Sebastian. "Bring that one, and come with me."

Sebastian felt lightheaded. Was it talking to him? Why? "I'm not coming with you." His voice cracked, but he made himself look into the blank face. He clung to James as tight as he could.

The shade let out a wheezing sound, almost like a sigh of frustration. It reached out and wrapped one limb around Sebastian's body and the other around James.

Sebastian went blind with panic. The contact burned like ice. He thrashed and sent sparks flying wildly, but they didn't catch. They were swallowed by the shade's darkness.

He felt James being pulled from his grip. "No!" he screamed until his voice was raw. He was vaguely aware of Hazel and Eleanor trying to set the shade on fire, but it was no use.

"You will stay here where you're needed." The shade shoved Sebastian back, releasing him and sending him crashing into the wall. It held a boneless James in its other limb. "The rest of you may leave. I have chosen my sacrifice. His blood will cement the claim Beyond has made on this place, as per the laws of blood and bone magic in the living world. There's no use fighting. Go or die."

It drifted up into the air as Sebastian lunged forward. He grabbed for the shade but his hands closed around nothing. It floated out the broken window, taking James away.

CHAPTER TWENTY-FOUR

SEBASTIAN RAN out the front door and onto the steps of town hall. He looked up but couldn't see the shade or James anywhere. He swore his heart stopped.

He stumbled onto the sidewalk, trying to drag in breaths but not feeling like any air was making it to his lungs. Where had they gone? He needed to get James back. He couldn't live without James.

Hazel and Eli appeared at his side, their hands on him, pulling him up from the pavement. Sebastian hadn't been aware he'd fallen to his knees.

"Where did it go?" Eli's strangled voice broke Sebastian's haze.

"We need to find it," Sebastian rasped. "I'm not letting James go. He can't leave!"

"We know. We'll find him." Hazel gripped his shoulder tight. "But we have to be careful. Look." Her voice shook on the last word.

Sebastian blinked at her, confused, and followed her gaze toward the street. His despair-soaked mind hadn't processed the thousands of shades now packed into the town center. He sucked in a breath. They were f**ked. It was too many to fight by such a ridiculous margin that no room was left for hope, not even by the most delusional standards.

All the streetlights had been busted out, making it the darkest town had ever been, and looking up, it no longer seemed like night but like a void lay above them, empty and black. Everything else was a sea of shadowy bodies, eyes, and claws. The only space free of shades was the small patch of grass in the center of the road, surrounding the tall stone marking the founding of Moonlight Falls.

For an odd moment, it almost looked like the stone was glowing, the only light in a world of dark.

Sebastian pointed. "Do you see that?"

"The stone? So?" Eli sounded frantic. "How are we going to find James? Parker is in bad shape and Eleanor is insisting on driving him to the hospital in Apple Valley."

Sebastian couldn't stop staring at the stone. It wasn't exactly glowing, but something about it drew his attention in a way nothing ever had before. He felt like he was losing his mind.

"Why did the shade tell me to stay here where I'm needed?" Sebastian asked as his thoughts spun. "It's like it knew I couldn't leave."

"I don't know, Sebastian. Who cares?" Hazel tugged on him frantically. "We have to do something. We can't stay here."

Sebastian couldn't concentrate on what she was saying. It was like he'd fallen into himself and wasn't sure he'd ever get back out. He was in desperate need of action but unable to move. It hurt. Fuck, it hurt like nothing else in his life ever had.

He pulled at his hair, gaze locked on the stone. "Does it know I'm tied to the veins? Can it tell? If it used the veins to create its darkness, maybe it can see that I'm part of it."

Hazel and Eli didn't respond to his frantic questions, but Sebastian didn't care.

This invasion from Beyond couldn't have anything to do with his curse. His family had not created this problem, but that didn't mean Sebastian wasn't connected to it because of the veins. If he and the veins were one, and the veins were holding the darkness here just as they held Eli, Hazel, James, and Parker captive, then was *he* responsible for holding the darkness here too? Could he release the imposing shadow from the veins? Could he disconnect the spells that bound everything together?

"Look!" Eli pointed at something behind the stone.

The massive shade that had taken James appeared on the grass. It was setting something on the ground. Sebastian couldn't see clearly but knew in his soul that it was James.

Sebastian grabbed Eli's shoulders. "Does the stone sit on top of the vein running through town?"

"What?" Eli gave him a bewildered look.

"Does it?" Sebastian shook him.

Eli jerked away. "Yeah, it does."

The stone and the vein's positioning felt significant, but Sebastian wasn't sure why. He had to get to James. He had to use everything he knew to save him. He hadn't finally found the one person who'd chosen him, only to lose him like this. He would not let the good in his life be ruined. He needed James. He needed this town and the people living here to be safe. He was going to make his home here and live out his days with the man he loved, and nothing would stand in his way.

Sebastian deserved better than to lose it all like this. He'd been through hell and survived despite wanting to give up every day he'd been imprisoned. A horde of beasts from Beyond was nothing compared to the years he'd spent alone. He wouldn't let them ruin the life he'd fought so hard for.

Anger and determination burned inside him. There was a vein running underground a hundred feet away, and he was going to test Eli's theory and see if he could use it. He'd suffered through his curse, bound to the natural magic of this region, and now he was going to take his due. If the magic in the veins was part of him, he would force it to do something good for once.

He sprinted down the sidewalk.

"Where are you going?" Eli yelled after him.

Sebastian didn't look back as he lunged into the crowd of shades. They hissed and scratched at him but didn't grab or pin him down. He pushed his way through, running as fast as he could until he was level with the stone on the north end of the circle.

The vein was beneath him, and he was going to steal its power.

He knelt on the ground and splayed his palms on the asphalt. Shades pulled at his hair and others jabbed his back. He ignored them. He needed to find the connection that Eli thought was there. If he couldn't, he'd lose everything. He'd lose James and the life they were meant to have together. If he had to go through that, Sebastian would lose himself too.

Sebastian delved within, feeling his own magic. It was familiar, not very strong, and weakened from the day's fights. He prodded at it, trying to find the shape of it. Somewhere inside was a link to the vast power beneath his feet.

He couldn't find it. His arms shook from holding himself off the ground. His knees ached, pressing into the road, but it was no good. There was nothing there. He felt no link, nothing beyond himself, his aching body, frazzled mind, and mediocre power.

The realization this wasn't going to work paralyzed Sebastian with hopelessness. It reared its head like the mother of all the internal demons he'd been fighting for years had finally come to end him.

James was going to die. Sebastian would lose him, and so he might as well die too. He couldn't save James, and maybe in the end, that meant he wasn't worthy of good things. Because he'd failed. If he deserved better, then why couldn't he prove it and keep the one person he needed more than anything?

Sebastian wished the ground would open up and swallow him so it would be over. He hated that he'd found someone to love and lost them. It hurt more than if James had chosen to leave. It was like a taunt. A tease, showing him what he could have had. But all he deserved was to be buried in the ground like his uncle and everyone who'd come before them. Alone.

Sebastian pictured himself in the ground, not even in a coffin, surrounded by dirt, as tears fell down his cheeks. Something about the image felt right, like he was coming home. Like he'd always been underground.

Something stirred within him, responding to his envisioned homecoming to the earth. It was like a small crack. His magic quivered before giving way to a vast ocean of power.

The smell of dirt and decayed leaves filled Sebastian's nose. He didn't need a connection to the vein beneath him because he and the veins were one. He was beneath the earth as much as he was kneeling in the street. He felt himself and his vast power moving through the soil, and he clung to it.

He felt along the vein until he found something cold and foreign. He knew in his gut it wasn't part of him. He pulled on it, and pain shot through his skull.

"Fuck." Sebastian spat blood on the ground. He'd bitten his tongue without realizing. It had to be the darkness he'd felt, but he didn't know what to do about it. It was tied to him, but he didn't know how to dislodge it.

He shook himself. He needed to get to James first. Everything else could wait.

Sebastian pushed himself up. As he stood, he pulled the power of the veins with him. It flooded his human body like fire. He let out a pained wail but didn't stop drawing on the raw energy that was apparently a part of him, yet not meant for a human to possess. It heated his skin and sent pain down every one of his nerve endings.

Something blue crackled at his fingertips.

Sebastian stepped forward, unsteady at first, then with more confidence as he pushed the pain away. He moved toward the stone, breathing heavily like he'd run a marathon. The shades let him pass, some hissing and cocking their heads while others stared without blinking.

The large shade's voice filled his head, and he pushed himself to move faster. It was chanting unfamiliar sounds, and Sebastian could feel the magic of Moonlight Falls responding.

A nearby shade lunged at him. Sebastian grabbed it with his electric-blue sparking hands, and with a flare of bright-blue light, the shade burst into nothing. The ones around it screeched and grabbed at him. He fought them off, letting power loose from within him without restraint. He pushed the beasts out of the way, banishing them with sparks of blue energy, and no matter how many times he did it, the power within him never diminished.

Sebastian stumbled onto the grass in front of the stone and looked up. The dark form of the shade loomed above him. It had a stone dagger held aloft in one limb and clutched James in the other. It stood frozen, its faceless attention fixed on Sebastian.

Sebastian launched himself forward. A black tendril caught him around the waist, and he cried out in surprise. He grabbed hold of the tendril but instead of feeling icy pain, he only felt the hot power burning through him as he scorched the shadow away.

The tendril screamed and broke off from the rest of the writhing mass on the ground, bursting into nothing. Sebastian thrust his hands toward the shade holding James captive and willed power to flow out of him. He screamed with the effort, his head spinning sickeningly as energy tore through him.

The shade was saved from the onslaught by a swarm of tendrils rising to intercept Sebastian's blast. The air filled with their shrieks. Sebastian tried again, only to be met with more expendable tendrils. He couldn't get his power to reach the shade.

"Leave Moonlight Falls," Sebastian shouted. His head pounded. He searched the power within him until he came to that cold patch, clinging to the vein like a parasite. He directed all his concentration and energy toward it, burning it.

The shade in front of him screamed. Sebastian's ears popped and his concentration broke as pain stabbed through his head. He retched bile onto the ground and swayed, legs almost giving out. He felt nauseated and broken and was surprised his head hadn't literally split open. His vision went spotty, and he barely managed to stay standing.

The chanting sounds he'd heard earlier began once more. Sebastian looked up in time to see the stone knife swinging downward, aimed straight at James's neck.

He screamed, and it felt like his head exploded as he sent a stream of blue power at the knife. It hit with a clap like thunder, and the stone dagger shattered into a million small pieces that fell harmlessly onto James like dust.

It was only a momentary relief. The shade growled and tossed James to the ground. It glided over him toward Sebastian, who sent another head-splitting burst of power at the beast only to be intercepted by more tendrils.

Sebastian dry heaved, his vision blacking out for a second. He might never run out of energy with the veins at his disposal, but that didn't mean his body could do this forever.

He blinked away the fog of unconsciousness threatening him and lunged out of the way just in time as the shade tried to grab him. He needed to end this soon. James needed to be taken care of. Sebastian couldn't waste any more time. He concentrated on the tendrils of shadow writhing on the ground. There seemed to be a dark center that didn't move. He aimed for it, sending power into its depths.

As the blow struck, the shade grabbed Sebastian around the middle with both limbs and squeezed. The air whooshed out of Sebastian's lungs, but his hit had found its mark. All the tendrils burst, unable to break away from the center and save any one piece.

But it was too late. The shade was crushing him.

Sebastian dug his fingers into the dark limbs constricting him, sending power hurtling through his body and into the beast. The shade jolted. Its eerie yell pierced Sebastian's eardrums as it released him. Sebastian found his feet and turned to face the shade, wobbling and sucking air into his aching chest. He sent another jolt of magic at the shade, and without the tendrils to take the blow, it hit.

The shade staggered but didn't burst.

Sebastian growled in frustration and growing exhaustion. "Leave," he grunted and struck again.

The shade's yell sounded weaker this time as it staggered back farther. "I will come back. Beyond is not for the living. You can't kill me."

Fear gripped Sebastian, but he couldn't let it stop him. "How did you even get here?" he rasped as he gathered power, hoping to hit the shade with a ball of power larger than anything he'd cast so far.

The shade cocked its blank head. "You already know the answer to that, Gatekeeper."

Dread filled Sebastian, but there was no time to stop and think about it. He pulled as much power to him as he could and let it loose. Raw magic burst from his fingertips and hit the shade straight in the chest. There was no scream this time. The beast seemed oddly frozen as the power ran from Sebastian into its dark form. Then, it exploded in a burst of light.

The smaller shades crowding around hissed and shrank back. Sebastian's knees hit the grass, his legs no longer able to hold him up. Sebastian only had eyes for James. His James. The light of his life slumped on the ground.

He crawled forward. "James, babe, oh, James." He rolled James over and cradled his slack face. "James," Sebastian sobbed.

He needed to pull it together. James needed warmth, rest, and food. An IV would be ideal, but there was no hospital in this damn town.

An increasingly loud hissing sound broke through his worried thoughts. He looked up to see the shades all around him closing in. The ones farther back in the crowd had floated up, forming a domed wall of wispy bodies, claws, and onyx eyes. All Sebastian could see was shades in every direction save for the grass beneath him.

Sebastian clutched James to his chest. Even with the vein's power, there were too many shades. His body was wrecked from the magic he'd already done. He had power, but his head was throbbing so badly that it was getting harder and harder to see. He couldn't blast all these shades back to Beyond. It would kill him.

He needed light. Even the light-resistant shades hadn't been seen in direct sunlight. He needed to banish the darkness and bring back the sun, or else he'd never be able to get past these beasts and get James to safety.

He rested his head on James's leather-clad chest and breathed in his scent. It calmed him. James was who he was doing this for. He would do anything for James, no matter how hard or how much it hurt.

Sebastian found the cold darkness clinging to the veins and focused all the energy he had access to on that one point. Pressure built inside him, in his head, more and more, making him fear it would never end. Right when he couldn't take it, the power exploded, burning inside him and making him scream.

The air around him dropped to a bone-chattering cold. The burning power and the frosty air warred in a battle that seemed to go on forever. Sebastian felt his breaths growing shallow. He couldn't do it. The darkness's hold was too strong.

But the darkness wasn't part of Sebastian. It wasn't part of Moonlight Falls and needed to leave, and Sebastian didn't think he could stop trying to banish it if he even tried, not now that he'd started. He was stuck. He'd either succeed or die.

Blinding light burst in front of Sebastian's closed eyes. The power he wielded overwhelmed the darkness at last, and the thing clinging to the veins let go. He forced his eyes open and looked up, his whole body shaking as the stone turned white, light radiating from it in all directions.

The shades shrank back, and just when Sebastian feared it wasn't enough, the stone seemed to burst and daylight erupted around them.

A blindingly bright, clear blue sky shone above his head. Shades hissed and screeched, hundreds of them bursting into smoke instantly. Any that remained fled, seeking shadows or dark crevasses to escape the sun. Soon, the street was clear.

Sebastian blinked. The stone hadn't burst after all. It was still standing as tall as ever right in front of him. *Huh*, was his last thought before he lost consciousness, his head falling back onto James's chest.

CHAPTER TWENTY-FIVE

SEBASTIAN'S WORLD was warm and wrapped in the familiar smell of leather mixed with the faintest hint of chlorine. He was home. He knew nothing else, but that didn't matter.

He couldn't open his eyes and wasn't sure he needed to. Something brushed his hair. He leaned into it, nuzzling the skin of a callused palm. The smell of home intensified and he breathed in deep.

"Sebastian, sweetheart, can you hear me?" a soft, familiar voice asked.

James. Sebastian smiled. Of course it was James. James was his world, his everything. He expected to be nowhere else.

He kissed the hand cupping his cheek, wanting to be wrapped up in James's sweet-smelling skin forever.

He must be lying on a bed because it dipped and a hard body encircled him. "I've got you, sweetheart. Just please wake up," James whispered against Sebastian's temple.

"I'm awake," he mumbled, shifting so he could bury his face in James's neck.

A relieved whine escaped James's throat.

That made Sebastian remember he was supposed to be taking

care of James, not the other way around. Memories of shades, hot blue power, and the sight of James limp in the grass flooded his mind. Sebastian sucked in a panicked breath as his eyes flew open.

James held him so tight he could barely move. "You're okay. I've got you. Everything is fine."

"But you—" Sebastian gasped, unable to finish the thought.

"I'm fine." James kissed the top of Sebastian's head. "Rest, sweetheart."

Sebastian's whole body relaxed, going limp and accepting the firm hug James gave him. He breathed in the smell of the man, the smell of good things, and drifted back to sleep.

LATER, Sebastian woke up much more alert. He was still in James's arms and had no idea how long it had been since the fight with the shades or the last time he'd woken up.

At least the sun was still out.

"James," he murmured groggily, trying to stretch but unable to move much with the way James held him.

"Sebastian." James didn't sound like he'd been asleep. "How do you feel?"

James released his grip enough for Sebastian to look at him. "Fine."

James glared at him. "Fine?" A sob choked out of him. "I didn't know if you'd ever wake up."

Pain gripped Sebastian's chest at the anguish on James's face. "I'm here." He clutched James's shoulders. "What about you? You drained yourself so badly with all that fire. And then —" His words failed as he remembered the shade taking James away.

James ran a hand through Sebastian's hair. "I recovered days ago. Parker too. All we did was a bit too much magic, nothing we couldn't come back from."

"You didn't know that." Sebastian squeezed him. "You could have killed yourself. And I know you were trying to protect us all, but, James, I can't do this without you."

James brushed his lips against Sebastian's, tangling a hand in Sebastian's hair. "I know, Sebastian. But I can't do this without you either. And *shit*, what you did was so reckless."

Sebastian fixed him with a serious stare. "If I hadn't done it, you'd have been sacrificed. There was never a question of risking myself. I won't let you leave me. Nothing can take you. I'd rather have died trying to save you than lose you."

Tears fell down James's cheeks. "But you're not allowed to save me and then not wake up for four days. You aren't allowed to leave me either, Sebastian. I wouldn't survive it."

Sebastian's own tears clouded his vision. "I won't leave you, James. I will claw my way back from the worst kind of hell to get back to you. Promise."

James let out a pained sound. Sebastian kissed him, swallowing all his fears, and didn't release his mouth until he could feel James smiling. "I promise, James," Sebastian repeated. "Nothing is keeping us apart."

"Nothing." James agreed softly and wiped his eyes. "But let's not do that again."

"Fuck, no." Sebastian let out a tired laugh. "Was I really out for four days?"

James brushed the tears from Sebastian's cheeks. "Yeah. We've all been so worried. After the darkness broke, some disaster relief workers came in, and Hazel convinced them to treat us here instead of trying to take us to the hospital, but they're long gone, and we've been doing our best to look after you. Things around town are mostly back to normal now."

Sebastian raised his brows. "No shade attacks?"

James shook his head. "No, it's been quiet. I haven't left you, but everyone else has been coming to check on you regularly and tell me what's been happening. They'll want to know you're awake."

"We'll tell them." Sebastian ran his hands down James's chest. "Just not quite yet."

"No," James agreed. "Not yet." He pulled Sebastian into a rough kiss.

The desperation as James devoured him unlocked something wild in Sebastian. He needed James just as much as James needed him. He had all these overwhelming feelings threatening to burst out of him.

James must have felt the same. Sebastian could feel it in the way James touched him. It was as if they were both searching for reassurance that the other was still there and not going anywhere. They tugged at their clothes until they were naked, tangled in the sheets, their legs wound together.

Sebastian pried himself from James's lips so he could kiss and suck his way down James's neck instead. James panted, arching into Sebastian. When Sebastian captured one of James's nipples in his mouth, James groaned.

"You're everything to me, James," Sebastian murmured as he dropped kisses across his chest. "I want a life with you. I want to see you every day and feed you all your favorite foods. I want normal and quiet moments with you. No more curses or other-worldly magic, just a simple and straightforward *us*."

James tilted Sebastian's face so they could look at each other. "I want that too. It sounds perfect. I want to give you everything you've ever wanted."

"I've already got it. All I need is you. The rest of life is just details."

James gave him a radiant smile, and then they were kissing again. Sebastian pulled James on top of him. The press of hard muscle weighing him down made him feel safe and each brush of James's hands against his body reminded him he'd been chosen.

This was his life. The good hadn't ended. It had grown into something even better.

Sure, they still had problems coming out their ears, and working out the details would be more complicated than in any normal relationship, but none of that mattered now. They were celebrating each other. They'd face the rest later.

"What do you want?" James whispered in Sebastian's ear as he rocked his hips.

Sebastian ran his hands down James's back. "I want you to stay right here on top of me so I can feel you."

They kissed, hips rolling, hard cocks rubbing, slickened with the precum smeared between them. Sebastian grabbed James's ass, and he groaned into Sebastian's shoulder. Sebastian kneaded the muscles, guiding James's movements against him.

"Love this ass." Sebastian squeezed again, then let his fingers trail between James's cheeks. James's movements faltered, and they looked at each other. "Are you into this?" Sebastian brushed him gently. He'd never touched James there before.

James was flushed, his eyes bright with need, as he pressed back into Sebastian's grip. "Yes, oh god, Sebastian, please." He spread his legs wider. "Touch me."

Being the one James opened up to lit a fire inside Sebastian. He buried his fingers between James's cheeks, and James canted his hips into the touch. Sebastian found James's hole and massaged the tight ring of muscle, circling around.

James shuddered and rocked against Sebastian. His eyes fluttered closed, and he dropped his head against Sebastian's chest. "Oh fuck, that feels good. Feels so good when you touch me."

"I love touching you." Sebastian pressed against the tight ring of muscle but didn't penetrate. James whined, thrusting back into the touch. "I love you fucking me and eating me," Sebastian said, and James moaned his agreement. "But the best thing is watching you unravel. Seeing how much you love it too."

"I do. Fuck, being with you blows my mind. I didn't know it could be like this, Sebastian. Not before you."

"Me either, James. I never knew it would feel this good to be yours."

It felt like light and life and everything Sebastian had longed for all his life. He had his home, his James. He had a place in the world. As long as he had that, he could deal with the rest. He could face what his connection to the veins meant and the truths the shade had hinted at. Sebastian was done preparing for the worst. He knew he had hard things to face, but it didn't mean the end was coming. It meant the best things in his life awaited him on the other side.

James bucked on top of him, kissing and sucking on Sebastian's neck. Sebastian pushed the tip of his finger inside James, his muscles opening and pulling him in greedily. James moaned as heat enveloped Sebastian's fingertip. He bit down on Sebastian's shoulder and cried out, coming between them.

James's teeth on Sebastian's skin had Sebastian's orgasm racing through him. His pulse thudded, chest fluttering with every good feeling he'd imagined possible.

James had chosen him. He wasn't alone and didn't have to fear being left in the dark and forgotten.

Sebastian held James close as the sun streamed through the window, caressing their sweat-slicked bodies. The darkness couldn't claim them when they had each other to come home to.

The End

JAMES AND SEBASTIAN'S story continues in *Moonlight Falls Book Three: The Heart of Moonlight Falls*. They have each other, but will it be enough to face destroying the curse once and for all?

LOOKING for even more of James and Sebastian? Don't miss *Baking Bread*, a steamy bonus scene exclusive to my newsletter subscribers. Join now and get a spoiler-free peek into Sebastian and James's happily ever after.

HAVE you read Eli and Parker's story? *The Fall of Elijah Gray* is a stand-alone prequel novella to the Moonlight Falls trilogy, available now.

WANT TO KEEP IN TOUCH? Join my reader group on Facebook, Colette Rivera's Coven.

THANK YOU FOR READING THE
CURSED SEBASTIAN STORM

I hoped you enjoyed this installment of James and Sebastian's story.

Reviews are invaluable to authors. Please consider leaving a review for *The Cursed Sebastian Storm* on your favorite review site or the site where you purchased this book to help others find magical books they'll love.

THE HEART OF MOONLIGHT FALLS

In the end, the heart is all that matters.

James is ready to settle into the future he's always dreamed of, but he can't. Nothing comes easily for him and Sebastian while the Storm House curse haunts them and trouble continues to brew in Moonlight Falls.

Battling shades is a given. What James doesn't expect is the town turning on the man he loves.

Secrets get out and Sebastian must fight for his place in the community as he reckons with his connection to the magic of Moonlight Falls and what it means for defeating his family's curse and restoring the veins of power once and for all. While the answers he finds challenge his resolve, Sebastian knows nothing from this world or Beyond can break his and James's bond.

There will always be light in the dark, and together, James and Sebastian can make it shine. But will that be enough to get them through their final challenge?

ACKNOWLEDGMENTS

I would like to thank Abbie Nicole for her excellent editing and attention to detail. I have really enjoyed working on this series with you.

Many thanks to Sleepy Fox Studio for the gorgeous cover design. I absolutely love Sebastian and his unique magic.

As always, thank you to TK for your love and support. I could not build these magic worlds without you. I hope you enjoyed the fireballs in this one.

And thank you to all my readers. I appreciate every one of you. Your excitement for my stories keeps me going, and your messages about the Moonlight Falls books have really filled me with joy.

ABOUT THE AUTHOR

Colette is an author of queer paranormal romance novels. She loves to write couples who take care of each other and show their soft sides when in love. Sugar and spice are key ingredients in all her books. She's an avid PNR reader and loves all things magic. Colette once lived in the US but now calls New Zealand home. As a bisexual she has to resist making all her characters bi. When she succeeds you'll find a variety of representation in her books.

Colette can be found on Instagram @colette_rivera and on Facebook under Colette Rivera Author. She can also be found on her website coletterivera.com where you can sign up to her newsletter for bonus scenes and updates.

MOONLIGHT FALLS

The Fall of Elijah Gray

The Seduction of James Gray

The Cursed Sebastian Storm

The Heart of Moonlight Falls